INHERITANCE

ALSO BY

Nicholas Shakespeare

Fiction

The Vision of Elena Silves

The High Flyer

The Dancer Upstairs

Snowleg

Secrets of the Sea

Non-fiction

Bruce Chatwin

In Tasmania

Nicholas Shakespeare

Inheritance

Harvill Secker
LONDON

Published by Harvill Secker 2010

2 4 6 8 10 9 7 5 3 1

First published in Great Britain in 2010 by
HARVILL SECKER
Random House, 20 Vauxhall Bridge Road
London SW1V 2SA

www.rbooks.co.uk

Addresses for companies within The Random House Group Limited
can be found at: www.randomhouse.co.uk/offices.htm

The Random House Group Limited Reg. No. 954009

A CIP catalogue record for this book is available from the British Library

ISBN 9781846553158 (hardback)
ISBN 9781846553165 (trade paperback)

The Random House Group Limited supports The Forest Stewardship
Council (FSC), the leading international forest certification organisation.
All our titles that are printed on Greenpeace approved FSC certified
paper carry the FSC logo. Our paper procurement policy
can be found at www.rbooks.co.uk/environment

Mixed Sources
Product group from well-managed
forests and other controlled sources
www.fsc.org Cert no. TT-COC-2139
© 1996 Forest Stewardship Council

Typeset in Sabon by Palimpsest Book Production Limited,
Grangemouth, Stirlingshire

Printed and bound in Great Britain by
Clays Ltd, St Ives plc

To Jón

Everything that begins as comedy ends as a dirge in the void.
Roberto Bolaño, *The Savage Detectives*

WESTERN AUSTRALIA, 1960

THE GROUND CRACKLED BENEATH his boots and the air was thick with insects. He tramped on over the scorched plain, seeking landmarks on his map.

Behind him lay Marble Bar; to the west, the ocean; to the south, Perth – where she was, though it stung him to think of her. Ahead, if his calculations were correct, was the mountain range. He had seen it only from the air, and then for a flash in blinding rain. What shape it might have from looking at it straight on, he could not imagine.

The sun burned through his eyepatch. High up he saw a flock of birds, like seeds.

He pushed south over the hot tableland, stopping occasionally to take a photograph or to check his bearings, across dry riverbeds and rings of saltbush, threading through the scratching grass and into regions of himself. At the bottom of a clay pan, he came upon a tyre mark. It ran for fifty yards and disappeared, an imprint from some earlier rain. In the dancing heat, he was compelled to make his own track; one that would have betrayed his personality to anyone following.

The thunderstorm which had flooded Marble Bar evidently had not passed this way. A fine red dust tinged all objects with a colour peculiar to itself. It might have been the oldest landscape in the world. The bottom of an evaporated ocean out of which his earliest ancestors had floundered and unaltered by any life that had breathed since. He walked on, at the angle of a rheumatic finger, made crooked by the weight of the sun and by what he carried in his pack. Looking down the hard dark length of his shadow, as if the person he was had been thinned out of him into the parched red soil.

There was no wind. He could smell his breath, like spilled beer; could taste, with his thickened tongue, the dried spit on his teeth. His eye lost all connection to what lay in front of him. The earth glimmered as though it still held an ocean. In mirage-watered plains, he saw lakes perfect and distinct. And floating in the lakes: Cheryl walking up a church aisle in Perth on the arm of an Englishman; his grandmother in

I

a desert like this one, drinking from a puddle that her donkey had pissed in; and always on the perimeter the figure of Don Flexmore.

A fly flew into his ear. It buzzed and ricocheted in his eardrum with a noise louder than any he had heard since leaving the Land Rover. He flicked it out and trudged on, swearing at himself because he had never thought that he would have to walk this far.

The country grew rougher. His legs bled and his soles wore thin, cracked open by sharp stones. He was in a world of stones. He picked one up, the size of a fist and hollow. Studied it intensely. Then threw it aside.

One step in front of another. His feet blistered and his eyepatch chafing. But every time he climbed out of a flood-scoured riverbed with the hopeful expectation of seeing his mountain, his eye drove on past the furthest red rocks into the featureless sky.

The air was so dry that coming to an outcrop he dumped his pack and rowed into the shade, where he waited, siding with the rocks, and a wedge-tailed eagle glided above. The black of its shadow slipped over the earth and merged with the boulder down on which it flopped. It looked at him, head at the angle of Cheryl's mother, calculating how long before it might pick out his eye, and when he moved it flew lazily off.

On the second afternoon he came to the powdery edge of another table-land. Below, pink patches of earth and dark contours of bluish rock – and ahead, in the distance, a peak. But when he reached the top of the next escarpment he was disappointed not to see it. The sun was going down as he walked from the lowland into a deep gully where he camped for the night.

He prepared a fire from dried flood-wreck and boiled up a pan of tea. The tall walls of the gorge amplified the crackling of the flames and the sound of his slapped cheek. He picked a mosquito out of the water and stirred the tea leaves with a tiny bone he had found on the riverbed, the petrified shin of an animal. He was thinking of his grand-mother, who smelled of French cigarettes and who fretted with the silver bangle on her wrist as she spoke to him.

The tide of light had gone out when he tugged off his Blundstones, wincing as he withdrew each sore heel. Tenderly, he set down his boots by the fire as though under a bed. The ocean of earth had left salt stains in white ripples on the caps that had become separate and gawped at him. He peeled off his socks. Deep red under the toenails and wet blisters caked with a rusty paste. He bathed his ruined feet with the dregs of the tea-water – the soothing relief, as though the tea might actually do some good, tanning his hide – and bandaged them with strips torn from his shirtsleeve.

After the heat, the sudden chill made him shiver. He scraped a hip-hole to sleep in and laid out the tarpaulin, but termites marched up and down his spine, and so he broke a few mulga branches, some with the ghosts of leaves still on them, and made a spiky mattress and slept on that.

The following day, the sun rose red and undistinguished from the earth, save for the faint definition of fresh tracks. He squatted, examining them.

He had been followed. His billy was knocked over, tin cans dragged towards the bushes and fresh droppings nearby.

His lips came unstuck. 'Hello?'

Nothing.

He rolled his swag and hoisted his pack and tramped along the dried river flat. Lighter for the tinned meat that he had eaten and the water that he had drained from his canvas bag. The early morning warmth was delightful though short-lived, until the moment of realisation that it stood to be another roasting day. The sweat that had dried on him unthawed, and soon his face and neck were damp with it and his back was a coat of flies. The tortured boughs of a desert gum pointed him on.

Further into the gorge, he came upon rockholes filled with oily water and floating with goanna scat, in which he saw his dark eyebrows blonder for moondust. The ground was soft and his boots squelched into the earth. Green grass had shot up in abrupt, unlikely patches, and on steep banks, in bursts of mysterious pinks and yellows, garish bands of small donkey orchids were shrill with finches. Here, the recent rain had brought life.

The gorge petered out in a bluff from which he obtained a view of the plain he had crossed. He was consulting his map when he felt an odd current of air. A noise dragged his gaze to a twisted tree sprouting from the south side of a cracked boulder, and in the same moment he heard a cough. He stood, rooted. The cough came again, like a guilt. Or was it a snigger? And at the tip of his long shadow was another, and he saw the silhouette of two lupine ears.

Then, before he could cast around for a stone – there it hung in the distance, looming over the stunted tops of the spinifex and obliterating all concern for what it was that had vanished back into the dirt. His first thought when he saw it: *I'm looking at Mount Ararat.* One large peak, one smaller and both rising from the desert at the spot he had circled.

He muscled forward, oblivious to his mashed feet and the pricked-up ears, dominated by his hatted shadow that stretched out now in the direction of the mountain. Needles of thirst and the constant dialogue of flies. And all the time the peaks growing before him and the glare in that rolling eye overhead.

Through the haze, he saw ridges of drifted red iron-sand lapping the purpler slopes. They were part of a range of weathered hills crafted by wind and rain into spectacular shapes. He snapped a picture for his inevitable return. The rocky mass of his Ararat, as already he thought of it, gave the impression of a citadel more than anything, with ramparts, turrets, chimneys. It shone in the sun, polished by wind and wind-borne debris.

It took him the whole day.

He camped in a ravine at its base. The sky, formerly blue and lucid, had clouded over with banks of thick dark cumulus. Night came on quickly, but lying on his back he saw no stars. He heard thunder vibrating in the hills and waited for raindrops the size of pennies to fall hissing onto the earth.

A cool breeze blew up before dawn. It funnelled down the ravine, and he listened to it communicating with the saltbush, but it did not rain.

At first light, he scrambled over a jagged overhang of ancient conglomerate and picked his way along slabs the colour of dried blood. Moisture had revitalised the earth and given it a gloss, but in the grey light the sides of the mountain were not shiny as he remembered them. The only indication that he might be close – his distracted compass, fluctuating from one escarpment to another.

The wind breathed into his face and over his skin. Not scented, as in Perth or Aleppo. Dustless and clean and sweet. Without history. Earlier, he could make no sense of its gibberish. Now the wind had the sound of a beginning, he thought.

Twenty minutes later, he reached his destination.

He stood there, trembling at the knee. It was as though something had gulped at the rock face. He laughed, and his heart flapped wildly from one side of his ribs to another as he looked right and left, seeing rust everywhere.

The young man afterwards calculated that on that day he followed his shadow over 1,000 million tons of high-grade iron ore, stretching forty miles one way, thirty miles another. And all of it his.

LONDON, 2005

I

ON A COLD WET afternoon in February, Andy Larkham was hunched over his desk in the offices of Carpe Diem when a woman appeared in the doorway.

Some time passed before Andy became aware of her. He looked up and licked the tip of his pencil.

'Don't you have a funeral to go to?' she said.

'Oh, my God –' pushing back his chair and springing up. His watch read 2.35 p.m. He unhooked his father's blue suit from behind the door and started to change into it even as she stood there. One arm thrust into his coat, he asked: 'How long to get to Richmond?'

'In this weather? Half an hour – but you'll need to take a cab.'

Andy had reached the door when he remembered the card on his desk. Coming out again: 'Could I borrow twenty quid?'

'And the twenty you borrowed on Friday?'

'Please, Angela. It's Saint Valentine's Day. You know you'll get it back.'

'Do I?'

'First thing tomorrow, I'll go to the bank. Promise,' running a comb through his thick blond hair.

She gave him the money, as she always did, along with a sour look that he ignored, and he hared down three flights of stairs, past Errol in Reception, to the kerb outside.

Raindrops fell on the black-bordered card as he checked the details. The service began at 3 p.m. Chapel 8.

He did not have an umbrella and he stood there getting wetter. A bus splashed by towards Kensington High Street and a line of schoolchildren hurried down into the Underground holding their book bags over their heads.

At last a taxi stopped and a woman got out and Andy climbed in.

'Richmond Crematorium,' he said.

In the taxi from Hammersmith, as all the rain from the sky spattered down on the roof, Andy wondered who else would be there.

His first teacher, Miss Carron? A lovely lady – kind, fair. The next year, Miss Lightfoot had taught him. Young, pretty. He had really taken to her. Unlike the vicious former lacrosse player who followed. 'Stalin' Podhoretz had lasted only a term before a new teacher arrived: a tall, sturdy bear of a man, older than the rest of the staff, with silver curly hair and piercing eyes, and disarmingly passionate about a range of subjects, from Vermeer and Argentine tango to the stories of Flannery O'Connor.

This was Stuart Furnivall. He had taught for the past thirty years in schools all over Europe and, his French wife having died, had retired to Shaftesbury in order to finish a book. He had settled down to write when the school approached him with a plea to help out.

Furnivall was not one of those teachers who moved about with a blackboard attached to their heads. He knew what mattered, what was mysterious to know, and had a talent for making people lean towards him. He was a keen fly-fisherman and rugby player, and within a year was running the cricket first eleven in which Andy played; although in what he really wanted to do he was unfulfilled. He really wanted to be a French scholar.

It was Furnivall who helped Andy back on his feet in the marrow-less days following his father's heart attack.

Furnivall's instruction to Andy went beyond teaching him how to twist a ball through the air and what to read. Almost what Andy liked most about him was that he did not preach or give advice, but by his passion and engagement set off fires in his students; each of his thoughts cast out like his trout line, without effort, and landing at the right distance above your head to make you want to rise up and understand it.

Long after Andy left school, Furnivall's firm example was a drum that resonated to his thoughts. What would Furnivall make of this? How would Furnivall behave in a similar situation? Would Furnivall approve? Although they had not been in touch for months, his death shocked Andy.

Rain was still bucketing down when the taxi pulled up outside the crematorium. Andy thrust Angela's twenty-pound note into the driver's hand and, not waiting for change, ran off between the puddles.

The chapel he sought had a number 8 on a white tile over the door, and was situated in an alley of such chapels. He burst in to find the service well under way.

The excruciating sense of being late yet again.

He stood dripping, his eyes adjusting to the interior. A coffin on a stand. A crucifix above a pleated oatmeal curtain. And empty – but for two people seated in the front pew on the left. A man whose dark grey head from the back seemed of one piece with his suit: fiftyish, with round bi-focal spectacles, who turned and fixed Andy with a what-the-hell-are-you-doing-here look in his eye. And a worn-faced woman in a brown fur coat, who stared straight ahead at the coffin and who – when with a gasp she also turned and looked at him – bore no resemblance to the diminutive Miss Carron, and definitely none to Miss Lightfoot.

The only other person was a short, stout chaplain with a wide florid face and pointed chin who stood beside the coffin, delivering his tribute. That was all.

'. . . It is at moments like this that we pause awhile and reflect and maybe ask ourselves the age-old question – "What is it all about?"'

Andy took off his sopping coat and sat down in the back pew. He checked his watch – twenty past three. Another ten minutes before Furnivall's service ended and the next one commenced. Where was everybody? It could not be the weather. People surely turned up in the rain for funerals.

'. . . The only reasonable answer I can come up with is that the purpose of life lies in the quality of our relationships. How did I get on with my family? How did I get on with my colleagues? How did I get on with my fellow-beings? And if I have faith – how did I get on with my God?'

The chaplain cast a grateful gaze across the empty pews at Andy, who wiped the dirty London rain from his forehead and shifted uneasily in his seat. He realised with a pang that he had no clear picture of his God. The only image bizarrely to break surface was not the long-bearded figure from the Sistine Chapel roof; much less the multi-armed divinity on the wall of his local Indian restaurant. Instead, there came to Andy through the fog of a distant wintry afternoon the outline of a silver-haired man gesticulating from the touchline and calling in a stern voice: 'Your shorts, Larkham. How can you expect to run with them round your knees?'

'. . . If this makes sense, then his life had great purpose, because love, affection and genuine concern undergirded all these relationships.'

That described Stuart Furnivall. But the couple in front? Andy took a harder look. His teacher had once mentioned a bossy sister, with whom he had survived the Blitz in Wimbledon. Perhaps that was her. As for the bespectacled man in the suit, his expression was not mournful.

The chaplain's eyes were anchored on Andy.

9

'. . . Everyone here today is here because one way or another we have been touched and influenced by this gentle and special man.'

Andy had lost contact with Stuart Furnivall once he went to university. The school had been sold. The games field, the ugly Victorian clock tower, the 'san' where Miss Lightfoot dispensed her repellent cough medicine, formed part of an industrial park. All that survived of Barton School was contained in a sporadic newsletter which Miss Lightfoot circulated to alumni. It was she who had supplied Furnivall's address in Cornwall, to which Andy had written two and a half years before, after Angela requested a character reference. Furnivall had replied by return and renewed his invitation for Andy to visit. Ever since learning of Furnivall's death, Andy had beaten himself up for not having taken a day out of his life to drive down to St Buryan. He owed Furnivall a huge amount – not least his job. It was Furnivall who had planted the seed of publishing.

The chaplain burbled on, but Andy was ten years back in the centre of Shaftesbury. A surburban Edwardian stucco with a monkey puzzle outside and a smell of piss that assaulted him as he entered for the last time to say goodbye. The old ladies watching telly on the ground floor were leaky, but Furnivall did not have that trouble. He lived upstairs, a room to himself, with a metal bed and a marble-topped table on which there lay a single volume, spine up, on the riffling hitch. There was a shelf for his CDs and art books; a row of hooks on which to hang his fishing gear, and on the wall a studio photograph of his wife Christine and, beside it, a reproduction of a charcoal sketch by the Delft painter Leonhard Bramer to which Andy's attention inevitably drifted during their tutorials: of a man and a woman lying on a raft, floating on an open sea. He looked at that sketch a lot.

The black silk gown shimmered in the subdued light.

Andy remembered his teacher saying that when Stendhal had died in Rome only three people had come to his funeral.

'And now let us pray and give thanks for the life of . . .'

He groped for a hassock and kneeled. The curtain opened, and there was a humming noise and the coffin began to glide on unseen rollers through the cavity. The sound of the recorded hymn made Andy want to raise his finger and press PAUSE.

'. . . of our brother . . .' consulting the service sheet.

Andy closed his eyes. He would never see Furnivall again unless he closed his eyes. And into his mind, as he tried to find somewhere to rest his elbows, flashed the memory of their first encounter on the river bank below Sutton Mill –

'. . . Christopher Madigan.'

Christopher Madigan? opening his eyes and sitting up.

Andy grabbed his coat, made to go – then realised that even if he did manage to locate the right chapel, it was too late.

He remained seated, considering his options. He didn't want to draw attention to himself. And it was rude, sacrilegious even, to sneak out of a funeral the moment it was drawing to a close. Also, he could tell that Christopher Madigan, whoever he was, needed all the mourners he could get.

The curtain closed and there was another prayer. 'We brought nothing into the world and it is certain we can carry nothing out.'

The chaplain was saying 'Amen' when the grey-haired man stood up and advanced in quick steps past Andy, towards a table against the brick wall near the exit, on which he lay down what looked to be a condolence book, opening it.

Andy was all set to leave, but the woman in the brown fur coat was progressing down the aisle. Shorter than he first thought, with protruding eyes and a deeply grooved, pale face, rather thin. She shot him a stiff look as she went by.

The man stopped her at the door and said something. She shook her head and Andy heard her talking in a lowered voice. Her coat came down to her ankles. She appeared very loose inside that fur. 'He didn't have on his yellow cardigan,' sounding foreign and upset.

The other, while offering comfort, unscrewed a fountain pen and motioned for her to sign the book.

She hovered over it before writing. Then handed back the pen, pushed open the door and, after turning to give Andy another glare, hobbled out.

Andy made to follow, but found his way barred.

'Can I ask you to fill in your name and address?'

'Why?'

'Because I have been asked to keep a record of all who attended the service.'

Andy was on the point of explaining that he did not know the deceased when it struck him how embarrassing this would sound. Besides, what harm resulted from signing one's name in a condolence book? He had never set eyes on Madigan, but he had sat through part of his funeral and that in a sort of way bound them.

He took the pen and scribbled his name in a firm neat hand.

The man looked at him without expression.

'And your address. We need that.'

Andy complied. For some reason, he added as an afterthought: 'I am so sorry.'

He was about to walk out when the door opened and a gust of cold air swept through the chapel. A young woman, collapsing an umbrella and wearing a soft ochre raincoat with its collar up, looked around. White face, shoulder-length black hair and the brownest eyes, Andy thought, that he had ever seen.

She raised a hand to brush the rain from her head and the light caught on a silver bracelet. Her agitated dark eyes pincered him in their gaze. She could have been the age of his sister; a year or two older than him.

'Have I missed it?'

'I'm afraid so,' the grey-haired man said.

She took in the fact and closed her eyes, biting her lip the way one does to stop tears. She shook her head and walked over to sign the condolence book.

The man sprang forward and interposed himself between her and the book, slamming it shut before she could write anything. 'I'm sorry, madam. The service is over.'

Silence.

She gave him a smudged, blurred look, as though the man had been at her face with a rubber. Her chin went from smooth to choppy. 'I need to enter my name.'

But the man stood his ground, pressing the book against his chest. 'I'm sorry, you're too late,' in a rock-firm voice.

She gathered herself and stared at him again. And turned on her heel and marched out.

The rain had eased when Andy stepped outside into a low buzz of conversation. People waiting for the next service assembled in dark-suited clumps beneath dripping umbrellas, none of their faces familiar.

A large lady, her shoulders draped in a black Persian-lamb stole, peered with smallish, impatient eyes above his head: 'Here we are. Chapel 8.'

Andy was still holding the card printed with Furnivall's funeral details. A raindrop had distorted the number. It was Chapel 3 he had wanted, not 8.

The door opened, releasing the sound of a taped organ voluntary, and a pinkish grey face peeped out. 'All right,' the chaplain said, compressing his lips at the cold, 'you can come in now.'

On either side mourners streamed past Andy into the chapel. Until two people remained sheltering under the overhanging roof, studying the rain that ripped from the clouds.

The woman in the fur coat had become less imposing outside. Something about the way she held herself caused Andy to think that she knew the younger woman, who looked more irritated with herself than with the weather or with the incident that he had witnessed inside. They continued, all three of them, staring up at the sky, the colour of scattered ashes, until the worn-faced woman cleared her throat and said in a surprisingly tentative, kind voice to the younger: 'I have something I need to tell you.'

'There's nothing I wish to hear.'

The sharpness of the reply made Andy turn.

The older woman looked defenceless. Her wrinkled face reflected an indescribable sadness. In that moment, Andy saw an openness in her that he warmed to.

Before she could say another word, the man in the grey suit emerged and stood behind them, still tightly clutching his condolence book. The young woman stepped forward at his appearance. Cold wet marble grated beneath her heels.

A bottle-green Volkswagen Beetle was parked on the grass. She shook open her umbrella and walked towards it.

Andy looked at his watch. 3.35 p.m. He considered searching for Chapel 3. But chapels spread out to the north and south of him, one chapel identical to the next. Even if he did find the right one, chances were that another service was getting under way.

Further, he had no idea how he was going to get back into London. He had spent all he had on the cab fare.

She had reached her car and was opening the driver's door.

Before he knew it, he was calling out: 'Where are you heading?'

She turned and two dark eyes stared back at him beneath her umbrella from which the rain flashed up like silver filings flying off a drill.

'Holland Park any good for you?'

She did not introduce herself and nor did he.

They had passed Shepherd's Bush roundabout when Andy felt that he ought to say something.

'That was my second funeral.'

'I'm surprised he bothered to have a funeral.'

'It's important to have some sort of ritual.'

'The only ritual he liked was torture,' she said.

'You don't sound as though you were very fond of him,' unable to work out her connection to Christopher Madigan.

'Fond of him?' she snorted. 'No one was fond of him, except possibly you.' Her eyes flashed. There was something derisive in them.

'Me? Yes. Well – you can drop me here.' They were approaching the bottom of Ladbroke Grove.

He could tell that she was tempted to halt the car right there, outside Lidgate's butcher. But good manners must have kicked in.

'Where do you live?' glancing at him sideways.

Seen from a different angle, her face was more striking than before. Not beautiful, like Sophie. But definitely she had a magnetism.

'Hortense Avenue.'

'I'll drive you.'

'Really, you don't have to,' feeling her eyes on his father's faded blue suit.

'I know.'

She showed no further interest in him and said nothing for the rest of the journey. When he climbed out and looked back at her through the passenger window, she was yawning.

'Thanks for the lift,' he said.

'No trouble.'

And that was that. When he raised his hand, she looked straight through him as if he did not exist.

'Bye, then.'

Her car drove away. Until it was just a motionless speck among the other specks of rush-hour traffic on a rainy London afternoon in February. It had begun to rain again.

2

THE RAIN HAD STOPPED by the time Andy opened the front door to his building, shortly after seven o'clock, on his way to pick up Sophie. He was taking her to the Portuguese restaurant on Portobello Road where they had eaten the night they first met.

It was his best friend David who had introduced them at Ivo's Christmas party.

'Andy, meet Sophie Sobko.'

She stood there, shy and heaven-sent. She might have been the only female in the Polish Club that night.

The dryness that spread over his lips.

She had the whole room's attention. Green eyes, wavy hair the colour of wood shavings, a bearing that said *I am probably the best-looking woman you have ever seen.*

She was wearing a tight-fitting, blue-black dress. Andy asked her a question and she did not answer. He asked her another question. This time her eyes jarred with interest.

'Grand Forks,' in a broad North American accent. 'You wouldn't know it.'

'Grand Forks?' he repeated, and felt sad. And saw his father at the airport, his face against a thick window pane, his ointment leaving a mark on the glass, calling to a glamorous woman who did not hear, then racing around the barrier to embrace her while Andy stood there, waiting for the luggage. If he had never suspected before, he understood in that moment.

'I think I went to Grand Forks once on my holidays,' his voice slightly breathless as his father's had been.

Her eyes came alive, transforming her nervous, haughty face.

'No way! You are kidding me.' It was a sign for her to forget – instantly – everyone in the room but Andy.

David said: 'Come and meet Ivo.'

But Sophie was not listening. Not to him.

'Did you ever eat Easter brunch at the Westward Ho?'

'The Westward Ho?' The only *Westward Ho!* Andy knew was a novel by Charles Kingsley.

'You know, the hotel with the pool shaped like a cowboy boot,' and he could hear it in her voice, light and airy like pine. A homesickness for a shared memory.

'The pool shaped like a cowboy boot . . .'

'Noo! Don't tell me. You do remember!'

What he remembered was a gridded town of bungalows exactly the same, the streets like open cuts into the sunset, where the other boys, all shovel-chinned and baseball-shaped, made fun of his voice and the way he skated.

'Know what?' she said, biting a cushiony bottom lip. 'They tore it down.'

'They didn't! Bastards,' this time with emotion.

Something about his response must have appealed to her. She held her lips open a little. Above her smile, two huge green eyes were staring.

Since her arrival in London four months previously, Sophie Sobko had not met a soul who had been to Grand Forks. Let alone one who knew the Westward Ho. As it turned out, Andy had not been to Grand Forks. 'No, that was Grand Falls,' sighed his mother. By then, it was too late, he and Sophie were unofficially engaged, and Andy had to beg his mother not to tell Sophie the truth, which was that he had mistaken her birthplace for a remote village in Newfoundland, where his father had taken him on their last holiday, that is to say in another country altogether – not even close.

Andy's choice of fiancée did not go down well with his mother or sister, but it was not Sophie's fault that she came from the same hemisphere as the person his father had run off with.

Sophie's maisonette in Chesterton Road was a ten-minute walk from the first-floor flat that Andy rented in Hortense Avenue. He pressed the top-floor bell and waited for her to let him in, instead of which she came out and closed the door behind her.

'Hi.'

Her face hurried across the space between them to kiss him. 'Hi.'

She was wearing her chunky-knit chinchilla coat belted at the waist and, underneath, an orange cashmere jersey that he had not seen before.

'You look lovely,' he praised. 'Sorry I'm late.'

Why the faculty of running late was so highly developed in Andy, he was unsure. It was not something he was proud of. It was systemic – from his tenth year on.

'I'd never make a good prince,' he said.

Sophie did not answer.

16

The cold wind gusting off Ladbroke Grove flushed her cheeks as they set off for the Camões.

The restaurant was emptier even than the chapel in Richmond. On this Saint Valentine's Day evening, all those who normally ate there must have been sunning their guts in Praia da Rocha, save for a brown-haired young man four empty tables away with a book propped in front of him. When he saw them enter he looked up, and returned to what he was reading.

It was good to be inside, away from that snapping wind.

'Oh, I've been looking forward to this all day,' said Andy, rubbing his hands as Rui limped across with two menus.

Andy sought Sophie's eyes and his heart ballooned. He forgot the cock-up at Richmond. In that moment, everything shone with a pure enchanted glow; nothing could flourish except their love and the expanding sense of himself about to discuss their honeymoon in Cintra. The man across the room had his book. Andy had Sophie.

After Rui had taken their orders, Sophie said: 'Did you get your pay rise?'

'No,' Andy said. 'Not yet.' He worked in a small publishing house that specialised in self-help books: living with loss, grief, how to get through pregnancy. Plus a whole lot of syndromes that he had grown too jaded to joke about. 'Goodman said he'd sleep on it and get back to me tomorrow – but it's looking good. He gave me the afternoon off.'

'I'm sure you'll get it this time,' she nodded, not catching his eye.

'Even if I don't,' he smiled, 'we'll survive somehow.'

At the thought of their life together, their shared bed, Andy felt a sexual tightening. He brushed her knees with his, and though she did not move her legs away she did not respond either. He started to feel, not nervous exactly, but as if he had failed Sophie as well as Stuart Furnivall. He wanted her to know that she could rely on him. She was making the money right now, but time would come when the photo-shoots and freebies would dry up – and it would not matter. By then he stood to be an established publisher, running his own list. He would look after her. She would never fade in his eyes.

'Conrad fixed the front door yet?' she asked, although Andy had the idea that it was of no interest to her whether his landlord had repaired the lock. Neither did she appear to notice that he was wearing the Emilio Zegna jacket that she had given him on their first anniversary.

'Not yet,' he said. 'Jerome's sorting it out.' A drug-dealer who lived on the ground floor.

'What about the fridge?'

'An engineer's coming on Wednesday.'

She wrinkled her nose and stared straight ahead. She sometimes had that see-nothing look on the catwalk.

'Andrew?'

'Yes.'

Her cheeks were no longer pink. She was pale and had an odd expression.

'You know I love you.'

Her voice.

'I just wanted to let you know,' she said quickly.

But he himself was too much in love with the moment at hand to see that something vital was being left unsaid.

Rui limped from the kitchen carrying their main course, grilled cod for Andy, chicken *milanesa* for her.

'*Bom apetite*,' he said sombrely and left. The Gipsy Kings were playing and then they stopped and it was fado moaning from the loudspeakers.

Sophie was studying the cod on his plate. She opened her mouth and closed it.

'I don't know about you,' Andy smiled, 'but fado makes my toes curl up like a rose leaf.'

She put her knife and fork neatly together, gave a quick look round, and said: 'Sweet, I'm not coming home with you.'

He felt a moustache of heat form. 'Why, you have something to do?'

She stared in an abject way at her broccoli. But something had shifted inside her. Something very simple and important that explained her forgiveness-seeking smile. 'Andrew, you're far too nice for me.'

On hearing those words, Andy sat very still. 'Oh, I can be nasty if you like. How nasty would you like me to be?' But he felt a chilling shame spread over his skin, settling in a stone weight at the top of his knees.

'I don't want you to be nasty.'

'I'm too poor for you,' he tried growling.

'You are not too poor for me.'

She opened the menu. There was a cord running down the middle of it like the string on his mother's spectacles. Sophie plucked it in a desultory way, as though she intended to break into hoarse, aching song with Amália.

'Andrew, I've met someone.'

It was the opposite of sprouting wings. The sense of something caving in; of his insides – his beams and rafters – crumbling.

He sat even stiller. Persuading himself that there was an appropriate reply and if he waited a few heartbeats longer the right words would click into place. But nothing came. It was what he feared most. He was falling. Tumbling away from himself. Disappearing.

'Oh,' he said. And then again: 'Oh.' And then, to protect himself by saying the most reasonable thing he could think of saying: 'Well, if you love someone you have to let them go.'

'Which was a pretty pathetic response,' he would admit afterwards to David. 'No wonder she preferred to be with someone else. I mean, how sexually attractive is reasonable – or Jonathan Livingston Seagull for that matter? The odd thing was, I didn't feel angry. I was unsure what I felt, but anger was not part of it.' He was only aware that the room had altered shape; the photos of Cintra looked embarrassed; the sprig of lavender had turned away in disappointment. Even the invisible guitarist was having trouble playing fado, he was so busy straining to listen.

As was the young man at the table behind.

For some reason – and this was precise in his mind – Andy was becoming very aware of him. He had the impression that he was sliding backwards down a tube and the light was getting smaller and smaller, until all he could see was this man's face. So he resorted to a trick he had developed as a boy whenever he was unhappy, of trying to crawl out of himself and imagine he was Someone Else. He thought: *If I put myself for a moment into that person's shoes and force myself to believe that all this has been a joke and Sophie has been pulling my leg, maybe everything she's been saying will erase itself.* So that is what he did. He concentrated very hard on the only other person in the restaurant.

The young man wore a burgundy V-neck jersey and striped blue shirt, open at the collar, and was wiry and compact and had dark, sly features that he had not bothered to shave.

He was leaning forward, but his fierce involvement in his book was not convincing.

Sophie was saying in a small voice: 'It's not that I don't love you. But I'm fond of Richard, too. I haven't been able to concentrate on anything since I met him.'

Andy flushed. He wiped his face with a napkin. 'Who is he?' he heard himself say.

'He works at Lehman Brothers. I don't know how it happened. But it's unstoppable,' her voice rising to a defiant falsetto before it became small again. 'Do you hate me? I haven't been to bed with him. Say something.' Her red lip trembling.

He pushed his plate away. 'I'll get the bill. Or do you want pudding?'

'No, no, let me pay.'

He was opening his wallet.

'Andrew, put that away,' she said miserably, and looked for a moment as if the music had tangled itself in her hair. 'I can claim it.'

He waved his card at Rui. 'No, I invited you.'

By the time Rui came back with the bill to sign, Andy's eyes were too glazed to read the amount. The waiter stood there, a reassuring presence, as Andy worked out what to tip him. It had nothing to do with Rui, any of this.

The lines on Rui's face were expressive of the knottier chords of fado. He gave Andy a sympathetic look and tapped his Mastercard. 'Do you 'ave another one, *senhor*? This does not function.'

'It's the metallic strip. It's probably just been demagnetised . . . Try again.'

Not looking at Andy, Sophie said: 'Here, take mine.'

A moment later, she accepted Rui's pen and with a veteran's scratch signed her name, unreadable as a signature, but as credit-rich indisputable.

Andy pushed back his chair and stood up, waiting for Sophie to leave with him. He had not yet accustomed himself to the idea that they were not going to be together till parted by death. But it was turning into one of those evenings when insult to injury kept happening.

'Hey, where are you going?'

She had risen from her chair and was walking over to the other person. The angle at which she leaned over him was unusually solicitous and the man looking up at her seemed younger, his nervous unshaven face now filled with everything that Andy had been feeling when he walked into the Camões – joy, love, hope.

'Have you managed to eat anything? You must be hungry?' and she laughed in a thrilling way before turning back to Andy. That silver libidinous blade of a voice had never sounded so seductive, so charged with sexual possibility. 'This is Richard,' sticking it in to the hilt. 'I asked him to be here in case things got ugly. I should have known you'd be a gentleman.'

'Hi,' said Andy.

'Hi,' said Richard, who Andy could see was stingingly good-looking.

As for Sophie, she stood so close to Richard that there was no room for Andy to crawl between them. He wanted to beg. To make her feel sorry for him. He wanted pity to win her back. But pity does not win anyone the kind of friend he wanted Sophie to be. The abyss had opened. He was never going to cross it by wrapping his arms around her legs, his face against her knees, pleading.

'Well, I'd better be going,' he said after a pause. A gut-shot dog smiling to keep the tears in. And left them there, looking into each other's eyes with no sign of shame. Absolutely no sign at all. Just the lazy, besotted expression indicative of lovers the world over. And relief that he was letting them get away with it so easily.

'*Boa noite, senhor,*' Rui said, pulling open the door.

3

THE OFFICES OF CARPE DIEM occupied the third floor of a converted warehouse on the west side of Hammersmith roundabout, near the entrance to the Underground. It was a much reduced person who pushed through the revolving doors from the street next morning.

Andy walked past the meaty Caribbean presence of Errol like a calf with the staggers, plodded up the stairs and was barely through the door when Angela strode out of Goodman's office.

'You're late,' she pointed out, as she organised herself into her chair.

A curt nasal voice sounded from within. 'Who is it?'

'Only Andrew.' Who was not greeting her with the normal, 'Hi, Angela, how was your dowsing class?'

In a lowered voice: 'He's been waiting *an hour* to speak with you.' Then looked up. At the sight of his reddened eyes and his blond hair stuck out, like something torn up by the roots, she gasped.

'My God, what's happened to you?'

He felt a martyred expression enter his face. 'My fiancée just dumped me.'

'Oh, Andrew . . .' She stared at him, and then, abashed, down at the manuscript that she held. 'Poor you.'

'I'll get over it,' he muttered bravely, though unbelieving.

He had always found it a leap of the imagination too big to understand how people could die from love. Now he knew.

'Hey, Andrew?' came his master's tetchy voice. 'Have you a moment?'

'I'll bring you a coffee,' she promised.

A large man in green braces and with a rubicund face suddenly appeared, a sheet of paper in his hand and a Magic Marker clamped cigar-like at the corner of his mouth. He had a sizeable paunch and close-cropped dark hair, and the buckles of his braces stood out like gold teeth.

'Come through, come through,' in a voice tinged with the veldt, and shut the door behind them.

'Please sit.'

Andy dumped his satchel on the floor and sat down and after a while looked up.

On brown-painted walls hung framed homilies illustrating the benign rules of Goodman's publishing house. *If in doubt, smile. If you follow your bliss, your bliss will meet you half way.*

The daddy of them all was contained in an outsized frame behind Goodman's desk. Andy had stared at it on the morning of his first interview, two and a half years ago.

On that occasion, Goodman, pleased to note the direction of his gaze, had swivelled in his high-backed leatherette chair and together they read the message. Andy had the idea that Goodman was keen for him to understand how it constituted the doubly-distilled essence of Carpe Diem. Its motto, as it were.

Be assured that you are a grain of God who sprouted up in human form at the precise moment you were meant to. And as such you're entitled to a life filled with joy, love and happiness.

Swivelling back, Goodman had looked at him companionably. 'A life filled with joy, love and happiness . . .'

Goodman came from New Bethesda in the Karoo and he saw in Andy – at that first interview – an impeccable provincial like himself. Suspicious of Oxbridge graduates – 'Horace-quoting misfits,' he called them – who would be aware that a job with Carpe Diem was not a thing to be sighed for, he had reacted positively to the CV that Angela had placed on his desk and from which, from time to time, he refreshed himself, being impressed with Andy's three-year stint in a second-hand bookshop in Abergavenny and, before that, his degree in modern languages at a university in the south-west. His stomach lapped onto the desk and his braces gave his thumbs something to pluck at while he flashed Andy an appreciative look.

'I have found it a sensible policy over the years to treat all people who come to work at Carpe Diem as grains of God – including Angela,' he smiled. 'That goes for our readers, too. However, I ought to emphasise that being a grain of God is not the same as being a Christian. Not at all.' He leaned forward and looked again at Andy's CV. 'It says here that your ambition is one day to run a general list. What do you mean by *a general list*?'

'Oh, you know – fiction, poetry, biography, history, fishing, maybe even some religion,' Andy said brightly.

'Maybe even some religion,' Goodman repeated in a dubious voice. He picked up a paper clip and dropped it back into the abalone shell from which it had escaped onto his desk. 'May I ask, Andrew, if you're a Christian?'

'Not a practising one.'

His answer had seemed to relax Goodman. He sat back and thrust a thumb under each loose green brace and rotated them. 'You see, Andy, the way I see it, the self-help culture is the precise *opposite* of the Christian culture.'

To Goodman, the science of self-help was to the twenty-first century what geology was to the nineteenth and astronomy to the seventeenth, the battleground of old and new faiths. His governing principle towards anyone tempted to pick up a title with the Carpe Diem logo on the spine – a slumbering pussycat adroitly curled into the shape of a human heart – was to promise a contemporary model of salvation and a rescue from phobias and fears.

'If the Christian message is to lose yourself in the Other, the self-help ethos is about putting yourself first. Let me simplify. Here at Carpe Diem, we give our readers permission to be selfish sluts!'

Two and a half years listening to his pontificating, and Andy was aware that his boss did not extend the same permission to his staff. When Andy let slip to Angela that he intended to ask for a salary rise or else his girlfriend wouldn't marry him, her cold grey eyes had looked at him in an ominous way. 'This is exactly how long the others lasted, until they demanded a pay rise.' Money was never mentioned spontaneously at Carpe Diem.

When at the end of that first interview Andy had asked what salary he might expect, Goodman had squeaked forward in his chair, evaluating him. 'Tell me – Andrew, isn't it? – have you a private income?'

'Heck, no,' and he burst out laughing. Andy did not know anyone with a private income. But neither did he realise that the man seated opposite was a chiseller who would grind you down to the last penny on a deal. Andy had only to discuss an author's advance for Goodman to brush away his hand in front of his mouth like a priest making a sign at a curse. 'Journalists have to think of the headline, Andrew. Publishers, of the bottom line.' Andy came to believe that Goodman almost expected his authors to work for free. In Goodman's opinion they were serving in the ministry of books. Those who wanted to be paid were not the real thing.

A melancholy expression had passed over Goodman's mottled face after Andy revealed that he did not have a private income. He sighed, the spirit of his conviviality already watered with his concern for the bottom line, and said very well, seeing as Andy had no previous experience he would not be able to hire him as an assistant editor, but what about a position as an editorial assistant? A probationary period of six months to see how things worked out. And while he was not able to offer princely terms in the way of – his word – 'emolument', what he *could* offer was precious experience at the coalface of the publishing industry, something not to be sniffed at in present circumstances – publishers, like farmers, existing in a permanent state of never knowing things to be so bad.

'And what could be better than that?'

Andy took up Goodman's offer. £15,000 a year was small money in London in the first decade of the twenty-first century, but he reasoned that it was his first proper job. It was a start. He was a neophyte. At last.

While Carpe Diem was not everything Andy had hoped for, there was the smell of cherry blossom in the air and there were towering oak trees all along Hammersmith Grove where Goodman's publishing house, with its character as purveyor of dreams to those in desperation, had its offices.

The principal duty of an editorial assistant was to stick books into brown Jiffy Bags and mail them to a list, provided by Goodman, of journalists he knew. Once, Andy made the mistake of sending a copy of *How To Make A Million By The Time You're 30* to a literary editor he had met at a party who had been vaguely encouraging of his ambitions. Goodman had intercepted the package with a streak of alacrity that Andy had not previously suspected in him. 'Utter waste of time. No one reviews our books. He'll take it straight down to Obelisk's.' Obelisk's – Andy learned from Angela, Carpe Diem's only other employee – was a bookshop in Vauxhall where critics traded in their review copies for cash. 'And next time,' Goodman said, carefully peeling off a stamp, 'be sure to send it second class.'

After he had worked five months at Carpe Diem, Andy was promoted. Goodman was able to manipulate his face in such a way as to communicate the news that to be appointed a junior editor on the Guru List – Goodman would remain senior editor – was to have arrived at a significant rung on the ladder of Andy's ambition to run a general list: to settle the point, he was prepared to raise Andy's salary to £18,000.

'Let me tell you something in confidence about gurus, Andrew. One day you may apply the same rule to novelists, poets, biographers, maybe even to fishermen. Their most remarkable characteristic is that they benefit least from their own wisdom.'

Goodman sketched out for Andy one of the lists that he was prone to making. It made for sober reflection:

—Khalil Gibran (*The Prophet*), died of cirrhosis. 'A sponging and randy bore who couldn't open his mouth without telling a lie. He lied even about whether he liked to eat lobster.' Lobster, so Andy had gathered over his one and only lunch with Goodman at Wheeler's, being one of Goodman's favourite dishes.

—Jim Fixx (*The Complete Book of Running*), died while jogging, of massive heart attack.

—Dr Robert Atkins (*The Atkins Diet*), 258 lbs at time of death, clinically obese.

—Morgan Scott Peck (*The Road Less Travelled*), womanising, alcoholic chain-smoker, unable to relate to his wives or children.

'You are looking,' Goodman said in conclusion, 'at the most reliable bunch of losers that I have encountered in twenty-five years in publishing. And if you come across another, please tell me. As you'll discover in your new incarnation,' he said expansively, 'all human problems have a family resemblance.'

Goodman's problems too, it turned out.

Success in the self-help world, in which he was regarded as primus inter pares, had failed to bring Goodman the corresponding personal contentment that Andy had fully imagined himself to be on course to enjoy with Sophie. Goodman's unfulfilled desire, according to Angela, was to have a child. 'You want to know what makes him tick? Well, that's it.' But fatherhood had eluded him, despite a brace of marriages – to two loud, talkative women, both of whom had ended up in Vancouver – 'like every other lost soul I know'. His failure had had the effect of sapping his confidence with the opposite sex. These days when women pressed themselves on him, he talked in an increasingly exaggerated South African accent about his bad back and lack of money and watched the trails of dust as they drove away. But Goodman's childlessness was not a topic to be discussed, this after reaching a melancholy acceptance that the cause lay with him. Whatever illusions he peddled to others, he lacked none about himself. 'I abide by this rule,' he disclosed to Andy during their lunch at Wheeler's. 'If there's more than one thing wrong with you, it's in your head.'

What went on in Goodman's head was sometimes a great deal less easy to read than his books.

After five minutes, Goodman lifted his red face and said: 'How was your afternoon off? A funeral, wasn't it? No one close, I hope.' His eyes darkened as he narrowed them and Andy wondered if Goodman feared the sinister competition of Christianity.

'An old teacher of mine.' But what he was thinking was that his life was over, too, and nothing remained but cold and rain as on every other February morning in London, always.

Goodman rubbed his nose. 'One's teachers can be closer to us than our parents,' with the seriousness of someone contemplating whether there might not be the germ of a self-help book there.

He picked up the A4 sheet that Angela had laid on his desk and scratched his cheek. 'As for your other request,' he went on, 'nobody likes to reward success more than I do. But let's look at the figures, shall we?'

His eyes absorbed the list in his hand. He might have been a foreman of the jury charged with reading out a unanimous verdict of guilt.

'Your last title was the Gladys Peak?'

Andy nodded.

'Here we are. *1001 Ways To Reach Nirvana*,' Goodman said sepulchrally. 'Only 284 sales through the till.'

Before Andy could protest that it had not been his idea to commission Gladys Peak, an auctioneer's widow who lived near Goodman's weekend retreat in Fordingbridge, Goodman allowed himself a sharp intake of breath and looked up. 'Not to labour a point, Andrew, could you explain why I should pay you a penny extra at a time when I am losing a substantial sum *because* of you?'

Leaning back: 'Now had you published a bestseller like *How To Make A Million By The Time You're 30* . . . But 284 sales . . .' He put down the list and folded it along with Andy's dashed hopes into his in-tray. 'No, Andrew, not good. As I explained at the outset, what you are gaining here at Carpe Diem is experience – and what is better than that? Let's pluck a leaf from what we tell our readers. "Life isn't about getting, it's about learning to let go," eh?'

That was Goodman all over: when you asked him for a salary increase, he asked you to think of the readers.

In maintaining his flexible policy of despising his readers in the flesh, but also, when it suited him, of appealing to them in the abstract as grains of God, Goodman admitted no contradiction. Nor was anyone at Carpe Diem likely to contradict him. His readers had been there longer than Angela, who had less time for them even than Goodman. Andy could not forget the low throaty hiss that issued from Angela's lips when he asked if she could recommend to his sister the book he was stuffing into a Jiffy Bag. Angela had the disenchanted look in her eye of a black woman from Benin who was wondering why, if voodoo was so powerful, her family had been slaves for 400 years. 'Pah! If self-help books really worked, there wouldn't be so many miserable people.'

But the door was opening and Goodman's arm was on his shoulder and he was giving Andy his pet smile again. 'Perhaps if your next book makes a splash we can return to the subject. What are you working on, by the way?'

Andy stared at him vacantly. How would he feel when he got home and no one came up the stairs?

'Ruth Challis,' he mumbled.

'Ah, yes. I need corrected proofs by the end of today. Is that feasible?'

'Yes . . . I think so.'

'Good. That's all I want to know. You've got a lot on your plate. To which I regret I have added more. I've asked Angela to give you Enid Tansley's new manuscript. Oh, and another thing.'

Andy waited.

'You might get to work earlier in future . . .'

And then Andy was out of the door, leaving Goodman pulling down the tie from the hook on the other side of it and grabbing his jacket and overcoat from the sofa, an infallible sign that he would shortly be on his way to a long lunch at Wheeler's.

Andy's father, a pilot, would say that when an object or a situation is staring you in the face you do not always see it straight away. 'It's to do with the optic nerve being right at the back. You have to keep scanning the sky. If anything's dead ahead, you'll lose it for a sec – until it hits you.' When it came to Sophie and also to Rian Goodman, Andy had not had any peripheral vision.

He returned to his office, tripped on a drawer that stuck out, and knocked over the mug that Angela had placed on his desk. He hunted about for something to soak up the coffee that was seeping into Ruth Challis's proofs. But the weight in his chest made it difficult to focus.

The coffee was dripping onto the floor. He saw his future. Everything that from now on went wrong, he would blame on the fact that Sophie was no longer in his life.

He grabbed a spare roll from the toilet and began mopping.

The damp pages were the work of Carpe Diem's leading manic depression guru. Goodman, untroubled by the necessity of having to read it, regarded her prose as 'highly enriched uranium'. The job of making the word of Ruth Challis flesh, of checking her spelling, facts and grammar, was Andy's, like so much else at Carpe Diem. The editorial, foreign rights and contract department – Angela looked at it every time she remembered to bring Andy a cup of her tongue-burning latte, a powdered liquid that bore no relation, either through the father's side or the mother's, to a coffee bean. Another example of Goodman's miserliness.

Ruth Challis's soggy proofs brought to mind the wet newspapers that Andy's mother liked to plant her bulbs in. The coffee had stained the near-transparent paper, and print showed through from the pages beneath. Lines composed of words the wrong way round competed to be read with the lines that they obscured. The effect, heightened by granular streaks and brown bubbles, was of something in torment.

Andy peeled off a page and it tore. He stacked the first half of the manuscript on the radiator to dry and began at Chapter Five, 'Giving Up Your Personal History'.

The first line was vintage Challis: 'Refuse to allow any thoughts based on your past to defile you.'

Glumly, he checked the paragraph against the original typescript. Then he took a sharp pencil and crossed out the l in 'defile' and made it 'define'.

Perhaps his mother and sister had been right. There never had been a future with Sophie. Perhaps he had only fallen for her because she reminded him of someone else.

On his return from his summer holiday in Canada when he was ten, Andy told his sister that he had seen their father embracing a strange woman at the airport.

'What was her name?'

'Lynn.'

'What does she do?'

'She works as a pilot in Moose Jaw.'

His sister looked at him. 'You're making this up.'

He could see that the woman's laugh made his father happy.

'What did she look like?' pressed his sister a year later, by which time their father was living in Canada.

'I've told you.'

'Again.'

Andy had not formed a proper impression. Only from the back. Her amber hair gathered in a tight ponytail. Oval face. And that laugh.

'She wasn't in uniform. She had a blue turtleneck and a black shawl over her arm.'

But he remembered where he stood, just as he remembered the position of certain sentences on a page. Near the conveyor belt, watching the mauve knapsack that his mother had bought in Salisbury shudder towards him. While opposite, in dislocated words that he would not be able to relate to himself or make sense of until years later, in the Polish Club, they talked.

'There's my bag,' unlocking their eyes.

'I'd better go,' muttered his father.

She touched the edge of his mouth, moved away.

When Andy asked him who she was, this woman whose wrists had encircled his neck, who caused him to look back at her so yearningly, his father took him by the arm and hugged him close, crushing the present from his wife, some pressed snowdrops from their garden wrapped in blue tissue paper in Andy's shirt pocket, and said, the first time he had spoken to him as a grown-up, 'Someone I used to fly with.' He wore a dark green polo shirt and striped socks and was quite out of breath.

Someone he used to fly with!

He grabbed Andy's knapsack and they went out to the car. A tube of cream on the front seat and a packet of dried pears, which he offered to Andy as he rubbed something into the corners of his mouth. His face had a grey boiled look. But his eyes were abnormally clear.

Shortly after five o'clock, Andy stretched two thick rubber bands around *Learn To Make Your Black Dog Your Guide-Dog* and carried it down the corridor to Goodman's office.

In the slumber produced by his reorientating lunch at Wheeler's, the owner of Carpe Diem lay across one of his sofas, snoring.

'Anything urgent?' asked Angela, appearing at the door and impeding Andy's view of a lobster-fattened waistline.

'He wanted this as soon as possible.'

Angela, irritated and yet partly calmed by Goodman's snoring, took the manuscript. 'I'll see he gets it.' Then looked at Andy in a curious way. 'What?'

Only now did it hit him. How would he get through the next couple of months? He had needed the extra income to settle a sheaf of bills, not to mention the rent outstanding on his flat.

'I don't know how to say this —'

In a shredding voice: 'You need to borrow more money.'

4

ANDY DID NOT RECALL much about the rest of that week. Goodman's refusal to raise his salary was of a part with the mess that his life had become since missing Furnivall's funeral.

He did not eat. He could not sleep. Pimples sprouted on his chin.

Everything was unbearable: the office; the instant coffee that Angela brought him out of a sense of pity; the lock on the front door that did not work – he pictured his landlord's response: 'I call it: I'm keeping the lock buggered like that until you've paid me'; and once he did manage to gain entrance, his flat strewn with envelopes – each stuffed with another rejection from a publisher or crimson reminder from London Electricity or refusal from the bank to extend his overdraft; the fridge that needed repairing; the sound of Marilyn Manson thudding down from the floor above; his bedroom with the chunks of plaster missing from the ceiling.

Then there were the holes in his vocabulary. He fell asleep counting the words Sophie had ruined for him, that he would never be able to use. *Sophie, model, chicken milanesa, Cintra, love, marriage, America, Richard, forever* . . . all words from now on that he would not be able to read or hear without a stab.

On the Wednesday after Furnivall's funeral, the telephone rang in his office and he seized it.

She used to ring about now, to brief him on her plans for the day. He saw her sitting on the arm of her outsized Conran sofa, her shoulder strap down and the blonde puff of hair between her legs . . . His hands never again to touch her.

It was Miss Lightfoot, wanting to know why he was not at Furnivall's funeral. 'Everyone was there.'

He felt an enormous sense of isolation. 'Something came up at work,' he mumbled.

Patricia Lightfoot commiserated: Stuart would have understood. She had visited him in the hospice in Barnes where he spent his final weeks. He had spoken warmly of Andy, his interesting work. 'He was waiting to hear back from you. He had great faith in your judgment. He was too modest to say so, but I think he hoped you would publish his book.' She described their last outing together, to a one-day cricket match at Lords. It was as much as she could do to walk Furnivall arm in arm from the ground to the taxi. 'I have to confess I cried when I heard that he had died.'

After she rang off, Andy sat staring at his desk. He had no idea what to do. His eyes fell in a blurred gaze to a pile of pages that he had thrust to the back.

Another moment before he realised that the letters he had been staring at spelled MISSING MONTAIGNE.

The manuscript, bound with a ginger rubber band, had arrived at Carpe Diem a week before Christmas, along with the covering letter that Andy now slipped out and unfolded. He felt a tightening, a sudden rawness in his gut as he began to reread the even-spaced handwriting.

> *Dear Andy,*
>
> *I won't beat about the bush. I've been suffering these past three years from a terminal illness and I learned long ago that the best resource against pain is diversion.*
>
> *Don't groan. I have – enfin! – completed the project that I embarked on in my twenties. This book (really an autobiographical essay) is my excuse to get in touch. It's a dreadful intrusion even to ask this, but might you possibly consider taking a look at it for me? I'm just so baffled as to what to do, and an impartial, clear, not to say distinguished set of eyes would be invaluable. But I'm sorry even to ask, both when it may be that the book is dreadful and unreadable, and when I know that you are deep in your own work as I write this. So please don't for a minute hesitate to tell me this is not the time. I'll totally understand.*

There followed a few paragraphs in which Furnivall outlined his project. Andy skipped to the end.

> *If, as I suspect, the result doesn't suit today's prurient climate, don't wrinkle your forehead over it – as the Great Man said: 'the worst writings of my time have won the greatest applause.' I've been through enough hedges. I fully expect to hear from you that* <u>Missing Montaigne</u> *may be of some interest to Montaigne scholars,*

but other than a brief reference to penis size (small) it will be of little interest to anyone else.

With fond regards,
Stuart
PS Cornwall is not so far from London – five hours by car.

It had taken the briefest glance to realise that *Missing Montaigne* was 'low box office', in Goodman's phrase, and unsuitable for Carpe Diem. Andy had not progressed much farther than the first page, which was riddled with quotes and schoolmasterly in a way that Furnivall never had been. Andy had put the manuscript aside to read later. But it was like accepting an invitation ahead: he hoped in some miraculous way it would go away. He had still not replied when Miss Lightfoot wrote with news of Furnivall's death. At least Furnivall never knew that his book was unpublishable. He died with it still a possibility.

Down the corridor a door opened and a paper lifted on his desk.

Andy was reaching the end of the first chapter when Goodman came in.

'My commiserations about your girlfriend.'

'Angela told you?'

'Don't worry,' Goodman said. 'As Thomas Moore put it better than I: "You have the opportunity to be close to another in a more profound way." How's the Enid Tansley, by the way?'

'Sorry?'

Goodman gave him a reproachful look. 'The Tansley, the Tansley,' clicking his fingers. 'Didn't Angela give it to you?'

'Oh, yes . . .'

'Well, have you finished?'

'Nearly.'

Goodman exploded. '"Nearly" pulls no man off his horse, Andrew. I need it marked up PDQ,' and glowered at his desk. 'Is that it?'

'Not exactly.'

'What is it – *exactly*?' Suspicion told him that Andy was being ideologically lax.

'Just something I was considering,' his voice more defiant than he meant, though not as defiant as he felt.

Goodman sprang forward, seizing what Andy had read and leafing impatiently back through it until he reached the title page.

'*Missing Montaigne* . . .' his mind working quickly. 'What's it about?'

'A French philosopher.'

Goodman pondered. 'Modern, is he?'

'Sixteenth-century.'

32

'What's his shtick?'

'He believed that in each one of us can be found the whole pattern of human nature.'

'Did he now?'

'He also believed that the state of the world is created by the individual actions of each of us.'

A strange look came into Goodman's face. Grizzly bears have this look just before they swipe off your head. Ever so slowly, he put down the pages. The sharp blast of his disapproval, the wind that blows over the Karoo, reached Andy across his desk. 'I think not, Andrew. We don't want another fiasco, *merci beaucoup*. I shall need the Tansley by Friday afternoon, absolute latest,' and he left the room.

The Valentino Alfresco Sex Guide by Enid Tansley was the latest addition to Carpe Diem's Valentino list, the titles of which were reliable in this respect: in thirty months not a single one had produced in Andy a smidgen of erotic stimulus. Goodman's fiat of minimum expenditure meant that a cousin of Angela's had taken the photos. Dominic's beaming young man and woman (students on the same art course) looked at first glance to be advertising garden products. Closer scrutiny revealed that they posed for a series of 'daring' outdoor positions, each accompanied by a caption containing sensible Tansley advice. 'A bird-bath is the ideal height for upright sex, but make sure it's secure.' Or: 'Inserting fresh fruit is no more dangerous than inserting a dildo, but best to avoid spicy plants (red chillies, peppers, ginger).' Or: 'Use a code word like "Basingstoke" to stop.'

In the early days Andy would have joked with his friend David about this, but he was now immune. Tansley was like every author in the Carpe Diem catalogue. The advice she gave was daft, though not so daft as people had to be to take it. He picked up a pencil and was marking the first page when a phrase brought him up short.

In Andy's hard-earned experience, most self-help books contained at least one marshmallow of truth. This was Enid Tansley's – lifted, no doubt, from Ruth Challis, who had clearly pinched it from Montaigne: 'Above all, be yourself.'

But who was he?

The self he had been had vanished that night at the Camões. Taken from him by a man in a burgundy V-neck. His dark hand on her breast . . .

The door opened.

He could only think of her.

The rain cracked down and there was the sound of a body collapsing heavily on a sofa.

He could only think of her.

Andy heard from the snores that it had been another good lunch.

But he could only think of Sophie.

Sod Basingstoke, he thought – and reached for the telephone.

Sophie was not at her agency. She did not answer her mobile. He tried her flat.

'Hello?' said a voice he thought he recognised.

'Is that you, darling?'

'No, it's darling's mother.'

Andy had not yet met Mrs Sobko, although they got on well enough on the telephone. Sophie had failed to mention that she was visiting London.

'I hope the fraternity houses are behaving themselves,' he said with a plausible attempt at excitement. He had had to become something of an expert on Grand Forks.

'I'll get her,' in a new acerbic tone.

'How is she?'

'She's sure in a mess, but you know how it is . . . Wait, here she is. It's him.'

'Hi.'

'Sophie?'

'Oh, hi.'

His heart spiralled to hear her voice. He had hoped to be holding her, but he was grateful to be holding the telephone with her voice coming out of it.

'How are you doing?' she said.

He could not bear it any more.

'Were you so unhappy with me?'

'No,' sounding miserable. And started sobbing as though she had been unhappy and had not understood this till now.

'Goodbye, Andrew.'

And put down the receiver.

When he listened to the tone in which Sophie said goodbye, as if he were some cowboy developer who had bulldozed her holiest site into its interestingly shaped swimming pool, Andy knew that the rupture was final.

There did not seem a lot else left to do in the world except consecrate himself to Enid Tansley. Oblivious to the city outside, he sat correcting her manuscript for the rest of the afternoon. There was a steady, oppressive rain. He could see the glare of the headlights refracted through it onto the wall above his desk; the lights raking the glass, illuminating the words *Release the need to be unpleasant to others.* By the end of the day he came to life for a moment, even felt quite content. But then despair returned in greater force.

He worked until midnight and missed the last bus. He walked with bent head through the dark, glossy streets, to his flat. What you needed to be to live in London was an umbrella, he thought. The darkness pressed in on him. Black and bitter and damp. Like the inside of a bird.

A month after his father failed to return from Canada, a letter arrived from Moose Jaw for his mother. She stood there muttering to herself, then ran up to her room. She did not open the letter for a week. Keeping it in her handbag like a grenade.

She sat with her light on after reading it.

The information fluttered into her lap, less explosion than dead leaf.

'But isn't he already married to you?' Andy said when she explained what his father wanted.

'Not any more he doesn't wish to be,' flashed his sister.

'Stop it, you two!'

His mother could not remember the best age for children, when they were supposed to be easy; whatever it was, it kept shifting, first ahead of where she happened to be; then a long way behind.

Such a coward. Not to look her in the eyes and tell her.

But she refused to denigrate their father in front of them. Her public position: 'Every so often it happens. You meet someone. You meet someone and you don't want to go back.'

Fighting words. His strangely loyal mother. Who would go on missing the letter-writer. His big brown burly head. His optimism. Do what people tell you and you'll be hunting fish in the woods – the line that had made her laugh when they first met. The man of many women who had dreamed of going into space.

Tongues wagged. Word got round that this time George Larkham was not coming back. His new wife was to be a Canadian. All true. Except that she ran off before he could divorce.

When the divorce finally came through Andy would hear his mother turning in bed upstairs. It was the overriding tone of his childhood. His mother's restless sadness.

Then, the autumn after his father's doomed visit home, after Lynn had rejected him for a pilot more her own age, Andy's mother fell in love, with – of all things – a Japanese elm.

Everyone has a Phase One and Phase Two of their lives. His mother's defining moment was seeing a red and gold *Zelkova serrata* in an arboretum near Romsey. 'Someone had struck a match on it – it had all

35

the colours of the bonfire.' She might have discovered a new star that did not exist for anyone else but sent his mother into her own happy heaven. For too long everything in her life had moved at a helicopter's pace, her husband up in the air always. The first time she set eyes on that elm, its gorgeous shape and colour – the shape of something that needed to stay put – she understood how badly she wanted to come back to earth. It grounded her, that elm.

She had tended the garden during her husband's extended absences, finding positive delight in being outdoors and getting her hands dirty. Now, she began to work with plants professionally, in a nursery near Gillingham, where she exhausted herself moving pots, bringing them in for the night, and, if it was raining, sticking them outside. If the weather turned cold, she would rush out in a worry that her darlings needed to be wrapped up. She could not bear for her plants to be hurt or damaged. Plants were her children, almost as much as her children were.

Andy had never seen his mother so involved. One evening after work, she took a piece of paper and sketched a large oak. She made a long line under it and drew the oak again, upside-down, like a reflection. 'Plants have anchoring roots which correspond to branches in the air,' she told him. 'If you dig down, you'll find a similar branch-pattern in the fine feeding roots that take in water and nutrients, like the veins and capillaries in our own bodies. As above, so below. It's in the Bible.'

Her husband had ripped out a whole arterial system, leaving her bloodless and pale in the sunless English weather. She would not fall into that trap again: of wanting to please.

After the Japanese elm, a rare coastal beard-heath that was impossible to make flower – until she was told a trick by a German woman at the nursery.

She packed the coastal beard-heath into a garbage bag and added a teaspoon of white wine vinegar and tied the bag up. Then left the plant alone for three months, until what came out was a stinking, rotting, horrible mess.

'Some seeds have to go through a bird before they germinate.'

Andy was present when she unknotted the bag. He watched her cracked hands with enormous tenderness remove the beard-heath and wash it, and then she planted it and – lo and behold! – a few days later it blossomed. He remembered small flowers and berries that started off green and finished white. Whenever he was in a bad or unhappy mood, one he could not escape by imagining that he was Someone Else, he tried to reach beyond it by telling himself: 'I'm going through the bird.' It never really worked.

5

NEXT MORNING, EARLY, STILL dark, the doorbell.

Sophie! She had woken up to what a loser Richard was and, like the penitent they once observed together at Fatima, had shuffled the length of Hortense Avenue – on tattering knees – to plead with Andy to accept her back.

He rose from his briny bed and crawled through the tip that his flat had become to the intercom. 'Yes?' he croaked with simmering hope and peered through the window.

Outside, an overcast sky quarried by a wind that raised the white pebbledash of the facades opposite into goose pimples.

From below, the postman's voice. 'Recorded delivery.'

Immediately, Andy regretted answering the bell. Right at the bottom of the list of things he required this Friday morning was a summons.

Months before, David had educated him in the practice of deferment. 'Those bills? You write back: "Because of a hereditary dyslexia, I require a slightly different form, with the As reversed and in Hindi, because I am seeking to become one of the last Tasmanian Aborigines."' This had bought Andy six weeks' respite with the Royal Borough of Kensington and Chelsea, but it no longer kept British Telecom at bay.

Linoleum goes very cold in a London February. Andy dashed across the icy floor and propped up the envelope on the shelf as he brushed his teeth. His apprehension sharpened when he read: *Vamplew & Whelan, Solicitors.* And heard the judge's voice: 'You shall be sentenced to seven years' transportation to a place beyond the seas.'

The letter was short.

Dear Andrew Larkham,
I represent the estate of the late Christopher Madigan. As you may be a beneficiary of his will, can I confirm that this is your permanent address?
Yours sincerely, Godfrey Vamplew.

It was not a summons. Andy felt such a flood of gratitude that he resolved to telephone Godfrey Vamplew and clear up this mess before it got bigger. The letter gave him the courage to act as he should have done at the crematorium.

Once dressed, he made a cup of tea and went into the living room and called the number at the top of the page. A young-sounding woman put him through to Vamplew.

'Yes, Mr Larkham. What can I do for you?'

Andy recognised the grey hair in his voice. 'I've just received your letter,' he said.

'I take it that is your permanent address?'

'Yes, but it's not why I'm ringing.'

Vamplew sounded oddly uninterested.

Andy continued: 'Listen, there's something I'd like to say. I didn't know this man Christopher Madigan. I shouldn't have been at his funeral.'

Silence.

'You see, I should have been in Chapel 3,' Andy babbled on – he wanted to help him, 'but there was rain on my invitation and I misread 3 for 8.'

The voice at the other end was polite, but firm. 'It doesn't matter whether you made a mistake or not. You've fulfilled the terms and conditions.'

Andy really was at sea. He licked away the skin of milk sticking to his lips. 'Terms and conditions?'

There was a sound that might have been a sigh. 'Mr Larkham, these are rather unusual circumstances. If you come to my office this afternoon at 2.30, I shall do my best to explain.'

'How long will you be?' Angela asked suspiciously.

Andy found himself wishing that she would go lose herself in a pothole. Angela often left early for her dowsing class, and did he say anything?

'No more than a couple of hours.'

'You *do* know he's expecting the Tansley,' she said officiously.

'It'll be ready.'

She needed to get it off her mind. 'And you owe me a hundred quid.'

'First thing Monday.'

He grabbed his coat and made for the Tube.

Thirty-five minutes later, Andy followed a self-possessed young receptionist along a carpeted passage, past coloured prints of Worcester Cathedral and the Oxford college where he supposed Godfrey Vamplew had studied law, to a black painted door.

38

His name was in double pica letters on a small brass plaque. The receptionist knocked twice, and when she heard 'Come in' opened it. Shelves of blue-bound legal codes. A huge desk inlaid with maroon leather. And sitting on the far side, the silver-headed figure who had asked Andy to sign Christopher Madigan's condolence book.

With the slow and considered motion of a man whose blood did not flow briskly, Vamplew continued filling his Mont Blanc from a bottle of blue Sheaffer ink, and when he had completed this operation glanced up.

'Ah, Mr Larkham, here at last.'

'Sorry I'm late,' without thinking, as he had said it a hundred times before.

There was another person in the room, who sat in one of two mahogany armchairs facing the desk.

That pale, wrinkled face, now wearing spectacles.

Vamplew stood to introduce them. 'This is Maral Bernhard. Mrs Bernhard, this is Mr Larkham I was telling you about.'

She was dressed in the same brown fur coat as at the funeral service and held a straw shopping basket in her lap.

'Larkham,' she repeated, not getting up. She peered at him, an expression of obscure resentment on her face, as though she did not believe that Larkham could be his name.

'That's right. Andy Larkham,' and held out his hand.

She gave it a squelching look and moved her chair away.

Vamplew returned to his seat and reached for a file on his desk, untying the tape that bound it.

'Kate getting you a coffee?'

'She is,' sitting down.

'You won't change your mind?' to Maral Bernhard.

She shook her head and picked at her basket, slumped in an attitude of dejected preoccupation. From the rigid set of her shoulders, she had arrived in this room against her will and would much rather have been squeezing avocado pears in Vladivostok or wherever she came from. Andy knew where he would have preferred to be. With Sophie. Taking off her slip. Falling backwards onto a lavender sofa.

'Mr Vamplew —' he began, but the lawyer threw up a hand.

'I apologise if what I'm about to do appears old-fashioned, but I think the best way to proceed is for me to read this out. Then, if you have queries, I shall do my best to answer them.'

There was a knock.

Vamplew said nothing as the receptionist appeared with a tray on which there was a single small cup.

Andy decided to enjoy his coffee and wait until Vamplew had finished before explaining why it was impossible that he could be a beneficiary of Christopher Madigan.

'And, Kate' – they exchanged glances – 'no further calls.'

The door closed. Vamplew filled a tumbler with water from a cut-glass decanter, took a sip, and opened the file, removing from it the condolence book. He put this to one side and next withdrew a stapled document.

'This should not take long. It is couched in legal jargon, but for all that self-explanatory, I hope.'

He rifled through the pages until he came to a page with a blue Post-it note.

'There's a preamble which need not detain us. If neither of you objects, I shall skip straight to the will itself.'

Andy glanced over at Maral Bernhard. She was straightening a strand of straw that had come loose from her basket. He gave her a nervous smile, the back of a hand for a dog to sniff. She turned her eyes to him, filled with venom.

He looked at Vamplew.

The lawyer took another fortifying sip, cleared his throat, leaned forward, and began reading aloud.

'I, Christopher Leonard Madigan of 11 Clarendon Crescent, Holland Park, London W11, hereby revoke all wills and testamentary disposi-tions heretofore made by me and declare this to be my last will.

'One. I direct that my Trustee as hereinafter defined shall cause my body to be cremated after a service in accordance with Clause Three hereof.

'Two. I appoint Godfrey Vamplew of Vamplew & Whelan, hereinafter called "my Trustee" to be Executor and Trustee of this my will.

'Three. I direct my Trustee to arrange at the expense of my Estate a funeral service at Richmond Crematorium as soon as is practicable after my death and to give not less than ten days' notice of such a service in the London *Times* and *Daily Telegraph* and *London Gazette*.

'Four. I require my Trustee to attend such a service throughout and to take and keep a full written record of the full names and current addresses of all persons attending such a service who are present at the final prayer (excluding my Trustee and the officiating clergy, organist and choir and any attendant funeral directors and their staff) and such persons so recorded are hereafter called "the Attenders" and I direct that the decision of my Trustee as to what constitutes an Attender shall be final and binding herein.'

Vamplew raised his eyes. 'I did suggest to him that an Attender ought to be there continuously throughout until the service's end, but he insisted that provision be made for those who might be late.'

'He was always late,' Maral Bernhard interjected, merging for an instant with the mysterious beast whose coat she wore. 'Always!'

Vamplew looked from her to Andy with a difficult, apologetic expression. 'It was really to cut out any tramp who might wander in.'

He found his place and resumed.

Andy drank his coffee – a huge improvement on Angela's – and interested himself in Vamplew's desk. This legal language, it had the effect on him of Carpe Diem's book contracts.

'Five. Subject to the payment thereout of all my debts and funeral expenses and all taxes payable by reason of my death I give all the remainder of my real and personal property whatsoever and wheresover situate to the Attenders in equal shares absolutely – provided that if there shall be no Attenders then my Trustee shall hold my said property upon trust for The Donkey Sanctuary in Devon absolutely.'

Vamplew looked up. 'It is surprising how much the enormously rich do leave to local animal charities. That won't be the case here, obviously.'

What was he talking about? Andy grasped that he had said something important.

'One last clause.'

Vamplew raced through it.

'My Trustee shall allow Maral Bernhard a period of up to eighteen months to remain at 11 Clarendon Crescent, she paying the outgoings thereof, before disposing of the property and its contents.' He looked at her. 'He did not know you were going to be a beneficiary, although it was his express wish that you were to be invited to the funeral.'

Vamplew put down the will. He opened the condolence book and studied the two signatures, his formal smile replaced by a different smile, not in his control, when he read *I am so sorry*.

'Well, as Christopher Leonard Madigan's sole Trustee and Executor I am able to confirm that Maral Bernhard and Andrew Larkham constitute the definition of Attenders – and in accordance with his will, his estate shall be divided equally between you both as the residuary beneficiaries.'

There was another silence, longer this time. It was evident from her face that Maral Bernhard was no more knowledgeable about the law than was Andy. She had no sense of property whatsoever to judge from her appearance.

Her shopping basket creaked as she bent forward.

'You mean he and me, we own the estate?' in a crusty voice.

'Correct.'

'And it is worth how much, his estate?' a little less grudgingly.

Vamplew sat back and gazed across his desk at her. In that moment, Andy saw him playing Sudoku on the train from Maidenhead, his lunches that lasted one hour, his scrupulous dealings with his Polish, Sikh, Estonian clients that formed the bulk of his business. He saw him at weekends trimming his hedge in red leather gloves, and over it discussing the barn owls in the Saxon tower and calling the General's wife by her Christian name, and eating pistachios with his Saturday night pint at the Lamb.

He smoothed his chin. 'After lawyers' fees, funeral expenses and taxes, I estimate that you will each receive a figure in the region of seventeen million pounds.'

Andy stared at him. The room was swaying. Vamplew was speaking, but whatever he said Andy could not hear it.

6

ON EALING BROADWAY, OUTSIDE Vamplew's office, it had stopped raining. A blue rent had appeared in the clouds and the air was warmer. Andy looked at Maral Bernhard, but she was tying on a charcoal head-scarf. She picked up her basket and he could see big blood oranges through the weave. He half expected her to thrust out her hand and say '*Prost!*' But she gave him another sphinctery glare and crossed the road in stiff arthritic steps.

Andy stood on the pavement struggling to make sense of it.

Seventeen million pounds. For turning up late. There had to be a catch. It was a test – a sort of secretly filmed reality show designed to measure moral integrity. Well, he would do the right thing and refuse it. Vamplew had insisted that the money was legally his, but he would give it to charity. Maybe not to the Donkey Sanctuary, but Save the Children. Or a cancer hospice.

Thoughts of renunciation lightened his mood. On the train back to Hammersmith, he felt reminted, newborn. What had Vamplew called him – an Attender?

The carriage swayed like Vamplew's room. He stared out of the window at the tunnel going by. On the platforms there were people, no longer dead-looking. Their faces and clothes, the bright colours of the material – all had a vitality, a freshness. He smelled pine. The distress of the past week receded. Perhaps he would watch Sophie come back to him, won over by his selflessness – or, at the very least, in awe of it. Although the scenario required a liberal amount of imaginative tweaking. Most likely, she would think it stupid. His sister was right. Money mattered a lot to Sophie Sobko. Which is why, perhaps, he might be better off without her. They were made of different stuff.

By the time Andy returned to his office, he was in an excellent mood.

7

ANDY'S BEST FRIEND DAVID was six-foot two, twinkling-eyed and bald, with a pepper-and-salt beard and a ski-slope nose. He wore his shirt as often as not inside out and walked around with his bootlaces undone until he discovered Crocs. He was popular, high-spirited and something of an obsessive. He owned the tapes of every film made by Eisenstein, Vertov, Tarkovsky and Waters, and a collection of beer cans that occupied four narrow display shelves. His car was a 1953 Riley Pathfinder and he had a permanent girlfriend, Julie, who worked as an occupational therapist.

Andy's arrangement to meet David this evening had been made before his dinner with Sophie; they had not spoken since.

Outside the Knopwood, a man was yelling at the night sky: 'Okay, I get the point! Give me a break!'

Andy walked past him.

It took a moment for the relaxed, shambolic figure in the corner who looked up from his newspaper to recognise him. 'It's quite unlike you to be so early.'

'Yes,' Andy nodded, able to acknowledge the truth of this statement. 'What are you drinking?'

David went on gazing at him. 'Or to stand me a drink.'

'You are absolutely right.' Ever since he had started going out with Sophie, all his money went on her.

David checked his watch. He had to leave in an hour – to interview Robert Altman – but he had time for a pint of Tisbury pale ale, he said.

The bar was noisy. Men in coats. Girls laughing. On a stage a pony-tailed man wearing a black leather waistcoat plugged in a guitar.

When Andy came back, David took his glass and held it up to the light and scrutinised it. 'I shall enjoy this.' He clinked Andy's glass and drank. 'Mmm. Mud to a pig: delicious.' Then he sat back and frowned at him. 'So, Andy, how are you?'

'Up and down.'

'Is that papal code for down?'

'I need to tell you something.'

David rested his hand on Andy's forearm. 'I heard.'

'You've heard?'

'Well, actually, yes, I have.'

What surprised Andy was how little pain he was feeling about Sophie. A few hours ago he would not have believed it. She was the person he had come here to discuss, but she hadn't crossed his mind.

The pain surged back as he told David the details. Until David, after listening and nodding in the appropriate places, said: 'Be a big boy. Forget her. She loves someone else.'

With a hurt that he wished he could shed, Andy said: 'I was going to ask you to be my best man.'

David stretched an arm around his shoulder. 'And I can still be your best man.'

Andy listened with only half an ear.

David was talking. 'I can say this now, but I never imagined you two together.'

'Why not?'

David placed his glass down on the table. 'All the time you were together did she once read anything that was not a fashion magazine?'

'Yes. I mean . . . Well, no.'

He remembered her asking: 'What's that?'

'A novel, Sophie. A very good one. Like to read it?'

Her rolled eyes: 'I should live so long.'

David glanced at him. 'Andy, enter the palace of truth . . . Did you see yourself growing old with Sophie Sobko in a Zimmer frame and slippers?'

'David, if you don't mind, I'd rather talk about something else.'

'I quite understand. Let's talk about something else. But I thought you wanted to talk about her.'

'Not any more.'

He thought of a line from Furnivall's manuscript: *When true friends freely criticise you what they are doing is giving you a remarkable proof of their friendship.*

'David –'

'The thing about you, Andy, is that you're too trusting, too open. You didn't have to be so honourable. You just had to have fun. Anyway, she's over. We can now reclaim you. What are you doing on Sunday? Julie has to work, but why don't I treat you to lunch at the Ship's Lantern. Another?'

'No, let me.'

'Whoa! Steady, boy . . . Two beers in five minutes?' David picked at his beard that he had grown after going bald. 'Can you afford it?'

Andy stood up.

'Hey, Andy, I was talking.'

Andy took their glasses and went to the bar before David could think of anything more idiotic to say. He had known David since they sat side by side on a blue plastic mat in Semley Nursery School.

David worked as the film critic of a national newspaper. He had tried, unsuccessfully, to write screenplays, but his journalistic instinct helped him to be a critic of distinction. Aside from his knack of knowing what was going on and the fact that he rubbed along well with everyone, he always needed to have his teeth clamped into something – and never let go. It used to infuriate Andy, whether football cards as a four-year-old or films as an undergraduate or – his latest – beer cans as an adult. He would not rest until he had hunted down the grail of beer-can collectors: a Sydney to Hobart commemorative can released by the Cascade brewery in Launceston the summer that the ferro-cement yacht *Helsal* set a race record that stood for another thirty years. Once you understood this about David, you knew how the filing system in his mind worked.

Andy came back from the bar with two more beers. He sat down and said: 'What's your position on taking gifts from strangers?'

'Why?' David peered into his glass. 'Is that what this is?'

'I heard something at the office today.'

'What?'

Instantly, Andy regretted his impulse. 'Oh, long dumb story, don't worry about it.'

'I don't mind long dumb stories. That's why I can still be your friend. Come on, Andy – share,' and winked.

'Sod off. It's a true story.'

David drew up his chair. 'Better and better.'

'You might find it hard to believe, but it's as true as I sit here.'

'Get on with it.'

Andy pretended that he had heard it from Angela. She knew someone who knew someone. Who knew this vagrant in Reykjavik, who had stumbled into an empty church to get out of the rain and sat in the back and was given a service sheet.

'This is what she said to me. But . . .' Andy stopped. 'I'm not telling it very well.'

'No, I like the way you're telling it,' David said.

'Well, it doesn't sound logical – but this rich Icelander left everything he had, the whole lot, to anyone who turned up at his funeral. Seventeen million krona . . . something like that.'

The only difference: in the story Andy was telling David, the tramp had taken the money.

David nodded, meditating on his Tisbury pale ale. 'Of course.'

Andy shook his head. 'Still. To think that some lowlife who just walked in off the street would accept it.'

'That's not lowlife. That's fair and square. Life's a lottery. A lot of things I could do with seventeen million anything . . . Iraqi dinars, for Christ's sake. It wouldn't change the way I lived, but I might buy a car that starts without me having to ring the AA every frigging time.' David's Riley was parked outside the Knopwood.

'So you'd take the money?' But it was too late. By telling David, he had planted his seed of doubt.

'I'm not certain that I totally follow,' David said slowly. 'Wouldn't you?'

'I don't know.'

'Listen to him!'

'No, tell me. Why would I?'

'Andy?'

'What?'

'About this Icelandic tramp . . .' David said. Then looked at him sharply. 'Oh, my gosh.'

'Oh, my gosh is right.'

A blue jersey spanned David's chest. Andy lowered his eyes to examine its weave and told him everything.

To David, it was a story from the age of fable.

'Seventeen million quid! For turning up at someone's funeral. Let the twelve thousand virgins of Santiago de Compostella get up from their knees and hosannah you, Andy. When do you see the money?'

'In six months, the lawyer said.'

'All you've got to do is wait?'

'That's it – unless someone contests the will.'

'Any disgruntled family members?'

'Not as far as I know.'

David pulled his chair further forward, excited. 'You know what you've got to do?' He put a hand on Andy's shoulder and stared at him full square. 'Embrace it, Andy. Take the money.'

Then he laughed through white-flecked lips and raised his glass to a future that Andy wished he believed in.

8

OUTSIDE THE KNOPWOOD FORTY minutes later, a yellow van with lights
flashing parked beside David's car.

'Pegasus won't budge?' said the AA man. He eyed the rust patches
like worn fur and recommended a Toyota. 'We never get called out for
them.'

Andy watched him jump-start the Riley and David drive off to
interview Robert Altman.

Feeling hungry for the first time that week, he went into a Spud-
U-Like and ordered a baked potato with an egg filling. His mind strayed
back to Sophie and Richard. Something else Andy had noticed since his
Saint Valentine's dinner: his most unpleasant thoughts came to him when
he ate.

Abandoning his potato, he made his way home.

His friend's voice reverberated in his head: *You've earned it, you need
it, it came at the right time, it's yours.*

David had a point . . . Andy had attended Madigan's funeral out
of fundamental decency, but when faced with the fundamental decency
of seventeen million pounds, how decent was he? In his bloated state,
Andy began to perceive merit in re-examining his impulsive decision to
donate the money to abandoned street children.

This is freedom you're being offered.

David's words made even more sense when Andy discovered a brown
envelope glaring up at him from the doormat with the venomous words
'British Telecom'. He looked at the envelope and was reminded of how
difficult it was to kill a rat. As he struggled to close the front door and
wiggle his key loose from its iron teeth, a new ferment took hold.

Andy, David had said very firmly, *you were late for a* reason.

He went into the living room and tossed the final demand onto the
mantelpiece, between a letter from the town hall, promising to look
further into the particulars of his dyslexia, and a bank statement
reminding him that he owed £11,832 at 6.25 per cent interest. At
the sight of other envelopes, like autumn leaves everywhere, the
thought recurred that he could in one swoop pay off these bills, buy

a mansion in Holland Park and live off the interest for the remainder of his days.

He went over to the window. In the street below, a black man walked by inexplicably wrapped in plastic.

Yes, there were a lot of things he could do with seventeen million pounds. He stood thinking about how he might spend it, before drawing the curtain.

It was not yet nine o'clock. In his satchel in the hallway was the manuscript that he had brought home to work on. Despite his promise to Angela, he had not finished copy-editing *The Valentino Alfresco Sex Guide*. He ferreted it out and sat down to do battle with chapter six. He was tipsy and tired, but he was not ready for bed.

His eyes dragged over the type, but the lines on the page disappeared and other words took their place.

Different voices started up inside him, back and forth.

'How can you refuse Fortune after she hands you this piece of luck when you most need it? It's an answer to your prayers.'

'Of course I can refuse her. I've never put money top of my list.'

'You've done nothing wrong. It's above board. Can't a man dispose of his wealth as he thinks fit?'

But who was this man? And why had he done this?

Sick with himself, sickened by his own excitement, he put down the manuscript.

A voice that he decided was Enid Tansley's insinuated itself: 'Don't worry about Madigan – whoever *he* was. Seize the moment!' A refrain that was taken up by Ruth Challis and Gladys Peak. Until all three were beating the sides of his chair with their carrots and knotty roots of ginger. 'Seize the moment, seize the moment, seize the moment . . . BE A SELFISH SLUT!'

He switched on the television and sat back. On screen: the latest cabriolet from Mercedes-Benz. Silver. Cutting through a green alpine scenery that dissolved into a red, horizonless desert that dissolved into a blinding polar ice cap. A creepily good-looking man at the wheel, a smirk on his tanned, unshaven face that said: 'Rain? Frost? British Telecom? Sorry, folks, never heard of 'em.' And why would he? He was driving forever in perpetual sunshine and stopping in Tuscany to pick up a beautiful woman beside a Renaissance church.

'That could be me,' Andy slurred aloud.

The clouds tore open. The sun poured down. He sat up, no longer bloated but light-headed. The weighted medicine ball inside him a helium balloon.

The television acted on him as a portal. Through it he passed – out of this cold pigsty of a flat, his ridiculous job, rain-sodden England – into an imaginary landscape of the kind that he used to invent for himself, aged ten, in Shaftesbury. The feeling that had tormented him, of life's cruelty and deceit, was fading; the world was bright and honest again. Had he ever lived a moment other than this one? He had thought that his life was over, but it was not.

He would take it.

The buzzer rang.

9

ANDY WENT DOWNSTAIRS TO tussle with the lock. Minutes later he swung open the front door. But not Sophie.

Someone for Jerome perhaps – a cantankerous rapper from St Lucia who rented the ground-floor flat.

Black hair, he saw, and a pale face and defiant brown eyes.

'Hello,' collapsing her umbrella.

A reedy female voice interrupted through the intercom, climbing over the sound of rock music. '*Who* was it you wanted?'

'All right, Marina,' Andy turned and shouted back. 'It's for me.'

'Sorry – thought it might be Sophie.' Marina had a stud on her tongue and looked like Marilyn Manson, her god.

The music cut out. Leaving Andy to face the person standing there.

'I gave you a lift,' she said. 'Jeanine Pyke.'

She had on her raincoat, buttoned to the chin, and was wearing blue gumboots as if she had been striding towards him through a puddle of ink.

He released the breath that had been caught in his throat. 'I remember.'

'What's your name? We never introduced ourselves.' The words came sharp and unexpected.

'Andrew,' he said.

'Just Andrew?'

'Andrew Larkham.'

She knew where he lived. She had hunted him down.

'Hello, hello, who ith it?'

'It's okay, I've got it, Jerome.'

'Yo, Andy, that you, man? Shit. I hoped it was the man to fix the daw.'

'No, it's a friend of mine.'

'I'll get on to Conrad again,' said Jerome, who had lost a couple of spaces in his teeth after a New Year's Eve deal went sour – since when there had been a noticeable upgrade in his security consciousness.

'Whatever you decide, Jerome, I'm behind you.'

He turned once more to the young woman. Her sudden appearance sobering him back to how he felt after he crawled out of bed that morning to answer the doorbell.

'I didn't know which bell you were,' she said, and stepped past.

Andy followed her up. She was waiting for him in his kitchen.

'Can I take your coat?' he asked.

'No.'

'A drink? I have a bottle of wine somewhere.'

'I'm not staying.'

Hands on hips, she stared at him. 'So, Andrew Larkham . . .' in an aggressive way that reminded him of his sister. 'Who are you?'

Her question flashed quivering through the air, a living brown trout that she tossed at him.

'Who am I?'

'That's what I asked.'

Andy looked away. The cramped kitchen had the aspect of his general mood since Monday evening. It required no fortune-teller to read his prospects in the coffee grounds fermenting in the sink. This was his life.

He felt a pinch of terror in his gut. 'Hey, why don't we go into the next room and talk there?'

She turned and strode into his bedroom.

'No, no, the living room's that way!' Andy cried, although not before she had taken a long hard look at his piled-up duvet, and he had a flash of Sophie's legs and his entwined.

She cast her eyes to the ceiling. The lightning cracks in the paint-work, as if someone had gouged it with black fingernails. The gaping chunks in the plaster. The ominous music. Before Andy guided her across the corridor.

He raced ahead to turn off the television. She swept her eyes over the packets of aspirin scattered on the mantelpiece, the torn-open envelopes, the row of spent joss sticks.

Her gaze dropped to the floor, sucked into a chaos of slashed cushions ('*If you feel angry, hit a pillow or cushion*' – R. Challis). But she kept her thoughts to herself. His flat was a dump where filth combined with sadness to produce an odour like a hung pheasant. Andy had the wit not to explain that he had been reading self-help manuals.

'Sorry about the mess,' he said.

She pivoted, unsure where to sit – so he cleared Sophie's chair, the one he still thought of as hers, that he had bought in a Habitat sale two years before and not got around to covering. Clumsily, he gathered up an armful of *Vogues* and *Marie Claires* that Sophie had left last time she was over, several weeks ago now, since she did not as a rule like to sleep here.

'There you are,' he said.

Taking a step, she tripped over something.

'Oh, that's where you got to . . .' he said in a tender way, and lunged forward to pick it up, in the process kicking over the cup of tea that he had made that morning before he telephoned Vamplew.

From her perplexed look, Jeanine could not fathom what the furry brown object was that Andy held up in a small, sad gesture of triumph.

'Just something from Portobello,' caught between his relief that he had found it and embarrassment that he should care, and put the velvet duck-billed platypus on the mantelpiece. ('*Cuddle a pet or soft toy*' – *R. Challis*.)

'So,' rubbing hands before the empty fireplace, 'what was it again you wanted to talk about?' And turned.

She was staring at the manuscript that Andy had left on top of the television.

'Avoid grinning and don't stare at her cleavage,' she said.

He stopped. Able – suddenly – to make out every word that Marilyn Manson belted through the ceiling. 'I'm sorry?'

'That's what the caption says.' She contemplated the photograph. 'What is it?'

'A book I'm editing.'

'Lie for the moment,' she read aloud.

'A typo,' he said, and relieved her of the manuscript. 'It should be "live for the moment".'

Whether it was the photograph or the music or the carrion smell, there came into her face the kind of look that only extreme disturbance can produce.

She folded her arms. She was not going to sit.

'I'm still waiting for you to tell me who you are.'

Andy felt his blood-pressure rising. He had no idea who this girl was in his flat, but one thing was clear. If he was going to be the man in the car ad, he had to get Jeanine Pyke out of here.

He met her stare and tried to hold it. 'Who are *you*?' he countered. He would punish her for despising him.

'I'm his daughter,' her voice flaming with emotion, 'but who the fuck are you? Maral Bernhard, I can understand. I'd have understood if he had left it to a donkey sanctuary. But you – why *you*?'

'His daughter?' he swallowed. He would never have guessed it from her attitude in her car. But if anyone should inherit from Christopher

Madigan, it was the man's own flesh and blood. Not someone who had never heard of him until 3.21 p.m. the previous Monday.

'I understand that you and Maral have divvied it up. All because I wasn't there at the final prayer.'

Andy nodded and reached to the mantelpiece for support. 'Your father's conditions did come as a surprise. To each of us, I think.' He searched himself. It was not a lie. He could speak on behalf of both Attenders. He felt.

'Why were you at my father's funeral?'

She was looking at him. Her eyes had the silver-brown colour of meteorite. An expression that did not properly belong to this world, but came hurtling from an asteroid belt.

Had Andy not consumed three pints of Tisbury pale ale followed by half an egg-filled baked potato, he might have better gathered his thoughts. He opened his mouth. 'Why was I at your father's funeral . . . ?' trying to smile her question away.

He remembered the fate of Alfonse Daudet, struck down in the middle of a sentence. Even so, he could not go on.

'Yes?' she said. She was waiting.

A car went by, siren blaring.

His life as a multi-millionaire was minutes old and already it was drawing to a close. But he was anxious to cling to it for a few seconds more. He had not yet come to terms with having to observe the vision that had only recently been granted him – viz. Andy Larkham as Selfish Slut – roar off.

He was aware that his breath had speeded up. Stirring deep within, he felt a resurgent energy. He felt it swirling up his throat. Then, in the voice of an exaggerated tough guy – the voice of an Attender: 'Why weren't *you* there?'

She winced. 'None of your business.'

'*None of your business.*' With grotesque haughtiness he mimicked her. 'You barge in here uninvited and have the gall to ask me why I was at your father's funeral when you didn't bother to be there yourself – *you, his own daughter.*'

She looked momentarily crushed by his powerful new character. 'I'm sorry, I just wanted to know why he made you his heir.'

He picked up Enid Tansley's manuscript and tapped it on the top of the television to tidy it.

'Because,' he heard himself say, locking eyes with her, 'I was a friend of your father's.' That is what he said. That is the answer that escaped from his larynx. It was not merely that he was one of his Attenders which stimulated Andy to speak up for Madigan. The same feeling had come over him in the chapel. An inexplicable kinship to a person he had never met.

He studied his nails. They were, frankly, rather dirty. 'A very good friend,' he heard himself add in a tone that impressed even him. 'And now I'm going to have to ask you, please, to leave.'

THE SHIP'S LANTERN OUTSIDE Marlow was run by Nigel, an affable Sandhurst type and friend of minor royalty.

In a corner, egged on by an ecstatic crowd, a small-chinned man with a pot belly was singing 'If I Had a Hammer'.

'This looks all right,' David said.

'Karaoke?' Andy frowned. He remembered the place when it had pickled eggs in jars.

David had booked a table in the adjoining restaurant, a room of panelled oak warmed by a log fire. A Latvian waitress lit candles and informed them, with a discreet jerk of her biro, that the person at the end of a long refectory table was 'Princess Tizzy'.

Their eyes caught each other and formed a chain of suspicion. David peered over the top of the menu at a girl with butterscotch hair, a ping-pong bat of a nose and the kind of peachy English voice to which, were he a woman, Rian Goodman might have aspired. Ten faces held onto her words with the attention of people clinging with their eyebrows to something that had begun to crumble.

'Last time we were here,' David recalled over an avalanche of polite laughter, 'was to celebrate you getting a job in publishing.'

Presently, he put down the menu and looked across the table at Andy. 'So have you decided?'

'I think I'll have the roast beef.'

'No, you oaf. About whether to take the money.'

'I'm afraid there's been a new development.'

'Oh?'

'Madigan has a daughter.'

Sparing few details, Andy described over lunch how Jeanine had stormed into his flat.

David gave him a concerned look. 'What did you tell her?'

Andy licked his lip. 'I said that I was a friend of her father's.'

'Andy?' David said, seeing his face.

'All right, I said I was a *good* friend of her father's.'

'Remind me what we know about her father?'

'Not a thing.'

'You've Googled him?'

'Right away. There's nothing.'

David stroked his beard. 'Where's there's a will, there's usually a relative. But why didn't he in the ordinary way leave anything to her?'

'I don't know.'

'And what's he done in his life that only one other person should show up at his funeral?'

'Exactly,' Andy said. 'Why would a man give away his wealth on the whim of whoever turned up, making it possible to exclude his own child?'

'If you ask me, it's definitely a loyalty test. A crude and yet efficient reward for some sort of loyalty.'

'Even though it's only for ten minutes?'

David was pondering it over. 'Has it crossed your mind that Jeanine could be a heist? A girl at Vamplew's office who overheard something, and because of some last-minute cock-up arrived at the funeral later than you? It would explain why in her car Jeanine was reluctant to ask you anything about her father – she didn't know herself.'

Andy was unpersuaded. David had been listening to too much Robert Altman. He pushed his plate away. 'I bet you anything that Jeanine is Madigan's daughter.'

'Okay, say she is. But let's get this straight. As of this moment, you, Andy Larkham, stand to inherit seventeen million pounds from a dead man of whom you and Google have never heard – just so long as the will is not contested. But you have now learned of the existence of someone who has every reason to contest it. Namely, this man's daughter.'

'That's about the sum of it.'

'The question is: How to stop her litigating and taking off with your money?'

'I agree.'

'It seems to me your one hope is to convince Jeanine that you actually were a good mate of her old man – and therefore every bit as entitled as Mrs Bernhard to benefit from his munificence.' David rotated on his padded stool. 'By the way, who do we think Mrs Bernhard is?'

'My first thought is that she was Madigan's housekeeper.'

'Then we may have to discount that possibility,' David said. 'Your powers of deduction have been, to date, abysmal. Whoever she is, I would say that she is of less concern to you than Jeanine. Right now, you must do everything you can to stop Jeanine contesting the will.'

'But how do I ward off a claim?'

'How indeed?'

Behind them a log slumped, sending up a comet trail of sparks.

'Do stop scratching that beard,' Andy said with uncharacteristic impatience.

David looked at him. 'She's a woman, a daughter, but money's not the issue. It slightly is, but not really. It's about a whole lot of other things. Her relations with men, most of all. She is angry, not because of the money, but because you may know more about her father. She hasn't seen him for seven years. How come *you* got ahead of her in his affections?'

'Then what, David, is your advice?'

'I think you've got to do two things. You must avoid seeing her again at all costs. Meanwhile, you must find out everything you can about Christopher Madigan – so that if by grotesque chance you do bump into Jeanine again, you can waffle your way out of it. Your only chance to keep these unimaginable riches is to continue with the fiction that you are who you claim to be.'

At that moment a man with a military bearing approached the table. Printed on his T-shirt were the words IF ASSHOLES COULD FLY THIS PLACE WOULD BE AN AIRPORT.

'Pudding, anyone?' Nigel barked. 'Specials are over there on the blackboard.'

'Andy?'

'After that roast beef, I'm not sure . . .'

'Go on. I'm putting this on expenses – just as long as you give me the story. It'll make a terrific movie,' he said, and pushed him. He was joking. Andy thought.

'Then I will have the bread-and-butter pudding.'

David smiled. 'That's more like it. Welcome back to the Land of Hope and Glory, *muchacho*. And should anyone ask, you are Mr Robert Altman.'

The light was failing when they left the Ship's Lantern. In the next room Princess Tizzy was singing 'I Believe in Miracles', a favourite, as she had sung it several times. To their joint relief, the Riley started first time.

'You okay to drive?' Andy asked.

'I think,' David said.

They motored back in a contented mood. David soon stopped waving his hands back and forth – in emulation of the three windscreen wipers that he dubbed The Andrews Sisters – and Andy fixed his eyes sleepily on the road ahead.

It was pitch-dark when the Riley pulled up outside his flat. David's voice followed Andy to the front door. 'I'll see what I can dig up about Madigan. Meanwhile, you go and see his lawyer again.'

'Thanks for perking me up,' Andy called back. 'I feel much better.'

ACROSS THE VASTNESS OF his desk Godfrey Vamplew looked at Andy through his unsettling bifocals. It was the following Tuesday morning.

Andy began nervously. 'Last Friday, you led me to understand that I shall shortly be very rich.'

'Once probate is granted,' Vamplew said in a formal voice. 'And subject to any claimants. And depending on your definition of "rich".'

Andy summed up his predicament. Creditors pressing. Insolvency looming. Credit card stopped.

Vamplew folded his arms. 'And in your judgment a lawyer's letter explaining your monetary expectation might persuade your bank to reconsider its position?'

'I was hoping you would write me such a letter.'

Andy's situation was one plainly familiar to Vamplew. 'I don't see why not. I'll get something off this afternoon.'

Andy risked another question. 'Can you tell me the source of my wealth?'

Vamplew's overlapping eyes gauged how nervous he was. Andy had considered with David everything from an office-cleaning empire to fruit machines and nappies. At the same time, he was braced for brothels and casinos.

'I understand that the bulk of my client's estate was initially invested in mining shares. But he took care before he died to transfer these into a spread of insurance policies. He had already given much away to a charitable foundation with which he was connected.'

Andy's relief was evident in Vamplew's almost-smile. Without quite being able to say why, Andy had the feeling that the lawyer wanted him to have that money. Just looking at Andy, he understood something about him.

'Is there anything else you can tell me? If I'm to inherit his money, I'd like to learn more about my benefactor. How well did you know him?'

'I didn't know him at all.'

Vamplew spoke precisely, but with obvious pleasure. Christopher Madigan had come in one morning last November. He sat where Andy was sitting. Mrs Bernhard had sat outside. 'He didn't wish anyone to overhear our discussion. No one but me was to be involved. And then, if I did agree to act for him, I myself would have to type out the will and any correspondence.'

'Did he give a reason?'

'He had decided, after a long association, to change his solicitors because he wished to alter his will.'

'Why did he come to you?'

'I was in the papers, which is not often the case, and it caught his eye.'

A client had left everything to a charity for the blind. An in-law contested, one ground after the other – fraud, undue influence, insanity. Each time, the judge found in favour of the deceased. In his summing-up, he had commented on Vamplew's integrity and propriety throughout the proceedings, and the clear way that he had drafted the will and presented his evidence.

'Mr Madigan was interested in the subject of wills because he was brooding on his own. He rang the Law Society to ask where I practised, and offered to pay me handsomely to protect his last wishes with the same "tenacity".'

Vamplew sat back.

'I asked several questions to make sure that he wasn't completely insane. He then revealed his conditions. When I put forward my reservations, he threatened to go elsewhere. Since I didn't want to lose the business, I agreed to act for him. I did, though, recommend that he appoint another independent trustee – his accountant perhaps – so that we could watch each other, and there would be less risk of collusion. We lawyers know how people can behave. He told me that he'd already considered this, but he was clear in his head that the smallest number of people must be involved. He was happy to appoint me sole trustee and executor. I had "form in defending the dead". That's what he said. After that, we haggled over fees. I added a bit more for typing the will out – for irritation, basically.'

'Did you ask why he wanted to make such a will?'

Vamplew shook his head. 'I never enquire of my clients their motives. I only caution them that if they are minded to use their will to slander others, there is a risk that their estate will be depleted by claims of damages arising out of slander, and their testamentary intention may be defeated.'

In drawing up Christopher Madigan's will, assuming he was sane, Vamplew had to ask three questions only.

'First: is this will contrary to public policy because of the strange-ness of the request? If Mr Madigan had left everything to Al-Qaeda, possibly it would have been treasonable, certainly seditious. I didn't consider his wishes either immoral or contrary to public policy.

'Second: is this will void for uncertainty? Had Mr Madigan left every-thing, say, to all red-headed males in England, it was likely to be struck out by the court.

'Third: is this will open to challenge by a beneficiary such as a spouse, a child or anyone who is dependent on him? When the deceased first explained his testamentary intentions, I anticipated that there would be claimants. I advised him that he was inviting real trouble.'

Vamplew paused. He was making his point.

Andy moved in his chair. 'What kind of trouble?'

'It is remarkable how long-burning fuses will surface on death. Emotions that have been stored up are laid bare and put before lawyers like me. I'll have people in my office in a livid fury. They've gathered round to find out what the old bastard's done for them, and it's gone to "someone unexpected". Thankfully, I have a broad desk.'

After thirty years of watching people across it, Vamplew was able to testify that patterns of human behaviour were dispiritingly unshifting.

Vamplew leaned forward, not so stiff now.

'When a client says: "It's a matter of principle" – my reaction is: "Oh good – the gravy train has pulled up at the station – here we go."

'Good Godfrey says: "Please don't." But Bad Godfrey has become more and more cynical. He has to meet targets.

'Another wonderful phrase: "It was a gentleman's agreement." As soon as they say that, I know they're going to stuff each other. A gentleman's agreement gladdens the heart of any lawyer.'

Inevitably, the worst quarrels occurred within families.

'Strong parents suppress all dissent. Once they're gone, it erupts. Often, the disputes are fuelled by nursery quarrels. "Mother always liked you better." This kind of resentment plays out in terms of money.

'When that money is left to someone unexpected – grief and shock. Especially if the "someone unexpected" is a local cat's home. Furry animals – old maiden ladies love them! Green and furry and cancer. The blind not so much. That's why the case which alerted Mr Madigan to me was crucial for the charity to win.'

With this in mind, Vamplew had questioned the deceased as to his family. His wife had died and there was only one person who might be regarded as family – a daughter with whom he had lost touch.

'I could see straight away that she was going to be a problem.

I emphasised that in order to head off a claim under the Inheritance Act, my client had to make reasonable provision for her. He maintained that he had already done so. It's not so simple as I'm about to say, but basically he had set up a trust fund with his former solicitors which she was to come into upon turning twenty-one. Trusts are normally irrevocable. However, in this case he had reserved to himself a "power of appointment" which enabled him, as Settlor, to reorganise the trust provisions. This at the very last moment he had decided to do – deferring his daughter's entitlement to capital until after his death.'

'So she *didn't* come into it at twenty-one?' Andy said.

'No, but she becomes entitled to it automatically now.'

'Did he mention why he deferred it?'

'It was something that pained him too much to discuss. The only person he wished to know about his funeral arrangements was Mrs Bernhard.

'I said that I wouldn't put in the will his sentiments, but it would be good if he made his intent known to me by private letter.'

Vamplew took some paper-clipped sheets out of a drawer. 'He wrote this to be included as a preamble. It's not unprecedented. I've seen one like it in verse – a first essay at rhyme, I suspect. Another took the form of a sermon. They are uncommon now, but usually they rant against the pernicious virus of socialism which has infected this country since the beginning of the last century and are an expression of a client's determination that not a penny of their hard-earned money shall go to the State. I see no reason why you, as his beneficiary, can't read Mr Madigan's preamble. I kept it in reserve for any proceedings; otherwise it just causes trouble. My secretary can run off a copy.'

'Maybe it will explain everything.'

'Maybe.'

'You might not have questioned his motives,' Andy said, 'but surely you asked yourself why he made such an extraordinary will?'

'It depends what you mean by extraordinary, Mr Larkham. Compared to many, Christopher Madigan was a pretty conventional testator. When he originally outlined his intention, I was put in mind of the Padua lawyer who disinherited anyone who wept at his funeral, appointing as sole heir "whoever laughed *most heartily*". That was in the fifteenth century, but you might recall the recent example of a Portuguese aristocrat who asked his notary for a copy of the Lisbon telephone directory from which he then plucked seventy names at random, declaring that he wanted to sow confusion by leaving everything he owned to strangers.'

Vamplew laughed to himself, his testiness gone. He had found his rhythm. 'Your case is less arbitrary. You at least showed up for his funeral. You at least were *there*.'

'But he must have had friends.'

'Evidently not.'

'What about that chaplain? He seemed to know him.'

Vamplew shook his head. 'Some "crem cowboy" appointed by the funeral director. The term, I believe, is a Dafa – Do Anything For Anyone. A twenty-minute slot, £100 a throw and no questions asked – except those he asked of me. He rang up before the service to find out three things about the deceased.'

'What did you tell him?'

'He loved his family, gave a lot to charity, enjoyed many different interests . . . The usual platitudes.'

There was a silence. Andy said: 'If Madigan wasn't mad, why did he do this?'

'He had certain beliefs, I would say.'

'What kind of beliefs?'

Vamplew's various eyes examined Andy. 'How old are you, Mr Larkham?'

'Twenty-seven.'

'And your profession?'

'A publisher.'

Vamplew made a vague motion at his shelves. 'I have often wondered if there might not be an anthology to be compiled from these cases.'

'I'm sure there is,' Andy said. 'And you could do worse than Carpe Diem.' He needed Vamplew on his side. It was how Goodman had seduced his wives, offering to read what might more sensibly have been kept locked for all eternity in a sock drawer.

Vamplew took off his spectacles and polished them with a Kleenex. He looked different; his face no longer ordinary. Andy saw the dark hair, the brighter eyes, the bushier tail of the young solicitor from Worcester. His voice, too, was different. It was a voice you wanted to listen to. All at once, the room was alive with what he was saying.

'I don't know if this is your experience in publishing, but when I started out as a lawyer I was reasonably optimistic about the human condition. Now, I find, it's rare to come upon a client who's honest. That's why it is sometimes nice to see people get what they deserve one way or the other.'

He put his spectacles back on. It may have been a trick of the angle from which he studied Andy, but his eyes seemed suddenly aligned, no longer concentric.

64

'You ask me what kind of man my client was, and I understand your curiosity. That's why I regret I have so little to tell you. I met him twice only. I couldn't say what made him tick. I'm not even sure I would recognise him from a photograph.'

Vamplew dropped the Kleenex into his waste-paper basket and closed his eyes, as if trying to narrow his thoughts on what he had decided to say.

From his brief acquaintance with Christopher Madigan, he had formed the impression of a close, solitary, mistrustful, slightly deaf man who kept to himself, lived simply and was careful with his money, except in a couple of areas – he liked very good shoes and fine wines, to judge from the claret that Vamplew had received from him. On the other hand, he was not a malevolent testator.

Vamplew would go further. Madigan seemed an exceptionally truthful man who did not indulge in too much self-deception. He had thought about how to dispose of his wealth. His instructions were designed to frame his will so as to allow the least room possible for dishonest emotions to play their part. At the same time, he did not wish to slam the door on random chance – on the same slender crack of luck, as it were, that may perhaps have formed the basis of his own fortune. Vamplew stressed that Madigan never said as much; this was his inter-pretation. And it led him to speculate whether some painful experience or disappointment had occurred in Madigan's life to make him dis-believe all subsequent protestations of affection, loyalty or love. Vamplew was even more convinced of this when he read Madigan's preamble. His desire for solitude seemed to be that of a man of maimed integrity who had suffered an extraordinary hurt. He was tired of people being inter-ested in him for his money alone, and was exacting his revenge by giving away his fortune to anyone who took the trouble to attend his funeral.

'He probably anticipated that his daughter would not do so, while at the same time secretly hoping that she might. When she turned up, late, and I refused to let her sign the register, I considered that I was interpreting his wishes.'

'Did you know she was his daughter?'

'She never said so at the time. My suspicion was confirmed when she telephoned the next morning to enquire if she was a beneficiary. I told her that she was not. She then ranted at me. I told her she should take separate advice. On Thursday I received a request from Bennett & Blaxworth, acting on her behalf.'

'What did they want?'

'They were writing as a matter of procedure for me to courier over a copy of Mr Madigan's will. I sent them a copy of the relevant provisions. But only after I had divulged their contents to the beneficiaries – the reason I invited you to my office.'

'So that's why she came round to my flat . . .'

Vamplew glanced at Andy. 'If she learned you stood to inherit his estate all due to an accident, it might stimulate her to litigate. You should avoid that if possible.'

'But I did tell her that I knew her father.'

To this, Vamplew said nothing for a moment.

'From a legal point of view you had no need to say anything. I told you before, the money is yours.'

What had prompted Andy to say that he knew her father – to come leaping to his defence, with all his flaws? What old tic?

'Maybe I was thinking of my own father.'

Vamplew nodded. As though in watching Andy he had guessed a few things about him. 'Well, let's wait and see what she does with that information.'

'But could his daughter challenge the will?' Ever since Jeanine had said who she was, this was what Andy had feared.

'It rather depends.'

'On what?'

Vamplew sat back, his hands laced together and his thumbs chasing each other like gerbils around a wheel, considering.

He still liked to regard the law as an eighteenth-century siege operation, he said: you sap a bit, open a battery up, and summon the opposition to surrender. In other words, go through the correct motions in a civilised way. But then you had twenty-first-century lawyers whose priority was to massacre you and build up the costs, who would exacerbate any situation and string it out so that a fat portion of the estate ended up not in your pocket but in theirs.

'From what I know of Mr Madigan's former solicitors, they are ballsy cost-wasters. They would be pretty raw to have been left out of this juicy probate.'

If her lawyers wanted to irritate, they might freeze everything by slapping a caveat on the will before it came to probate – if they thought something was dodgy or undue influence was exercised or the testator was mad.

'Once probate is granted, they'll have to go for any subsequent claim on the basis of reasonable provision. She is, after all, his only living relative. And because she's his daughter, the court will give her a right to be heard.'

'And then?'

Vamplew's fingers stopped circling, and started rotating backwards. And then he could see it being argued that she was entitled to her father's estate. If she was grown up and self-supporting, the courts used not to care so much. But looking at more recent cases, Vamplew could not guarantee what position a judge would take.

'She'd probably get something. And if she hires a sharp QC in the Chancery court who can lead the judge from soup to nuts she may get rather a lot, although this could depend on what the judge had for breakfast.'

'But she is getting something. She's getting her trust fund.'

'Oh, she'll get something. The more interesting question for you to consider is whether, as sole descendant, she decides to claim the rest of the estate.'

'What happens if she does challenge the will?'

'You must understand, Mr Larkham, that as the executor I'm not fussed – I don't care how the estate is distributed because I get paid. The golden rule for executors is that they must remain impartial in any dispute between beneficiaries. For as long as the dispute rumbles on, the estate is likely to pay everyone's costs.'

'Then what would you advise me to do?'

The half-smile left Vamplew's face. His neutral eyes looked at Andy through the bottom half of his glasses. 'I can't personally advise you, although it strikes me the less suspicion you arouse in Mr Madigan's daughter the better. She ought never to suspect that you were at her father's funeral by accident.'

THE AIR SMELLED OF hops and the road pointed straight and empty before them. He remembered chevrons of geese and rhubarb clumps and ziggurats of baled straw. Once he saw a bald eagle perched on a fallen aspen. The flatness was confounding, with no variation for the mind to dip into. It was like a child's steady gaze.

They had crossed the provincial border and were driving east into Saskatchewan when his father gripped the steering wheel and said: 'I've had a marvellous life, I don't regret a moment of it.'

George Larkham was not a demonstrative or confessional man. Simply a romantic one. His obituary in the *Blackmore Vale* would say of him:

'When he left school he went to RAF Chilmark with a letter from the Prime Minister extolling him as an astronaut, with Winston Churchill spelled Winstin Cherchill.'

About his life, he rarely talked. Once, Andy overheard his sister question him about his brief first marriage, to a woman called Avril. He had looked glumly away.

'The past is a door you don't want to bang open, love, not unless you've got a meat-cleaver in each hand.'

He had the secrecy of a cat who crept away from trouble and yet caused a lot of it.

'Your father – he was a character,' Andy's mother would say, and give a short laugh and start looking around for her secateurs.

Andy tried not to think about him. He left too much smell of burnt hair. But then, springing out of nowhere, a memory would catch him at the back of the throat.

Much as he concealed it from himself, he missed his father terribly. For several years after his death, Andy unconsciously played out the possibility that his father was watching. Reading his name in the paper. Impressed by something he had done. He had wanted to live for him, this man he remembered as tender, impassioned, overwhelmingly positive.

His mother and sister had protected Andy from the truth. He was a pilot and therefore unfaithful.

There had been plenty of women, apparently, but this Canadian one had unbalanced him.

'What did she have?'

'Youth,' rasped his mother, who had gone white when he was seven. 'And flying.' She had suddenly lost patience with Andy's fantasy.

His mother had been the more forthright parent. She could not stand life as a service wife, just hated it. Her feelings got to be so bad that when Andy was six his father resigned from the RAF and found work as a civilian helicopter pilot. Among his incarnations, he was a heli-logger and firefighter. His job took him away for long periods.

When Andy turned ten, it took him to Newfoundland, where it was arranged for Andy to join his father over the summer holidays. A place called Grand Falls.

'How was the flight?' as they drove from Gander Airport.

'Not so bad,' Andy said, admiring the spacious back seat.

He had been nervous about flying on his own to Canada. Down a crackling line, his father had made every effort to calm him. All the pilots had to do was to take off, punch in the IFR flight plan, and even if both pilots fainted the plane would still land and taxi to the end of the runway and turn itself off. 'If both pilots drop dead, you'll probably have a better flight than if they were alive.'

Andy, flying with one other unaccompanied minor, had had a stewardess to pamper him.

'Well, what did I tell you?' his father said, looking at him in the driver's mirror.

'You were right, Dad.'

The back of his father's head was clearer than his face; the hair on his neck going grey and longer than in the days when he used to come home in an air force cap.

'And your mother?'

His mother and sister had preferred to stay at home in Shaftesbury.

'She sends her love,' and remembered the gift in his pocket. That he fished out and handed over.

'I've missed you,' his father said, laying the squashed blue tissue, still unopened, on the passenger seat, next to the packet of dried pears and the anti-inflammatory cream. 'I've missed you all.'

His hands beat against the wheel as he whistled a calypso: a sure sign of danger.

Then he started coughing, a stridorous wheezing that altered the whole musculature of his face.

'Are you okay?' Andy said when he had stopped.

'It's nothing, nothing,' touching the corner of his mouth. 'It's just that I'm not good on terra firma. Bit like a ship's captain – get me ashore, I can barely drive a car.' And took his hands off the wheel.

'Dad!'

'All I know about cars is to be sick in them,' he said cheerfully.

They participated in a salmon festival. They walked the Corduroy Brook Trail. They went ice-skating. One morning, they flew in a helicopter over a forest – 'so you can tell your mother and sister what I've been up to.'

It was the first time Andy had been in the air with him. His father described how he would sit in this cabin seven hours a day, lifting black spruce and yellow birch to the log-landing on a spur of the river. 'Last month, I was picking a turn when a tree slipped out of the jaws of the grappler. Will never forget that sight.'

Andy looked down at the river and pictured a log falling, falling until it hit the water, exploding on impact into two-by-fours.

His father's favourite timber was the yellow cedar. You did not find it in Newfoundland but in British Columbia, where he next took Andy. 'The yellow cedar's a lovely tree. You can still pull them off the hills when they're sixty years old and lying on their side. Worms don't get into them and they last forever.' Andy leaned out of the helicopter bubble and looked down, watching the grappler taking hold. 'Grey ghosts,' his father called them. The trunks had an alabaster grain and were much prized by the Japanese for temple logs, he said.

As summer wore on, his father himself turned into a bit of a grey ghost, a shadowy presence whose attention came and went, a helicopter whirr on the grass, ruffling his hair, 'I just need to make a call,' beginning the process that would see him vanishing into the cool, grain-scented air of Manitoba.

Because all at once they were driving east through fields of wheat and wormwood sage and switchgrass. His father had decided to show Andy the place where he had learned to fly Sikorskies, on a pilot-exchange programme for NATO and allied air forces. Moose Jaw was one of the most important places in the world from a geopolitical view, he said, to excite Andy's interest as they motored over the flattest country Andy had ever seen. His eyes sparkled like the tin foil he would put up against the windscreen to stop the glare.

Moose Jaw was where his father's friend Lynn lived, in a Tyndall stone duplex on Wildwood Crescent, though Andy never again saw the young pilot with amber-bleached hair for whom his father was to give

70

up family and home. When he thought of the last days of that holiday he remembered missile-launchers trundling by and a summer parade with ethnic pancakes, and going for a walk in a field that went on forever and was full of blue grama grass that gave him hayfever. Through puffed-up eyes he watched his father coming towards him with an armful of wild flowers. 'For your mother.'

On the last day of the holidays, his father drove him to the airport. 'I'll be here another month and then I'll be back. Another month, tell her.'

Andy nodded.

His father drove on in silence.

Over the radio a Canadian voice talked about the competition for university places.

'I went to no university.' His father stuck his arm out the window and pointed at the sky. 'That's my university.'

He caught Andy's face in the mirror and smiled. His face was the colour of the capsaicin cream that he kept applying to the edges of his lips. 'When will I be back?'

From the back of the spacious car Andy groaned: 'In a month, Dad.'

It would be another three years before they saw each other again. And then only for a final few moments.

13

THE CHERRY TREES EMERGED through the fog like graffiti.

Andy had worked late to make up for his absence. It was eight o'clock by the time he returned home. Hortense Avenue was slippery with black ice. Preoccupied, he picked his way along the pavement and up the steps, and failed to notice how smoothly the front door opened. He had reached his landing when something moved on the stairs to Marina's flat.

'Hello,' in a voice of ebony, dark and sinuous.

She stepped down into the light.

'Jeanine . . .'

'Jerome says to tell you that your landlord's fixed the lock.'

He looked at her. Not knowing what to do. Except to go on standing there as though her appearance outside his door was a reliable fore-runner of someone's demise.

Why was he unlocking it and inviting her in?

He helped her off with her raincoat.

'Thank you,' she said. Then slowly turned to face him.

Outside it was minus four degrees, but under her coat it might have been spring. Low-cut jade top. Black mini-skirt. Stockinged legs above the boots.

A woman with a perfumed smile has a stronger chance than a woman who scowls. Nonetheless, there was something blatant about Jeanine's expression that prompted in Andy a moment of circumspection. Her smile did nothing to erase the incurious face of the woman who had driven him home on Monday afternoon. Still less the image of those thrashing eyes that had focussed on him on Friday night in a glare so fierce that he worried in case his skin turned black and started wisping smoke. Now, she smiled through eyes the colour of brown shot-silk in the way that Sophie had smiled at Richard, as though she wanted to peg him to the sisal floor.

'I've got some red wine open,' trying to rescue his gaze that was entangled in her décolletage.

'Red wine would be great,' she said.

*

He returned to the living room with two glasses quickly rinsed and the bottle of Jacob's Creek that he had opened after her previous visit.

She was sitting in Sophie's chair.

He poured.

She peered at the rim of her glass. 'Cheers,' and sipped.

He raised his glass. 'Cheers.'

Andy did not find it odd that they had settled down like this, before he had asked why she was here. From the way she kicked off her boots and drew up her legs beneath her, there was an intimacy that they already shared, and which he regretted and yet felt powerless to thwart.

'So, Andrew . . .' after her eyes had completed another circuit of the room – which he had spent the whole of Saturday tidying up. This time, above the smile she aimed at him, he saw the outline of a telescopic sight.

He stared into his wine. He felt no urgency to speak. The moment you talk, you say less of what you are. Plus, he was warming to the person he was about to be.

Something was digging into her thigh. She took it out, inspected it.

'Here, let me have that!'

He returned to his seat brandishing the last trace of Sophie. She must have planned her departure for weeks. His only souvenirs of their relationship – the jacket in the cupboard, a pile of fashion magazines. And this hair-clip.

'Sophie's?' as if reading his thoughts.

He nodded. 'She's . . . she was my fiancée.'

'No longer?'

He shook his head.

She crossed her arms, chewing the inside of her cheek. 'I apologise for my behaviour on Friday.'

Andy made what he hoped was a sympathetic noise and looked at his hand. 'I'm sorry about your father.'

'I hated him.'

'Oh, he wasn't so bad . . .' The words slipped out.

'He was. Every bit of him.'

'Come on, no one's that bad, surely. Not when you get to know them.'

Jeanine put a hand to her forehead and stared at the floor.

'He never let anyone get that close.'

'I'm not so sure about that,' Andy said. His own father had found intimacy tricky: a hand on the shoulder, a quick kiss on top of the head – his way to demonstrate affection.

'Well, I am,' she said.

He waited for her to go on, but her eyes had left him, were travelling into some icy past.

'Even so,' he conceded, 'I can see how difficult he may have been.'

His message miscarried.

'Difficult?' sitting perpendicular. 'He cut me off – freezing my trust fund *two days* before I was due to come into it, and letting me know through his lawyers that I could have it only when he had died and not a moment before. That was how he kept in touch!'

Andy had only been trying to say something nice about a dead man.

She went on: 'It meant I had to earn a living, which was no bad thing.'

But the spell was broken. There was something stubbed out about her face, as though where she had sat a maiden aunt of hers was staring with cheeks the colour of ash.

His finger dialled the rim of his glass. 'Is that why you missed his funeral?'

She frowned. 'Maral left a message on my machine. My first re-action – So what?' Her voice had the hard scraping sound of his sister removing the burn from toast. 'But at the last moment I changed my mind. I thought: *Fuck it, no one's going to go. It's pissing with rain, my father's being cremated and not a single person except Maral will be there to register the fact that he has ever lived.* Despite everything he had done, I couldn't bear the idea. But I didn't take into account the London traffic. Or you.' She gave a desultory laugh. 'All I had to do was make it for the final prayer . . .' And stopped. 'Odd, that.'

Andy scrutinised the hair-clip, his fourteen months with Sophie reduced to two blonde hairs. 'It happens to a lot of people at the end, so I've read – discovering God.'

'I suppose,' she said. 'Although I don't remember him having a religious bone in his body.'

They each took another nip. Maybe it was the effect of being four days old, but the wine tasted like Andy felt, ferrous and stale and cheap.

'More?' he said.

'I'm fine.'

She pulled at her bracelet and moved her hand through her hair.

The way her legs looked, tucked up under her, encouraged Andy to give the rest of Jeanine a covert glance. She was attractive, but it was a darting beauty; she gave no impression that she derived pleasure from it herself. Maybe it was because she was a firstborn, like his sister. All those scratches on her prow where she had had to break through the ice.

Turning her head, she caught his glance and brought it back to her face, and he knew that this was someone who preferred to have him look her in the eye than at her body.

'That will was typical of the man. He was so cynical. You really must be some sort of miracle not to have fallen out with him. Are you gay?'

'No.'

'That's not why Sophie left you?'

'No!'

Staring at the glass that rose to his lips: 'Was my father gay?'

He drank too fast. 'Now why would you ask that?'

'You said you were a good friend. That's news to me. My father had no friends.'

Andy kept in his head Vamplew's image of a close, solitary, slightly deaf man. 'I saw no evidence that he was gay – or that sex played a large part in his life.' He sounded stilted even to himself.

'So if you didn't have sex with him, how well did you know him?'

'Oh, reasonably,' feeling trapped. 'I only met your father recently – that is to say in the last few years – but I got to know him quite well,' he gabbled. 'He wasn't always so cynical, you know.'

'Then he must have changed a lot.'

'People do change,' Andy said quickly. He had to say something.

'Not to that extent. Where did you meet him?' she asked abruptly, her chin thrust forward. Something not adding up.

'Where did I meet him?' he laughed out loud.

'Is what I asked.' A lethal look had entered her face. 'Why do you always repeat other people's questions? It's very irritating.'

'This is a long time ago now, Jeanine.'

Up flared the dark brown eyes. 'Would you just tell me?'

His brain whirred, splashing the water to deter a circling hammerhead. He raised his eyes to the ceiling as though an answer might appear through the cracked plasterwork.

A voice. Marilyn Manson. But sounding like Furnivall.

'I remember . . .' sitting up. 'I met him first on the riverbank.'

It was the weekend after his father's visit home. Andy was walking along the path below Sutton Mill.

'Your father was sitting on a bench, peering upstream . . .' And there appeared on the ceiling, like a Dutch painting within a painting, the face of a man in late middle age, dimly with joy.

Eager to share his excitement, the man beckoned Andy over. Moments before, an otter had swum across the mill pool – right at a time when

75

it was feared that otters had vanished from this part of England. Stuart Furnivall – as he introduced himself – was tying on a fly when the otter's wide, sleek head had looked at him and continued swimming upriver, 'undulating like the Loch Ness monster'. And then the head went under and he did not see it again. Not even a ripple; only an odour.

'You can still smell him if you come down here.'

Andy followed to the river's edge and the pair bent over a rock covered in golden brown moss and a blackish-grey sediment, and sniffed. The very strong and distinctive scent reminded Furnivall of the fish counter on Shaftesbury high street, with musk in it. Andy did not know what it smelled like, but he would know it for ever.

The scene presented itself to Andy on his ceiling with the clarity of one of Furnivall's favourite Bramers, and he conveyed it to Jeanine. She wished to know about her father; he would tell her about the person he had met on the banks of the Nadder, who less than a fortnight later walked into his classroom to replace 'Stalin' Podhoretz, his face breaking into a smile when he caught sight of Andy: 'We've met before.'

'After that, we often went fishing together.'

'I didn't know he fished,' Jeanine said slowly – the first time she had taken an interest in what he was saying.

'It was his passion – towards the end.'

'Fishing?' she said, stupefied.

'What he loved most,' he said to her, 'was to catch small wild trout with a Muddler Minnow.'

She shook her head. 'He couldn't fish.'

'When did you see him last, Jeanine?' very quiet.

'About seven years ago. I told you, we were estranged.' It was hard for her to come up with the right words. 'I left home when I was ten. I only met him again – briefly – when I was twenty-one. During his last seven years, I didn't see him at all. Not once.'

'Fishing is a sport many men retire into.'

On the calico chair she continued to hold herself tensely. 'But how did he see in order to cast?'

'I don't follow.'

She looked at him and smiled. A little too exultantly, he felt. 'Well, having only one eye – it can't have been easy.'

He pondered this. Vamplew had not mentioned the Cyclopean aspect. Possibly, he hadn't noticed. But a river mist had descended.

'Well, it wasn't *always* easy. Especially at dusk. But taking his partial blindness into account, he did cast remarkably well.'

She was listening.

'I always stood on – was it the right or left side?'

'You don't remember?'

'I can be a bit dyslexic about things like that.'

She nodded in apparent sympathy. Then moved her hand from her chin to her right ear and began to tug at the lobe, reflecting. 'I wonder what happened to his rods?'

His previous answer, Andy intuited, had been too ornate, like explaining to his mother why he had not been down to Shaftesbury. He would have to tread carefully. 'Won't Mrs Bernhard know?' dipping a tentative paw in the water.

'You're right. Maral will know.'

'He didn't spend much on himself. Except on shoes and wine.'

But she was still sceptical. 'If you were such a good friend, did he tell you what he got up to in that tower of his? Did he tell you if he was writing a book?'

A closet author. Andy brightened. He sensed the hardening outlines of terra firma.

'That's how our relationship developed. I must have met him shortly after you last saw him. He discovered that I worked in publishing. I offered to take a look at his book. One thing led to another . . .'

'So he *was* writing a book?' Her eyes stirred. 'I was just joking. What happened to it? No, I can guess,' with a cold laugh. 'Before he died, he asked you to take it into the garden and douse it with petrol and spread the ashes, along with his own, under the copper beech.'

'You guessed well,' and gave her a conspiratorial smile. 'But in the battle of Art against the Artist, I side with Art. If Virgil's executors had listened to him, we would have no *Aeneid*. If Max Brod had abided by Kafka's wishes we would have no Kafka.'

'What are you saying – my father was Kafka?'

What was he saying? It came out before he could think it through. 'What I'm saying . . .' he said in an earnest voice, rescued by the image of his teacher's still unread manuscript at the back of his desk, '. . . is that I took the precaution of making a copy.'

'You made a copy of his book!' She was impressed, despite herself. 'Was it any good?'

Andy cast his eyes down, coughing. It was one of those plunges. You pinch your nose and you jump. 'To be honest, no.'

'Just as I thought,' slightly relaxing.

He had not anticipated her reaction. But his frank assessment of Furnivall's manuscript gave him an authority he had not so far enjoyed, he could see that.

'If he'd had more time –' he suggested.

'Pah! He had all the time. He had nothing but time.'

'It's always hard . . . with philosophical memoirs.'

She swivelled her head. 'Philosophical memoirs? He wasn't writing a history?'

'He began with that. But I encouraged him to go more personal. To find his voice. To get at the inside story – and through the inside story the wider history. Through the personal comes the cosmic,' he blathered.

'I had no idea he was interested in philosophy . . .'

'God, yes. He was particularly taken by the works of Montaigne.'

'Montaigne? The French writer?'

He had been carried away.

'That's right. Montaigne gave him the reason to go on living, he told me. His favourite line – "Our greatest and glorious masterpiece is to live appropriately." In his last seven years – and I say this without fear of contradiction – your father lived appropriately.'

Jeanine put down her wine and stared straight into Andy's eyes.

'What does that mean, *to live appropriately?*'

Andy's answer was a stone to stick under a tottering cart. 'It's no good me telling you, Jeanine. You'd have to read it for yourself, what he wrote.'

In her expression, incredulity and anger mingled with curiosity. 'At the end . . . how did he strike you?'

'Complex.' Then added for good measure: 'There was really no one like him.'

'You obviously knew him better than me.'

'Not necessarily,' his eyes reverting to the ceiling. But he was aware of a sadness in her voice beyond the sarcasm.

'Look at me. I want to know what he was like.'

Every problem, they say, is new. Here he was, lying to an upset girl about her dead father, not a dilemma catered for in any of the titles on the Carpe Diem list. The only way of escape was to plunge on, towards the figure of Furnivall. At least Andy had a body to work with. And now a manuscript.

The only true authority he had possessed over a book. One by a dead man that no one was likely to read.

In his desperation, he continued to describe the character of his teacher. He could not lay claim to someone he did not know, but if he pictured Stuart Furnivall, it was easy to resurrect Christopher Madigan.

Across the room, Jeanine regarded Andy with a look of unguarded re-evaluation. She repeated in a husky voice: '"English to his toe-nails"? But he had this thing about coming from Armenia.'

'Armenia?'

'Yes, but don't think he told me, I had to find that out myself.'

Andy swallowed. He, too, was having to assimilate rather a lot.

What did he know about Armenia? The massacre for one, not that he had any idea of the details. He ransacked his mind. He remembered that Armenia was the first Christian state and that Byron believed it to be the site of Paradise and that the country that today called itself Armenia was considered not a patch on the original. And that Charles Aznavour was Armenian, as was Khachaturian the composer. That was it. Sum total.

'Being Armenian was certainly important to him, but so were other values.'

'Like what?'

He took a long breath and again sought Furnivall in the ceiling above. It struck him that Jeanine not having set eyes on her father for seven years, much might have happened to Christopher Madigan. He could have gone into therapy and become a terrific bloke. He could have started reading Montaigne in the original. He could even have written a book. It might be hard for her to believe, but practically anything was possible. Each of them possessed only the haziest portrait of her father. All Andy had to do was to make it plausible.

Pointless to tread water any longer. He submerged his head.

'Your father, Jeanine, believed in the power of empathy.'

'Of *what*?'

On her face that expression of adjusting to a revelation still more astonishing.

He breathed out, clinging to the memory of his teacher. '"Stand in my shoes, see with my eyes, feel with my heart" – that was one of his mottoes.'

'Really?'

'Another was: "Life is mostly froth and bubble, two things stand out like stone. Kindness in another's trouble, courage in your own."'

She shook her head and laughed, but with an edge of uncertainty. Like many daughters, Jeanine had felt that she understood her father better than he did himself, despite not having spent time with him since she was a small girl.

'You've got the wrong man. My father didn't have a heart.'

'That was his business face, Jeanine.'

Her hand rose in a tentative motion and fell. 'You . . . you did business with him?'

'I didn't myself, but I observed him with others.'

'Tough. I bet he was tough as guts.' She looked at her stockinged feet. 'It takes three Greeks to get the better of a Jew, but it takes three Jews to get the better of an Armenian. I read that recently.'

'You could trust your father with business, but no one enjoyed doing business with him. If it was a fifty-fifty deal, he'd take the hyphen.'

She nodded to herself, her head at more of an amused angle. 'That would be him. Still, from what you say, he did change a lot . . . The person I knew – thought I knew – wasn't worth knowing.'

'Nonsense!' chucking the hair-pin on the floor. 'That's ridiculous!' Now he was being heedless, but she might have been talking about himself. This was how Sophie had made him feel. How his sister had talked about their father.

'Andrew, *please*. You were his friend – probably his only friend. That's something worth discovering. I thought he was incapable of friendship, of love . . .'

'What about you?'

It was a simple phrase tossed off. But something in her swam towards what Andy had said. His eyes found hers and he had this mystical flash. The floor was a raft and they were floating on it, and the world outside was the mess.

'I thought he had no redeeming quality whatsoever . . .' in a fractured voice, her face tender as if the slightest touch would hurt it.

Andy dropped his eyes. Up until now he had got away with the assassination of Christopher Madigan. He put down his glass and stood up. Before he blew it. Before he had time to dwell on that flash. But he would not forget it.

She was looking up at him. 'Oh, don't worry, I loved him too, adored him – until I found out how he treated my mother. It's what killed her in the end. She couldn't live with the truth.'

'Very few people can,' he nodded.

'What about you?' in a disarming way. 'You seem able to.'

'Me? Yes, well . . .' He was about to make such a fool of himself. 'Listen, there's nothing I'd like to do more than chat with you about your father, but I don't have time right now. Could we speak again?'

'When?'

'I'm tied up for the next few days. Why don't we meet later in the week?'

'Yes,' she said, pulling herself together. She leaned forward and released her legs from under her and twisted around. 'Because I need to tell you something important.'

'You tell me what you need to tell me, and I'll tell you about your father and his book,' he said pleasantly, and went to fetch her coat.

'What about Friday?' she said, buttoning it up. 'Could we meet then?'

'Friday would be good. I'll take you to my favourite restaurant.'

They arranged to meet at the Camões at 7.30 p.m. He wrote down the address. He was not thinking ahead. He did not ask for her telephone number or where he might contact her. He was in that much of a hurry to get her out of his flat. Out of his bloodstream, too.

Jeanine folded away the piece of paper and thrust her hands into her pockets. Still processing what he had told her.

'My father was so secretive. You've reminded me of how little I knew him.'

'Well, whatever I can do to help . . .'

She looked up. 'There is one thing. I would love to read his book.'

'And read it you shall,' in a careless tone, opening the door, surprising himself with what he had said. 'It's in the office right now.'

'Why don't you bring it with you on Friday?'

They were standing close to each other. Their shoulders brushed and they started back.

Before Andy could formulate his prevarication, Jeanine frowned, appearing to remember an important matter that she had forgotten. Her voice became stiff, her expression flintier.

'I ought to warn you, I am thinking of contesting the will. I spoke this afternoon to my lawyers – actually my father's lawyers, before he decided to leave them for this Vamplew character, of whom no one has heard.' In her pale face her eyes shone doubly brown. 'They say I have an exceptionally strong case.'

14

ANDY HEARD IT RINGING from the front steps. One last look at her Beetle driving off. Then he closed the door, making it in three bounds to the landing.

He ran into the living room and hurled himself at the telephone.

'Hello?'

No answer. He could make out a woman in the background singing *'Do you see, do you see, do you see how you hurt me, baby?'* before another voice he had known all his life said: 'Andy?'

'Oh, hi,' and slumped to the floor.

'I've been trying to reach you all week. Mum told me about Sophie. I'm sorry, Andy.'

'Thanks,' although his sister had never camouflaged her opinion of Pirate's Dream as she called Sophie ('as in sunken chest'). Another one who believed that he could do with more maturation.

In a bruised voice, she said: 'Maybe now you'll understand how I felt about Jeremy.'

Andy and his sister had a relationship of arrested development. They regressed in each other's company, picking up the old script they were working on in Shaftesbury.

When Andy was fifteen, his sister was exasperated into telling him at last about the pocket tape recorder that she had found five summers earlier in their father's desk. She had taken it up to her room and listened, embarrassed and mesmerised at the same time. Her father sounded unlike himself, his words charged with love, tenderness, consideration. He must have recorded the message on one of his furloughs abroad and posted the tape to their mother in a fierce fit of missing her, she thought. Until their mother's name should have been mentioned. And then, with a subtle alteration in his tone, the name of another woman, prefixed by the word 'darling'.

'She definitely wasn't called Lynn, who he was talking to. Probably it was Lynn's predecessor.'

The tape confirmed what his sister suspected and what their mother had tried to guard her children from knowing: their father's history of women. It was the reason why his sister had refused to accompany Andy that summer to Grand Falls. By the time she was able to make Andy understand that she had been trying to protect her little brother from the truth, George Larkham was dead and a pattern established. Andy thought that she was being extremely unfair about their father, while his hurt and furious defence of him got on her nerves.

Relations between them had remained pretty well insoluble.

Sometimes when exasperated Andy would let off bitter plumes of steam about his heart-sink sister. How large and gauche and glum she was, given to bouts of despair and biting her nails – the only thing she appeared to live on, he joked cruelly. What else could make her so prickly? No one had been able to work it out. Over the years, his friends had developed a lurid picture of a sit-by-the-fire who still packed her shoes at her mother's and preferred nothing more than to ferment in the countryside, curating her slights – 'some of them so ancient they could be carbon-dated', he complained. Often she was so lost to herself that she would shut herself in the toilet and sob and sob and sob. She was never embarrassed if Andy knocked on the door to ask what the matter was. And a nightmare on the river when fishing.

'She's been like that every day I remember,' Andy maintained blackly. 'She was probably born like that.' Like the reincarnated member of an errant Merovingian tribe. People were. That kind of scowl took time.

Still, everyone agreed: something was not right with her.

She could be pretty. She was almost pretty. Their mother kept telling her she could be beautiful if only she stopped dressing like a frayed sofa and did herself up and ate sensibly. Although that was being optimistic, Andy thought. 'It's hard to be beautiful while you're imitating a security guard at an incineration plant.' Her upper half was delicate, but below the waist she was a large-hipped mammoth. A tulip in a bucket, he joked. Or one of their mother's paint tins that she used for her plants.

His sister had challenged his affections for so long.

'Don't run away with the idea that I don't love her, I do. But it's no mystery to me why she's still on her own.' Nodding in a significant way to a tortured Canadian voice singing *I am on a lonely road and I am travelling, travelling, travelling*. That was another thing about her. She loved Joni Mitchell.

Which was why it was redundant when speaking of his sister to talk of a relationship. There was a horror Andy used to see in Shaftesbury, an unemployed collector of *Star Wars* memorabilia with hair tufted and gelatined, until he popped up in the shape of his sister's boyfriend.

Jeremy P. Tanyard, or Swamp Thing as Andy used to call him, was responsible for his sister's sole experience of romance to date, and not someone that he warmed to much. It was not simply his lunatic fringe; Andy did not trust him a foot. Quite right too, as events proved. His sister moved in with Swamp Thing, a council flat in Bell Street, but he ejected her after three weeks, no explanation.

After that his sister went back to living with their mother. She juddered around the place, hitting into walls, as if she was being directed by remote. But the mud she threw at Andy over time had cracked off and brushed away. All he wished for her now was to meet someone who might appreciate her good qualities.

Andy went through the motions of saying yes, he was able to appreciate how she must have felt about Jeremy, and was sorry that he had not been more sympathetic at the time, but he couldn't wait to get off the phone.

'Thanks for ringing.'

15

ANDY WAS SITTING BEHIND his desk the following morning – he had been there since 8.30 a.m., the first to arrive – when Vamplew rang.

Madigan's daughter had slapped a caveat on the will.

Andy's regret was mingled with relief. Walking to work, he had made up his mind: whatever Jeanine had to tell him at their upcoming dinner on Friday, it was irrelevant. He planned to confess everything. He had not known her father at all. His presence in Chapel 8 had been an accident. If that meant forfeiting his fortune, so be it.

But his resolve dissipated even as Vamplew continued in a level voice: 'As the executor, I have written to say that they must show grounds for this or back off.'

Andy struggled to recall their previous conversation. 'You believe they have grounds?'

'Unlikely. I believe it's a rigmarole to scare the estate while they decide whether to dispute the will. On which subject, may I ask formally what is your attitude to a claim by her?'

'My attitude?'

'Do you wish to keep all of your entitlement?'

'Why, do you think I shouldn't?'

Vamplew reminded Andy that in the event of any claim he had to be neutral and await the outcome of the court – unless a settlement was reached beforehand between the beneficiaries.

Andy described Jeanine's second appearance at his flat. He wanted to tell him the truth.

For a long time, Vamplew did not speak. At last, he said: 'Do you intend to see her again?'

'I've invited her out to dinner this Friday.'

There was no response. The traffic went by and down the corridor Goodman was greeting Angela good morning. Then that formal, distant voice: 'If you wish to preserve your entitlement to the estate, it seems to me you should not meet her again, but conduct yourself at arm's length.'

*

Nothing happened for the next few days. No midnight bells. No solicitor's letters. The only post the following morning – Vamplew's letter for Andy to show to his bank manager. The effect was instantaneous. Not only did Miss Obiora unblock Andy's credit card and increase his overdraft, allowing him to settle all his bills and pay back Angela her hundred pounds, but she urged him to consult with a private wealth expert, and offered to set up the appointment and even accompany Andy to the introductory meeting in Canary Wharf.

Vamplew had also enclosed a copy of Christopher Madigan's preamble. It was easily paraphrased. Life was absurd. An ugly game. A few paragraphs gave the flavour.

'I have no idea who you are. Possibly you are a person familiar to me. Or a casual acquaintance who receives this money as a reward for fidelity to habit and ritual. You might be someone I have never met. I'm not concerned. Knowledge is overrated . . .

'Whatever impulse caused you to be an Attender at the final prayer, I enjoin you to remember that an old man's sayings are seldom untrue. My fortune bought ease and convenience, but its own poverty, too. Nobody is suddenly good or suddenly rich. Nor are we suddenly loved. Before I acquired my wealth, no one but my grandmother, my parents and the woman I was to marry appeared interested in my well-being. After I became rich, that changed . . .

'All that money has taught me is this: If you believe in love, you are taking on an illusion that will kill you. The only reality is blind chance. It was luck that brought me this money. I distribute it now in the same vein.'

Andy read and reread the letter. It seemed written in a stilted style. He was going to have to find out more. His sole lead was the address in Holland Park which Vamplew had mentioned in the will. This was where Maral Bernhard was permitted to live for the next eighteen months, before it became hers to divide with Andy. Jeanine apart, Andy's fellow Attender was the only person who might be able to answer his welter of questions.

11 Clarendon Crescent was a substantial white house in a quiet street bumpy with sleeping policemen. Twice after work, Andy opened the low cast-iron gate, climbed the steps and rang the bell. The tall windows, four to a floor, remained dark behind their shutters and no one came to the door, which for a front door was rather distinguished, with stained-glass panels in the pattern of the zodiac.

On the second occasion, Andy walked down an alley to the rear of the house. A large copper beech dominated the back garden, obscuring a stucco facade the colour of clotted cream. The most noticeable feature was a brick tower – he expected to see a stream of bats fly out of it.

Not finding Maral Bernhard in residence, Andy was at a loss to know how to contact her. Nothing under her name was listed in the telephone directory and Vamplew remained scrupulous about not revealing her number. He was happy to pass on Andy's details and to tell her that Andy wished to speak with her, but she never got in touch.

All week the questions remained. Who the hell was this guy? And why such a misanthrope? And how had he grown so wealthy? And was there a catch? *Because I need to tell you something important.* Maral Bernhard had said the same thing to Jeanine outside the chapel in Richmond.

On Friday morning, David called him at work with a progress report.

'Sorry, Andy, I'm drawing a blank. The name Christopher Madigan is not attached to any mining company or charity and his name doesn't appear in our cuttings. You?'

'Nothing. Except that he might have changed his name. Originally, he was Armenian.'

'Armenian?'

'It doesn't matter.'

A beat. Then: 'What are you doing tonight?'

'I'm supposed to be going out.'

'Who with?'

Andy couldn't not tell him.

'Andy, you weren't seriously thinking of seeing his daughter?'

'Not really,' he said. Although he had gone so far as to book a table at the Camões. The truth was he did not know what he was going to do. He needed to understand why someone would behave like Christopher Madigan, even though every step he took to find this out placed his inheritance at risk. But he could not help himself. He had felt attuned to something in Jeanine, a vibrancy.

'That's good,' David said. 'Because the very last place in the world you're going tonight is the Camões. Instead, you're coming to the Knopwood where I shall stand guard over you like bleeding Cerberus.'

Andy could feel David's breath on the back of his neck as he ordered two pints. It was shortly after 7.15. The intense way David looked at him, Andy recognised from years past when engrossed in the side of an Ovaltine jar to obtain a Captain Midnight Secret Decoder Ring. David launched in immediately. 'He purchased his shoes from Ducker's in

Oxford and had an account with Berry Brothers in St James's, and a quarter share in a mare that once came fourth in the Derby. On the other hand, Farlow's have no record of any C. Madigan. Recluse he may have been, but no fisherman. Nor have I had luck with Armenian leads, although absence of evidence is no evidence of absence . . .'

Once David's interest was aroused, he was a tenacious bastard.

But Andy could not concentrate. He kept glancing at his watch. The time was approaching 7.30 p.m., and he was conscious that he should be elsewhere. A promise was a promise, even if it led to his undoing. Jeanine was waiting for him at the Camões, waiting to hear about her father; and waiting to tell Andy something important. He was often late, but you could rely on him to turn up in the end. This time he was not even going to turn up. On top of it all, an unwelcome sense of guilt affected him, as though he had violated an elemental protocol.

Over in the corner, the Dry Heaves struck up '*J'attendrai*'. Andy batted Jeanine out of his mind and drank the night away. He had no idea how he found his way to bed.

Next morning when Andy heard the postman come whistling up the front steps, he tensed himself for another recorded delivery to sign. Nothing.

All that weekend he was on edge. Hanging around in case the telephone rang – and if it did, not answering. Caught between a clutch of dread that Christopher Madigan's inheritance was on the point of being snatched away. And – in the next breath – a strange hope that it might be.

This unclear and awkward feeling did not disappear. Each time the buzzer sounded, it chilled him with fright. Even had he wanted to apologise for not turning up, he had no address for Jeanine. He squared it with his conscience by telling himself that she, on the other hand, knew where he lived.

Late one night he heard a hesitant noise outside, the engine of a questing taxi. He got up from his bed and parted the curtain. Not her.

Was it so unpardonable, what he had done? Was it any worse than driving through a red light on an empty road? Or was he being mercenary, unreasonable?

'What if I make a deal and give her an ex gratia payment?'

David advised against. 'She'll only change her mind. She'll come in all lawyered up and take the whole estate.'

And why should Andy give her anything? £17 million was, after all,

£17 million. A figure to which he had become accustomed. A recompense for his misery. It was his, thank you very much.

The following Tuesday, David invited him to a press viewing of the new Altman film. He went. He enjoyed the film. He went to another. But when David set him up with a couple of dates, he could only feign interest.

Another week passed. No challenge materialised.

He submerged himself in his work. There, at least, he had started to thrive. Goodman stopped giving him a past-tense look. Ideologically, he was back on track.

In the fourth week, the telephone rang on his desk. Vamplew.

'Just to let you know that we have warned off the caveat. Her lawyers have withdrawn. They didn't have the grounds.'

Andy was pleased by the 'we'. 'What happens now?'

'Let's sit back and see if they make a claim.'

While Vamplew busied himself cashing Christopher Madigan's insurance policies, accumulating money and putting it on deposit, Andy kept his head down. As another month came to an end, he gave himself leave to doubt whether she would ever contact him.

Meanwhile, life was improving. His credit card worked. He could open and close his front door. He was back in touch with his friends. In May, following unprecedented sales for Enid Tansley's *Alfresco* guide, Goodman placed him in charge of the entire Valentino list.

The days dragged by. The trees recovered their leaves, although he never seemed to be there when the lights snapped on or the cherry blossom appeared. He was editing Tansley's new book.

Until on a crisp, sunny morning in August, Vamplew telephoned to confirm that although the method adopted by Christopher Madigan did not commend itself to the judge, Andy's right of inheritance had been upheld. The will was proved. 'I am in a position to advise you that no claim has been made and I am therefore able to distribute the estate.'

THE WILL

I

'I'M RESIGNING,' ANDY BLURTED.

Goodman was thrown back. He had received the figures for the latest Tansley. He was about to offer Andy his own general list.

By ten o'clock, Andy had cleared his desk. He walked down the corridor, stuffing a manuscript into his satchel and looking for Angela to say goodbye.

She stood by the sink at her morning ritual, spooning granules from an unmarked tin into a mug.

'Goodman will be sad,' was all she said.

'Come on, he won't even notice.'

She turned to look at him. 'He's not just motivated by money, Andy. There *is* a good streak in him.'

Doubtless there was – or else why would she have endured at Carpe Diem? But it hadn't spread into his books. Three years Andy had worked in Goodman's publishing house, and the only book he felt inclined to take with him was *Missing Montaigne*.

Goodman appeared at the door.

'You may not believe this, Andy, but I'll miss you,' and rested a hand on his shoulder in an embarrassed, paternal gesture.

Andy had never felt lighter as he descended the stairs.

'Hey, man, what's that calypso you're whistling?'

'Before your time, Errol.'

He hugged Errol and stepped out into Hammersmith Broadway. Nothing prepares you for the first day you become rich.

With the assistance of Miss Obiora who had reclassified him as an 'ultra-high-net-worth individual', and asked him to please call her Ayodele, which in Yoruba meant '*la joie s'est entrée dans ma maison*', Andy hired the private wealth manager to whom she had introduced him back in March.

He bought his sister a cottage in Sixpenny Handley; his mother, her own nursery south of Shaftesbury. He was lavish with close friends, especially David who had agreed to keep the story out of his paper and woke one morning to find a black Toyota estate outside his front door, and, in the passenger seat, a parcel containing a thirty-year-old Australian beer-can and a card: *To complete your collection.*

Not that he stinted himself.

'What are your immediate plans?' Ayodele asked in a pleasant manner in the taxi back from Canary Wharf.

'Right now? I'm off to Bradshaw Webb on the Chelsea Embankment to take delivery of a silver CLK 63 AMG Cabriolet.'

Yes, he was a happy man. All his publishing ambitions swept aside in a flash flood of possibilities. He wanted to experiment, to experience.

Andy was aware that in buying his Mercedes he was enacting a cliché, but clichés contained truth and appetites are universal. *There's not a male alive who doesn't aspire to a great car,* he thought. And a bolt-hole. With a terrific sound system and a home theatre. A gigantic bed. And a white Fender Stratocaster guitar. After addressing the needs of his family and friends, Andy bought a flat with a minstrel's gallery in a private courtyard off Kensington Square. He equipped the main bedroom with invisible Sensurround speakers and a high-definition plasma telly. He ordered crates of the best wine and malt whisky. Smoked Cuban cigars. And threw a party.

He hired the jazz band from the Knopwood and invited everyone: his mother and sister, right down to Angela, Goodman and Errol. He asked David to bring his crowd, and to even out the balance he telephoned Sophie's agency and contracted Cassandra to send along a troupe of unattached models.

At nine o'clock on the night, Andy stood leaning over the minstrel's gallery. A fresh-clipped Partagas Lusitania between his lips. Below, the Dry Heaves playing 'Long Before I Knew You'. On the edge of the dance floor Ivo was talking to a strong-looking girl with short-cropped hair and – somewhat noteworthily – making her laugh. Angela was dancing in a frenetic way with her dowsing instructor, a furtive, blinking, toothy-looking man. David was in deep conversation with Andy's mother. Andy could not see his sister.

He had invited her, of course, but never for one moment did he expect her to show up. He had swiftly introduced her to the first un-accompanied male he could find – Goodman – which in retrospect was a wasted opportunity, given his history with women. He had not seen her since.

'Andy?'

He turned and there – in hippy-de-luxe jeans fastened by a whip of black ostrich leather with a gold serpent's head on a buckle – she was. Pirate's Dream.

'Hello, handsome,' as if the last six months had rustled away like maple leaves.

'Sophie! What are *you* doing here?'

'Cassandra put me in charge of the girls,' giving his shoulder a proprietorial, ball-wrenching squeeze. She stood back, gorgeous as ever. 'Here, let me take a squinny.' And the new monied Andy caught a look in her eye that was never there when he worked at Carpe Diem. 'Don't you look well!' she said.

'You, too.'

'I *am* well,' having signed up with a Paris couturier to model belts such as the one pulled tight around her waist.

'Richard?' peering over her shoulder.

She looked about. 'I say, Andy, this is one helluva place.'

He stubbed out his cigar and took her on a tour.

There were people – many of whom he did not know – crammed into corridors and bedrooms. Even the marble-floored bathroom.

'It's busy,' bayed a voice quite like Goodman's, followed by a familiar-sounding girlish giggle. Quickly followed by a whisper definitely like Goodman's: 'And what is better than that?'

'Let's go in here,' Andy said, unlocking a door.

They passed into his study. Sophie kicked off her shoes and lay down on a long chair. 'This is *so* comfortable.'

'It should be. It's a Le Corbusier lounger.'

Andy, knowing little about art or design, had hired a girl who had dropped out of architecture school. India had taken him to auctions and advised him on what to bid for and even who to invite to his party. A bit of fun, really.

Sophie had her eyes fixed on a portrait above the limestone fireplace. They flicked down to the signature and widened.

'Not Warhol as in?'

'The very same,' settling himself opposite in an Eames chair.

'Who's the dude? Napoleon?'

Andy mentioned the name of a former politician, currently in prison. India knew the man's wife who had had to sell the portrait to pay for his legal fees. 'I got it for a good price.'

In the main room, the Dry Heaves were riffing into a jazz rendition of 'In Dreams'.

The look on Sophie's face had deepened. Down the memory hole had gone her callous treatment of Andy Larkham, impecunious self-help editor. 'If you'd won a dime for every time I thought of you . . .'

'Do you want to dance?' he asked. There did not seem a lot else to say. What surprised him was how calm he felt.

She stayed on after everyone left. They had had lots of sex before, but this was exceptional.

Except, it was not the same. Even if Sophie manifestly thought that it was.

'You let me go and I'm back because I realised that I'm truly yours,' she said just before dawn.

She lay naked on her side. Her long lean body stretched out.

'Then why did you go off with that banker?'

Sophie swirled the thought and looked very tragic, as if it would not fit into her head. 'You got rid of me.'

'No, I took you to dinner to talk about our honeymoon in Cintra and you left with the other man.'

She shook her head and with her finger traced a pattern on his stomach.

'The thing is, Andy, you and I are very alike, and that's how it's always going to be.'

He repressed a snort of laughter.

She finished her hieroglyph with a full stop. 'Andy, couldn't we begin again?'

Andy looked down at her body, the waist to launch a thousand ostrich leather belts, and opened his mouth to agree when he heard himself like another person who lay beside him say: 'No, Soph, I don't think so.' He could see that the roots of her hair were dark. 'I'm with someone.'

He watched the snatched hands reaching for cover. 'How *dare* you . . .' she began. She arranged herself hastily into a modest position on the edge of the bed. 'Is . . . is it serious?' Not looking at him now.

'Oh, yes, it's serious. We're engaged. I just haven't bought the ring.'

'Do I know her?' She jumped from the bed and started pulling on her stonewashed jeans. Her buckle projected darting shapes on the wall like reflections from a knife.

'I doubt it.'

'Why tell me this now?' bustling into the bathroom. He recognised something hysterical on the edge of her words. It was how he had sounded at the Camões.

'Because I won't see you again,' said his voice.

*

96

It was a few days before Andy adjusted to the fact that he did not have to walk to Carpe Diem through the rain every morning in order to gag on Angela's instant coffee. Or drink a stale bottle of Australian red wine when he returned home. Or clench himself each time he caught sight of a rodent-coloured envelope. He had eleven million pounds in various accounts, with dividends and interest accumulating daily.

The fear that his new life might be seized from him at any moment began to fade. He still looked over his shoulder. But nothing happened. Jeanine had disappeared. He was in no hurry to pursue her. Nor, after anticipating this moment for six months, was he curious any longer about his benefactor. Jeanine was probably right. Her father probably was a bastard. Madigan, Maral Bernhard, Jeanine – he was pleased not to have to think about them.

Meanwhile, his life immediately improved in hundreds of small ways. Instead of the Tube, he took taxis. If someone recommended a book, he ordered it on Amazon, although he did preserve some meannesses – such as a list of books that he refused to buy until they came out in paperback. He adopted Goodman's habit of sending letters second class. 'Only poor people use first class.'

The unexpected gave pleasure. He wrote out cheques to his most deserving friends, with the condition 'under no circumstances tell anyone else how much this is for'. He could not be a big-league philanthropist, but it excited him to make anonymous gifts to strangers. Dining on his own in Launceston Place, he noticed a courting couple and from time to time glanced over at their table. The young man reminded Andy of himself in the way he ordered the cheapest items from the menu, while encouraging his companion to choose whatever she fancied. Andy had long departed the restaurant by the time the bill was called for, and had to imagine the young man's expression when the waiter said: 'That's all right, sir, there's nothing to pay.'

'What do you mean?'

'That gentleman over there' – pointing to Andy's empty chair – 'asked me to give you this' – and unfolded the piece of paper on which he had scribbled: *Stay together.*

Andy no longer had a girlfriend, but he believed himself to be as happy as that couple. It wasn't long before he understood the truth of what Christopher Madigan had written in his preamble. No one can be rich too suddenly. Obvious stuff, but Andy could not fully appreciate its meaning until it happened to him. And it started at home.

*

His sister was grateful for his help, but her jocular asides carried a new edge. 'Don't think because you've given me a house I'm going to start forgiving all the horrible things you've said and done to me over the years.' Not only had he bought her a pink brick Elizabethan cottage with a spare paddock for a horse. But he had managed to kick-start her romantic life by introducing her at his party to Rian Goodman, who the very next day had invited her for a lobster lunch at Wheeler's. Andy doubted that she had ever tasted lobster before in her life.

At first, he put it down to simple jealousy that people did not rejoice at his good fortune, and that his money seemed to act as a measure of everyone else's lack. 'You've been lucky. Why haven't I?' He started to feel himself the source of people's resentment and rage as well. They regarded him as lucky *only*. Had he worked his guts out in Richard's merchant bank, at least they would have nursed a grudging envy. But all he had done was turn up, late, to the wrong event. It should not have surprised him really. He would have felt the same way. What did shock him was to suspect these emotions in people he would never previously have dreamed of harbouring them. His personal relationships had instantly grown complicated.

One of the first difficulties you have to negotiate with wealth is what do you do with someone who has become a close friend. Popular at school, Andy had always placed importance on friends. His friends were his brothers. But now they disappointed him. They appeared unable to handle his success. It was not clear to Andy what to do about this. Ivo was too busy appreciating the girl he had met at Andy's party to show gratitude for the cheque that Andy had written him, while David wrote one lousy e-mail to thank Andy for the Toyota. Montaigne had it spot on. 'Benefactions are welcome so long as we feel we are able to return them. But if they pass far beyond that point, we requite them with hatred, not thanks.'

Especially, Andy began to see less and less of David. It was cumulative, but what upset Andy most was that all the time he was renovating his new flat, David did not come over. And why should David care? Because he was Andy's best friend, that's why. Of course, Andy did not mention it. David would have said: 'Oh stop it, Andy, you're being paranoid.' Andy did once say to him: 'Well, you haven't asked, but I'm very well, and my flat's almost ready. Since you didn't ask.' David had stared at him with a strange expression that Andy remembered from Semley Nursery. 'Are you all right?'

David's strained and vacant look made Andy feel that he did not want David around after all. It was the same with Ivo, who took one glance at the fireplace, gave Andy advice that he did not need, and remarked that he was extremely fortunate to have found such a good designer.

'Wait a sec. I picked the colours, the fabrics, the limestone. She didn't want to use Onondaga limestone' – because Andy had discovered not only an interest in design, but some talent. India told him that he had excellent instincts for materials. It hurt to realise that the people he cared about should be almost hostile in their indifference. He received no credit from anyone. The only credit he received was if he went with friends to a restaurant. Then when the bill arrived, he was the one they looked to. Andy did not begrudge them. Not at all. At least, not at first. But the occasional gesture – even a half-hearted one – might have been nice. Someone reaching for a wallet. Although to his credit David always e-mailed him the next day.

All this, Andy saw, was why the rich hang out with the rich. It was a tribal thing. When you wanted to have shared experiences and could afford the best, it was more comfortable to be with people of similar means. Who paid for what was immaterial; it would balance out. Nor did you have to downplay the fact that you had shelled out five times your previous salary on the car of your dreams.

But he found wealth an isolating experience.

Not long after his party, Andy took off. Only to his mother, when she pressed him, did he attempt an explanation of where he was going and why. He had a desire to see Montaigne's castle in the south of France and to read his teacher's book, he said. Had it not been for Furnivall, he would never have come into this money; and he considered it his duty, he told his mother – now that he had the leisure to give *Missing Montaigne* the attention it merited – to find some way to honour what amounted to Furnivall's last will and testament, before the grass grew over his name.

He did not think she believed him.

'Have you rung your sister?'

And when he did?

'What am I? Chopped liver?'

'I have been extraordinarily busy.'

'You're so anthropocentric.'

'How's Goodman?'

In an unfamiliar voice: 'He's right here. Do you want to speak to him?'

'Goodman?' Andy started laughing, but no sound came out. He composed himself. 'Not right now. I've got to catch a ferry.'

2

FROM SEPTEMBER TO AUGUST, Andy was a boy playing truant from school. He woke with his heart soaring at the prospect of the whole day to himself to do as he wished, although he was aware that he might grow frivolous if he did not get a plan in order. Which was why, wherever he stayed during those first days abroad, he made certain that there was a desk. The manuscript in a neat pile next to his laptop, his pencils and sharpeners in an RAF mug that had belonged to his father. But his one idea – to lose himself in *Missing Montaigne* – never happened. Each time he settled down with an intention to read it, some new distraction took over. There was lunch. Then dinner. The casino. The attractive – and available – women. There was bed. How else to explain that in nine months he did not get beyond page thirty-five? Often he would read a page and realise that he had read it before, and not just once. He began to feel like the man who works through the night to compose a single sentence that he erases at daybreak.

Four days after crossing the Channel, outside a hotel in Cluny, next to the monastery, Andy was showing off his new iPhone to a girl called Lenka, who had stopped to admire his car, when it vibrated.

Thanks for the party. Where did you & Sophie get to . . . ?

PS Your mysterious benefactor – I've discovered an Australian connection. In Oxford last week I popped into Ducker's & met his cobbler. Apparently, Madigan needed special shoes after prospecting in the Australian outback. Did he make his fortune there?

Andy was grateful when David had offered to discover all he could about Christopher Madigan. But following Jeanine's failure to pursue him in the courts, Andy had asked David to lay off his investigations. The subject was better left buried.

Lenka looked on, smiling – a lovely smile, it really was – as he texted back: *Don't worry, I've brought closure to it. What do I owe you for your trouble so far? Just send me the invoice.*

'My best friend,' he said, and showed her a photo of David in his Crocs, which did not impress. Then he took one of Lenka – in close-up – and showed it to her, which she enjoyed.

Their affair did not last long. From the initial vitality to the exit point of exhaustion: two weeks. But his experience with Lenka, a showstopper when it came to tantrums, set the tempo for the next eleven months. He was a stand-in for someone else who should have been there, not him. As David kept on reminding.

Sod you, Andy. I'm not doing this to be paid for it. I'm doing this because you were a friend and I thought it mattered to you. Problem is, now it matters to me. I'd like to know who this SOB was who's made you into such a SOB. Love, D.

Andy had left England with the idea that the whole of his life was a fresh canvas.

He gambled. In the past, he had dabbled with David and Ivo at black-jack and craps, which give the best odds. But his gambling instinct changed now that he had money. He preferred roulette, where the odds were stacked against him.

He travelled to Venice, which was crowded, and to the Alentejo, which was not, and to Havana (for a cigar convention) and to Switzerland (for a Bugatti rally). On previous trips, he had never tipped – and certainly never treated himself to that freshly squeezed orange juice in the morning. Every day in Portugal with Sophie he had thought to himself: *Can I make it?* Now, he could order what he liked, whenever and wherever he liked, and he wanted to do it.

Only with women did money get in the way, impede any progress beyond the surface gestures and games. Waiting for love to strike started to feel like trying to create a bird out of a bird-bath. He had fun, but nothing lasting. He met nobody he wanted to spend time with.

In Venice, he saw a woman having a drink by herself in a café. There was something familiar about her expression. Something nearly forgotten that he recognised as having to do with him, and yet which he had not encountered before, like facing his own bowling at cricket. He pushed it aside, but as he walked down the dimly lit street back to his hotel he felt a throttling sadness.

Every few days, Andy received another e-mail from David.

In Paris: *No Madigan is listed as owning any Australian mine. We need his Armenian name.*

In Munich: *Spoke to his wine merchant at Berry Bros. Madigan liked Tuscan red & Pétrus; & owned a small vineyard nr Lisbon.*

In the Casinò di Campione on Lake Lugano: *Spoke to a jockey at*

Epsom who rode for Madigan. M's father loved horses – his family bred
them in Turkey.

Christopher Madigan had become a replacement for David's beer-can collection.

To none of these e-mails did Andy respond. He had been interested at the time, but he had moved on. Surely, David had better things to do than sleuth around in a dead man's past. Andy did. As he ambled down to play roulette.

But still the e-mails kept coming.

C. Madigan was principal benefactor of the Cicada Foundation &
involved in philanthropic activities. Also a Cheryl Madigan on the board.
Jeanine's mother? I'm seeing the files tomorrow.

Until, feeling exposed, a slightly sick feeling, he stopped reading them. He created a new file: 'David's Unreadables'.

He drifted south. From Switzerland to Vienna. Cafés, piano music, warm puddings. Capri, Rome – a city of statues, as he wrote in postcards to his mother and sister. In Naples, he let himself be carried away. His nights warmed in the arms and legs of compliant young women with names like bootleg vodkas.

In Sorrento, he saw someone come towards him and involuntarily heard himself say 'Jeanine?'

His mother had dug a square hole before she planted her coastal beard-heath – 'or else the roots will spiral round and round in a circle and not go down.' That part of himself which was above ground was growing heavier and heavier.

3

THE END OF SUMMER saw him driving towards Florence with a girl called Gabriella.

Their romance was a fortnight old. 'Andee', she liked to call him. Never had she 'adored' anyone so much.

It was a late afternoon in August. They were hurtling through the Tuscan landscape at 140 kph, and he was telling her all the ways in which this car was an improvement on the previous model, but he could see her face in the driver's mirror. Of greater fascination than his spiel about the Formula One-derived traction control system was the odometer: it registered 99999 and she kept glancing at it with girlish expectation, fingering the garnet necklace he had bought her, waiting for all the digits to go round.

Andy had a sense of déjà vu. Hadn't he been here before? And then it came to him: he was the figure in the television commercial watched in Hortense Avenue a century before, only more unshaven and tanned, with an inflexible scowl beneath his shades.

Next to him, Gabriella stirred.

'Oh, look!'

It was Gabriella's habit, which in the first week he had found enchanting, of enthusing about whatever caught her deep-set eye. A fortnight ago, it had been him. With an immobile face he turned to her and saw that he had been supplanted in her admiration by a hilltop church.

Indulging her, he pulled over onto the shoulder and now he knew where he was.

In the gathering dusk, they mounted the steep steps and entered the interior of San Miniato al Monte: dark and cool, with the echo of subdued voices, and in the valley outside a chaffinch yelling.

Inside, the smoothness of certain coloured marbles. And an ottery smell.

He looked around. The last time he had stood in a church or chapel was in Richmond. He put a finger to his shades and lifted them.

A thickset man, late sixties, in a linen blazer was speaking in English to a group of elderly tourists. Chiselled, calculating face; intense blue eyes; flat grey hair slicked down with lubricant. A guide from the hour of his birth, Andy thought.

Blinking in the direction of the pointed finger, Andy saw – high up on a darkened wall – a painted figure in a scarlet robe, gold crown, holding a javelin and lily.

The guide continued in an Australian accent: 'The church of San Miniato al Monte is dedicated to the first Christian martyr in Florence . . .' Noticing Andy, he smiled. His eyes absorbed the light in a disarming way, lending them a strange tint.

Andy caught the drift. Young soldier in the Roman army. Becomes a hermit. Arrested on orders of Emperor Decius and thrown to the lions – who refuse to devour him. Cast in boiling cauldron, suspended from gallows, stoned and beheaded. Whereupon he picks up his head, replaces it on his shoulders and walks back across the River Arno to his hermit's cave on Monte alle Croci, site of present church. And then the interesting bit. 'He was an Armenian Prince.'

Giddy, as if spun around too fast, Andy stepped outside – the darkness that had fallen, the lights of Florence below – and took a deep breath. The mention of an Armenian had tugged him up a different hill. Christopher Madigan flashed through his mind. Something shifted when he said the name to himself; the pressure of a great postponement. He did not look up, and then he did and saw a round silver moon that reinforced his thought.

The thought did not go away as he waited for Gabriella. She ran up and slipped her arm through his – she had been chatting to the guide – and they walked back down the steps. The strong moonlight fell across her collar.

All that medieval brightness in the sky, in which everything beneath presented itself with ruthless and dramatic clarity – Andy saw it so well:

Madigan's will was no different to one of those three-card tricks that he used to see played outside Ladbroke Grove Tube. What he imagined would give him an unfair advantage had been a device for his own deception.

It was suddenly cool. Gabriella pressed closer, her chatter swishing the whys and whatifs. But in the moonlight one thing stood out clear. Unearned happiness was not happiness at all.

He would have liked his sister to be there. He heard her saying: 'When are you going to stop being a Selfish Slut?'

They reached the road and walked along it to where he had parked. He opened the passenger door for Gabriella and a line came and went from Furnivall's manuscript: *Luxury is more terrible in its ravages than war.*

Gabriella turned in her seat and the smell of the car upholstery lodged in his throat.

'I'm putting the roof up,' he told her.

He took off his shades and folded them into the glove-box and drove away in silence. If he could ask San Miniato one thing: why did Christopher Madigan make such a will? The question he had stopped asking himself, intentionally had put away, but which David had been constantly nagging him about all year.

His thoughts pierced by Gabriella's cry.

'Oh, we've missed it!' staring in a heartrending way at the dashboard, which registered 100001.

Behind them, a siren wailed. An ambulance raced up and overtook.

Andy drove on, breathing in the herby Mediterranean night. Rolling hills with the fragrance of cypress and the full moon reflecting on the ponds; and the boundlessness of the evening sky. They passed the edge of a reservoir. Caught in the headlights, a thick white vapour lay suspended above the water, coiling over the road.

He slowed.

The mist engulfed them and then thinned, and then covered them again.

From somewhere, a harsh cry.

'Is that a duck?' Gabriella said.

'Sounds more like a pheasant.'

She listened to the cry rising and falling. 'I never heard a noise like that before.'

Then they were out of the mist and he changed gear and sped on.

A while later they came to a village. There was a commotion in the main square. A carabiniere in a fluorescent yellow jacket stood flashing a torch, diverting traffic up a side street.

In quick succession, Andy saw a mangled black Vespa; a crowd peering from behind a tape; and the ambulance parked up on the pavement – rear doors open and lights blazing.

He glimpsed two bodies on stretchers – younger than him and slimmer, with a sapling quality. A boy and a girl. And then the doors were pulled shut.

Andy was absorbing the tentacles of grief that extended from the ambulance out into the square towards parents, friends, relatives, and failed to see the carabiniere waving him down. A loud rap on the bonnet brought him back. He was so disoriented that he accelerated before stamping his foot on the brakes.

The carabiniere gestured for him to wind down his window.

'Where have you come from?' with a sharpness in his voice.

A sick, nervous feeling spread through Andy, delaying his response.

Gabriella took over, answering in Italian. They had been at San Miniato al Monte. Sightseeing. There was a guide who could vouch for them. Yes, they were tourists.

The carabiniere listened absent-mindedly, flashing his torch up and down the sides of the car, the bumpers. Not finding what he was after, he spoke across Andy to Gabriella.

'He wants you to open the back,' she said.

Andy climbed out. The crowd had turned in his direction. Even as he inserted the key, he felt the dread that comes from having committed a terrible crime. He raised the boot expecting to find a body curled up inside.

The carabiniere poked the two suitcases without opening them. He thrust a hand into the holdall and flicked through the pages. Then indicated for Andy to close the boot. Gabriella had joined them and he talked to her in an angry way, too fast for Andy to follow, now and then gesticulating towards the crowd with a distressed expression.

He waved them on, but Andy did not feel pardoned.

'What was he saying to you?' he said to Gabriella.

'He was saying the other car didn't stop.'

An old couple sitting on a bench had witnessed it. The lovers on their scooter. A silver cabriolet going much too fast – foreign number plate, male face at the wheel – and then nothing more, gone.

'He ploughed into them and didn't stop.' She shook her head, nestled closer. 'What a prick.'

He went on driving.

The full moon rising was Madigan's single gimlet eyeball.

'Are you all right?' she said after a long while. 'You've done nothing wrong, Andee,' and patted his knee. 'You're a good man.'

'No,' he said, 'I'm not that good.'

'We all arrive in the end at the same inn,' the vicar had said at his father's funeral. That night Andy and Gabriella checked into a pensione in Ponte all'Asse. Its restaurant was closed for repairs and the manager sketched out directions to a bistro on a paper napkin.

Andy went through the motions of ordering, but he ate without conviction. The events of the past three hours had shaken him. First, a headless

Armenian saint; then, a couple of young lovers blotted out in a hit-and-run accident.

Dinner over, he walked Gabriella back to their pensione and had the sensation of being watched by another figure. If he looked in a window, there, across the street, she stood. When he took the stairs to their room, she followed a few steps behind, gazing with steady brown eyes, one hand above the other on her umbrella handle.

He escaped into the bathroom while Gabriella undressed.

In the mirror, he saw himself through her eyes. Tall, English, approaching thirty, with straight fair hair parted across a wide brow that had been out in the sun, a long narrow nose, and his mother's careful eyes, pale blue and estimating. But the thing he noticed – how his face had an interrupted look, like a book that's been flattened at a page. It was the exhausted, resigned face of someone unsure of his passion, or hiding it.

From the bedroom: 'Andee?'

A clandestine image stole back – Jeanine sitting opposite him in his flat in Hortense Avenue. He remembered the burn of recognition when he looked into her eyes. Wasn't she – of all people – entitled to the truth?

The question nagged at him long after their tired bodies rolled apart, disturbing what should have been his peace, like the sound of a phone ringing and ringing until it falls quiet.

Breakfast next morning took place in silence. Whenever he looked over his shoulder or across the floor of the room, there Jeanine sat with heavy lids, waiting for him. The raw flavour she had left was a lever prising open a crack. Gabriella observed how he was particularly jumpy and low, and left him alone.

He had intrusive thoughts about his life in London, his childhood. He was too depressed to drink or smoke and spent the day in a trance of irritability. He went to bed early and when he woke up it had passed.

Bright and rested, with the clear head of a ten-year-old, he flipped open his laptop. Another e-mail from David.

Haven't heard from you in a while. Are you OK? Am still on Madigan's trail. Guess what? You told Jeanine that her father was a good man – seems you were right.

PS Sophie sighting. On the arm of M & S boss. Hair colour – red

Andy began to drag it into 'David's Unreadables', when he stopped himself. Why was he angry with David?

He stood up and opened a bottle of spring water, trying to pinpoint the source of his hostility. As he drank, he heard David saying: 'Don't ask this pig not to grunt, Andy. You asked me to do this, remember?'

That morning, eighteen months after a chaplain in Richmond uttered the name Christopher Madigan, Andy sat down under the neon light of a not very good café in Ponte all'Asse and opened his 'David's Unreadables' file.

Once he had scrolled to the end, he realised that this was David being David. He was doing the work that Andy should have done, and would have done back in the days when he had integrity; or integrity enough to be curious.

Reading through David's e-mails – more than sixty – Andy felt reconnected. The time had come for him to return to London. But before he parted company with Gabriella, there was one outstanding trip to make.

They were driving after lunch across a plateau of scrubby pines where the Dordogne becomes the Gironde when a prodding noise penetrated his thoughts: his iPhone, on which he had stored his favourite images of the past year, trilling the first five bars of 'I'm Your Man'.

'Andy?'

'Oh, hi Mum.'

He tried to keep in touch with his mother once a week; usually on a Tuesday – her day off from the nursery.

'Where are you right now?' she asked.

'According to the satnav, about thirty miles east of Bordeaux. How about you?'

'I'm staring over the lake towards Semley.'

'What have you been doing?' he said.

'Planting something you've never heard of – and I'd never heard of till last week.' A Cardiandra from Taiwan. The colour of a hydrangea, purply, but with flowers on extended stalks that she likened to butterflies. She had bought it in a nursery south-west of Paris. 'Forget Chelsea. Go to Courson.'

At the sound of her excitement, his heart rose on a wave of affection mingled with envy. How much pleasure it gave her to find a new species, plant certain trees. Melaleucas and banksias, which fifteen years ago might not have survived in England, but now, because the climate was warmer, flourished in her nursery. He wished for himself even a fraction of her passion.

'And what about you?' she asked. 'Have you seen it yet?'

'Seen what?'

'Montaigne's house.'

'Not yet. But I'm about an hour from there as we speak.'

'Anyway, it's not about that I'm ringing. It's about your sister.'

'How is she? Found her heart's rest yet?'

'She's getting married.'

Andy closed one eye to make sure he was not hallucinating. 'Married?'

'In three weeks' time.'

'Run along.'

'I am not joking, Andy.'

'Who on earth to?'

'Rian Goodman, you dolt. Your old boss. Who wants you to be his Best Man. You can't begin to know how grateful he is to you – how grateful both are.'

'To me?'

'For having been Cupid.'

Andy was astonished. He was worried that if he opened his mouth he would start speaking in tongues. He had drunk two grappas on an empty stomach while waiting for Gabriella to return a dress he had bought her, and he could not tell if it was this or his mother's words that had sowed in him a queasy feeling like mountain sickness.

His mother went on: 'She loves him. They're very happy. I would like you to suspend your insults for once and be happy for her.'

'Then I'm very happy for her,' he said weakly.

'You'll be even happier when you see her. She's lost a lot of weight. A lot.'

'Good news?' said Gabriella.

Andy followed Gabriella into a thirteenth-century stone tower – the only part of the original chateau spared by a fire in the nineteenth – and climbed a circular staircase to the third floor. A custodian shuffled up after them to show Andy the little room where Montaigne hid when he heard anyone coming. The cold floor reminded Andy of his bathroom in Hortense Avenue.

The larger room was the library. Andy touched the bare whitewashed walls, imagining the five shelves where Montaigne had stacked his thousand volumes. He crossed the flagstones and stooped at the narrow window. The road along which Montaigne observed people arriving. The exposed hills. The forest where he set loose a stag for the King of Navarre to catch. Andy murmured: 'Just think. For three hundred years all this was English.'

Andy stood there, taking in the space where Montaigne had dictated his essays, the beams above his desk with fifty-four inscriptions in Greek and Latin that he had had burned into the wood when he retired from public life. One of them he translated for Gabriella: 'I am a man. I consider nothing human foreign to me.'

'How did you know that?' much impressed. She made him so sad, Gabriella.

'I had a teacher who wrote a book about Montaigne.'

And to the end of that road he came.

They stepped outside and stood on the grass beside the car. His bags were packed. He was on his way home.

'I want you to have this.'

She looked at the cheque, a twitch in her slow, serious, deep-set eyes. They widened to read the figure he had written. But, hell, it was only someone else's money.

'I'll drop you at the station in Bordeaux.'

Gabriella was staring at him.

You betray yourself in those moments. He felt sick at her eye contact. He told her, looking over her head at the round tower, its conical red roof: 'If you love someone, you have to let them go.'

MARAL

WHEN ANDY WALKED UP the steps to the Chelsea Register Office, an attractive woman barred his way. She wore a simple cream dress and had short fair hair. She smiled down at him.

'Excuse me,' in his politest voice. 'Are you with the Larkham-Goodman wedding party?'

'Hello, you poon.'

He did not recognise his sister in the slender creature who wrapped her arms around his neck, smelling of something French and squeezing him to her. The fact that she was smiling may have had something to do with it.

'When did you get back?' as she covered his cheeks with kisses. Lifted, the all-concealing burka of her gloom.

'Last night.'

'I'm *so* pleased you're here,' and leaned away to get a better look at him. She sounded as though she meant it, too. 'Rian was convinced you'd be late.'

'You look so –' but he could not find the right word.

'Andy! You made it!'

And here he was, the congenial goliath of the self-help industry, his well-ordered stomach encased in a blood-red velvet waistcoat, beaming at soon-to-be-wife-number-three and informing her that Andy was the best editor employed in the history of Carpe Diem, and the only bad thing he would continue to hold against him was that he had never let on about his sister.

Andy looked back at his sister from the depths of Rian Goodman's scarlet embrace, her eyes gleaming with the light of passion. Goodman was, he supposed, an improvement on Swamp Thing. Still, Andy could not help thinking that it would not be long before he was visiting her in Vancouver.

'Mum!'

His mother, a broad-brimmed straw hat on her permed hair, stood a little way off, preoccupied. Her hands were upraised as though in prayer and she peered down through them in the attitude of a postcard he had sent from Rome. *Oh please God!* he thought. *Don't make her have become religious.*

'Mum?'

Still she stood there, like Saint Teresa in an ecstasy. Then she clapped her hands in front of her face, opened them and stared with a satisfied look at something on her palm.

'Want to catch a fly, clap hands above it.'

When they left the Register Office an hour later, the sun was dazzling.

Even as Andy was acting the prodigal son, his ex-boss had seen clean into the marrow of what made his sister so witchy and spotted something that no one else had.

An underactive thyroid. That's what the trouble was. One of Goodman's authors was on *Woman's Hour* to promote Carpe Diem's latest health compendium, *Your Body, Yourself, You,* and while on a riff about the pervasiveness of depression in the modern female, so pervasive that doctors frequently failed to investigate underlying causes, she mentioned an immune disorder with a Japanese name. Goodman located the passage in the book and showed it to Andy's sister, and listened to what she had to say and then ordered her to take a thyroid test. One doctor thought that she might have suffered from a form of hypothyroidism her whole life, and it was this that caused her to be obese and lethargic, and when she was not being lethargic to be scrapping for a steel-cage fight with anyone she came into contact with; another doctor said that the disease was more likely to have kicked in as a young adult. In any case, the presenting symptoms were consistent with low thyroxine levels. A simple case of hormonal imbalance.

The upside was that within a month of starting treatment – just a daily pill – Andy's sister was no longer the size of a minke whale, nor her usual hysterical, maudlin self. All thanks to Goodman, she had joined the race of anthropocentrics. She felt normal and good about herself.

Her startling transformation set Andy thinking.

2

As I MENTIONED IN my last letter, when I came to Cornwall I resolved to potter around on a river bank, learn to tie flies, and read some of the books I ought to have read, and reread my favourites. Once I was diagnosed, I went back to Montaigne and 400 years had not passed. He was sitting in the same room, looking out over the same stretch of water where my reflections are at their liveliest. But then the strangest thing. I felt him taking me by the elbow and urging me back to my desk to re-examine the book that I'd abandoned umpteen times, about his essays and their relevance to today's world.

There's no reason you should remember this, and I don't want to blow it out of proportion, but the edition of his essays we have today was overseen after his death by his young disciple and adoptive daughter Marie de Gournay, who made many revisions. What always interested me was the earlier 1588 edition, annotated in Montaigne's own hand, and which mysteriously disappeared. This contained numerous insertions and changes in outlook, and there is evidence that he expanded it in order to be more personal and revelatory. For some time I have been obsessed with my own speculations about what Montaigne might have slotted in/taken out. Modelling my reconstruction on what he termed his 'fantasies', I had a go at supplying the missing bits: his meditations on marriage and money, on courage and betrayal, on the daughter he never mentions, et cetera, et cetera. I had no desire to add another book to the mountain (200,000 titles a year, do I read?), but as you see, my scribbles took flight.

3

TWO DAYS AFTER THE wedding, Andy combed his hair and put on a coat and walked out along Kensington High Street. It was late afternoon and his sister would be on honeymoon in Cape Town with Rian, as Goodman insisted Andy now call him. Following his speech at the wedding, the couple had presented Andy with a five-year diary from Asprey's. The inscription inside, written in a firm hand in black ink, read: *Thank you for bringing us together – with love from both of us*, and their signatures.

But the thought of Rian Goodman and his newest bride gambolling among the penguins at Camps Bay also irked Andy. He had had a year to think about his life and what he wanted from it, and what had he come up with? Nothing.

He walked and thought as he headed for his rendezvous. It was windy, but it was not raining, a typical September afternoon in London. Furnivall was fresh on his mind, and Andy was contemplating what his teacher might have made of his sister's metamorphosis when he heard voices yell out. Teenagers crouched around upturned flowerpots at the entrance to the Tube. 'Hey, mister, wanna guess which one's the Joker?' He walked quicker, ignoring the three playing cards.

Andy had finished reading his teacher's book the night before. He felt empty after coming to the end. Void and empty. As it stood, *Missing Montaigne* had no relevance here, in London, in the first decade of the twenty-first century. Had he, instead of hurrying past, approached those teenagers and asked them: 'Excuse me, but can I interest you in the life and reflections of a French nobleman who died 400 years ago?' – they would have looked at him with eyes pumped up on speed provided by Jerome and slotted him with a flowerpot and scarpered.

Montaigne had been correct to warn that 'he who commits his old age to the press is a simpleton if he thinks to squeeze from it anything but dreaming, dotage and drivel.'

Even so, Andy's thoughts kept circling back to Furnivall. It hadn't taken much to transform his sister from a minke whale into a minx. Might the same be true of *Missing Montaigne*?

His teacher's voice remained stubbornly absent from the text, but that was not all. Something vital was lacking, some hormonal imbalance, as it were. Whatever it was, Andy could not put his finger on it, and he was still puzzling it out when around about 6.30 his legs, which were making better sense than his head, carried him up Hobart Street and into the packed bar of the Knopwood.

4

'I KNOW YOU,' SAID the figure in the corner, who put down his paper and smiled, although his eyes were guarded: 'Didn't you used to be Andy Larkham?'

'David,' hugging him. 'David. How great to see you.' It was, too.

'Nice shirt,' rubbing Andy's collar between his fingers. 'Pima cotton?'

'I don't remember,' Andy said modestly.

Andy might have changed, but David had not. His salt-and-pepper beard and shirt hanging out and olive Crocs that looked as though he had never taken them off.

Andy bought a round of drinks. Beer had never tasted so good.

'Cheers,' clinking glasses, but David did not look him in the eye. He stared down at his paper. 'What swine we are,' and folded it. Another massacre in Iraq. One more in the Congo. 'Do you wonder why the words most commonly used with "humanitarian" are "catastrophe" and "disaster"?'

'You got my postcards?' Andy said.

'I did. I did.' But David's expression said you can kiss my Crocs with your postcards.

Andy sipped more of that excellent beer. 'I saw the Riley outside.'

'Yes, still on the road.'

Andy did not ask what had happened to the Toyota.

'Julie?'

'She's good.'

'You're lucky, David, to have her.'

'So, what frost has brought the pig home?'

They were on their fourth pint when David turned to him.

'I'm still waiting for your reaction to what I've discovered about Madigan.'

'To be honest, I haven't considered it,' he said, subsiding, ashamed.

'But intriguing, wouldn't you say?'

Andy shook his head. 'Incredible,' in a stronger tone. 'The story I told his daughter turns out to be true . . . He *was* a good man.'

He could see that David was listening and coming closer after keeping back.

'I'm not sure whether he's a good man or not is the issue. It's just the beginning.'

'The beginning of what?' Andy said.

'Is he good, is he bad, is he crazy? Aren't you foaming at the mouth to find out more? If not, you should be, because this is really about you.'

'About me?'

When David let rip he did so with all his heart.

'You didn't only inherit Madigan's money, you idiot. You inherited his story as well. As long as you refuse to investigate the legacy that comes with the money, you're going to be a miserable git. Why? Because you're paying the price of getting something for nothing. And the price you pay is that you're lost.'

Andy coughed.

'To yourself,' added David. 'I'm serious, Andy,' calling him this for the first time. 'You owe it to yourself to get to the bottom of Madigan's story, to understand why it's you and not anyone else who has ended up with his money. Because you won't know why it's you until you realise what kind of man Madigan was in the first place.'

He faced Andy, letting the words sink in. 'Remember I said you were late for a reason? You didn't receive that £17 million for free. Look on it as an advance that's been shelled out for a book you haven't written. Showing up was securing the contract. Since when, you've been doing what every charlatan author does: spending your advance. But you need to do some legwork. You need to sweat a bit in order to write your way out of whatever pit you've created.'

Part of David's cleverness was not to seem clever. Andy was trying to follow his line of thought when David said: 'This is something you've got to work out, Andy. I am not ghostwriting it for you – although I may be able to help.'

David made a quick inventory of the material he had amassed. He had the excitement of a boy talking about his collection of soccer cards. He was prepared to hand it over.

'I can give you most of the plot and the main characters. But I haven't been able to crack it all. There's Maral Bernhard. She won't talk to me. But you need to see her. She's the key who can make sense of this. What's more, there's an outside chance she might speak to you – being Madigan's only other Attender.'

The crowd had thinned and the barman was bawling last orders when

David looked at Andy in a significant way. 'You realise that in every-thing you've told me tonight there's one name you haven't mentioned.'

'Who?'

'Are you seeing Jeanine?'

Andy drained his glass. 'What makes you think that?'

'Stop blushing like a spanked bottom.'

'David, what makes you think that?'

'Ivo has this interesting idea that's why you haven't been in touch. Historically –'

'I haven't seen Jeanine since the night you and I sat at this bar and you threatened to rip my arms out of their sockets with the assistance of the Dry Heaves if I so much as got up off my chair.' He was seething. It just got to him.

'No bull? Not that I care whether you are seeing her.'

'I am not bullshitting you,' a little too quickly.

'Come on, lads. Door's thataway.'

Uninfluenced by Andy's inexplicable change of mood, David stood up. 'That stuff I've got – I'll dig it out when I get home. I can get you at your Kensington address?'

5

ANDY DROVE TO CLARENDON Crescent the following evening. But when he opened the gate, his courage failed. It was a colder night, and the white stuccoed house, shuttered and dark, looked more forbidding than on the previous occasion when he had stood here. Until his mother's words came back: 'Want to catch a fly, clap hands above it.'

He walked up the steps, pressed the bell.

The trees rustled in a breeze. But nothing moved behind the stained-glass door. He felt slightly uneasy.

Andy had already been in touch with Vamplew, who reminded him that he and Maral Bernhard were due to inherit this house at the end of the month – the date set for Mrs Bernhard to move out. Even were she in residence, she would be unlikely to answer the door, mistaking him for his obsessive friend.

He pressed again. Light from a lamp across the street fell on a row of tiles that he had not noticed before, glazed with the name 'Villa Marash'.

Andy turned the handle. Locked.

He walked around to the walled garden at the back. No one watching. He heaved himself onto the wall and sat catching his breath, peering at the copper beech.

A crack of light through the topmost leaves.

He jumped down, landing on a thick bed of grass, and began walking towards the house, expecting at each step an alarm to go off, security lights to blaze. But the only sound, the leaves rustling; the only light, in that window high up.

You didn't only inherit Madigan's money, you idiot. He started to understand what David meant as he approached the house. There was some fragment of his childhood in the walk across the garden, the pots of herbs and flowers, the unmowed lawn with its sundial on which he grazed himself after tripping over the roots of the tree. He reached the back door and knocked.

No answer.

He shuddered, rubbing his elbow. It was going to be an icy night.

The back door was locked as well. He looked for something to throw at the window. Only long, thick grass. Common sense and fear urged him to leave, but what he did was grab hold of a branch and pull himself up the copper beech.

He could see Jeanine before him as he climbed the tree. He gripped the next branch tighter. Ever since Ponte all'Asse, he had tried to shut her out, his back turned, deliberately avoiding her eye, this person who nonetheless had determined his behaviour by dint of the fact that his every action, every thought was predicated on not thinking about her.

Andy rose level with the window and crawled along a branch until he could see down into the room. He had decided that the house was empty and was not expecting what happened next. Below, a noise like a cough, and then a figure edged into the light.

That sight! His heart beat faster. Pale and drawn with a thin nose and a face lined with wrinkles as though too long in the water. And wearing a skimpy green dressing gown the colour of pine mulch.

He inched further along the branch.

She had inherited £17 million, but she looked crushed.

'Mrs Bernhard!'

She came to the window. In the moonlight he could see her, the dragon to Christopher Madigan's Hesperian garden.

His heart thumped faster than a voodoo drum. Was he serious about wanting to beard this creature in her den?

'Maral Bernhard!'

She pressed her face closer to the pane. A round mouth puttering to itself and two eyes gaping.

What was the matter? Didn't she recognise her name? Did she think he was a squirrel? 'Maral! Maral!'

She arched her eyebrows until they disappeared beneath her hairnet into her sparse grey hair. 'Krikor . . .' She stared at him. 'Krikor . . .' bare-gummed, with a look of indescribable anguish. His grandmother with her teeth out never scared him as much.

'It's me,' he waved, mooned on a branch, looking down at her through the leaves. 'Andy Larkham. Your fellow Attender.'

Maral Bernhard unlatched the back door and let him in.

'I thought you were him,' she panted, looking at Andy with a frightened, furtive expression.

She turned and slopped across the floor, barely raising the soles of her feet. He followed her bent shape, along the passageway, into a spacious hallway stacked with twenty or so plywood tea chests, marked 'Books', 'Papers', 'Paintings'.

'It's all right, I'll be gone by the end of the week,' she said in a strained voice, and shivered. 'Upstairs is warmer.'

She was so weak that she could take one step only at a time.

'Here,' he offered, 'give me your arm.'

'No, I can do this,' snatching it back.

Very slowly, she climbed a broad winding staircase that divided into two on the second floor, and into the room that he had gazed down upon from the copper beech. She sat in a small wicker chair after failing to shut the door. Staring at the brass doorknob, the light reflecting on it from the bare bulb overhead.

A wooden crate was the only other furniture. He dragged it over.

Andy's focus to this point had concentrated on getting into the house to speak with Maral Bernhard. Now that he was here, he had no idea what to say. It demanded little clairvoyance to see that she was in no fit condition to talk about Jeanine's father.

Her face was cracked like his mother's hands. He had an urge to stroke it.

'You must be sorry to go,' he began. 'How long have you lived here?' Once again, this strange sensation of wanting to be her friend, when so clearly he was repugnant to her.

Maral Bernhard looked down. The room smelled of feet and red wine. 'Twenty-nine years,' she said in a defeated voice, and rubbed her thin ankles as though she had cramp.

She was exhausted. She could hardly speak. The stress of leaving home, he supposed. Of having to pack up three decades of objects – in order that the house might be sold, along with those plywood boxes and their contents.

Climbing that tree had made him almost as shaky as her. He felt colder inside the house than out, and, stirred by the smell of alcohol in the room, unbearably thirsty.

'Do you have anything to drink?'

She volunteered to get up, but he said, 'No, just tell me where.' She mumbled something about the kitchen being across the landing, and he went in and found a light and turned it on. All that was left was a crate of wine with five bottles missing and a bottle half full with a cork in it and a glass upside down on the enamel drainer. He took the glass and bottle and came back in and he said, 'Pétrus 1982 – do you realise how much this costs?' and she said, 'I don't know, I was hungry,' and he said, 'Want some?' and she shook her head, so he poured himself a glass and sat there reading the label.

How long he sat there, drinking that superlative wine, Andy could not have said. It tasted as if the whole year and a half – since the first time he stood outside the Villa Marash – had filtered down into his glass, and he was tasting it neat.

Presently, he looked around. A high empty bookcase. Pale spaces on the walls where paintings had hung. And cold as the tomb. Funny, this was the sort of place he had envisaged for himself. Not any longer. It was like the inside of somebody's skull.

'It's a big house for two people to rattle around in,' he remarked after a while.

'He slept in the tower,' was all she said.

The wine was working its effect on him. He felt generous.

'Why don't you stay here?' he said suddenly. 'I don't need the money. Keep the house.'

She stared down between her legs.

'I don't want to stay.'

Her white ankles protruding beneath her dressing gown resembled the splayed claw-feet on his school bathtub.

'Where are you going to live?'

'I had plans,' she said, but very vaguely.

'Tell me.'

She looked up. Her dragon eyes on him, uneasy-making. His father had the same expression. Lying on his back on the front lawn, his eyes reflecting telegraph wires. His fingers raised on the grass in a tense claw before he scuttled away.

'You don't know, do you?' Andy said softly. 'You haven't a clue.'

Her chair made a noise as she sat forward. Murmuring something Andy did not understand, snippets of another language.

He reached out, took her hand. Icy. 'When was the last time you ate?'

Was she dying? The veins on her wrist like the insides of an old book and her face all hollowed out, as it would be if you had been living for weeks on Chateau Pétrus, even a 1982.

'Maral Bernhard, when was the last time you had a meal that wasn't wine?'

He noticed that she was not listening. Something about the look in her eye, it got to him. He put down his glass. 'You haven't been taking care of yourself. You need to see a doctor.'

'No, no doctor,' shaking her head. Nervous, she spoke louder.

'Listen, you need help.' He had made up his mind. 'You have to eat. You have to get some fresh air into your lungs. What about a trip to the seaside?' He did not know what made him say it.

124

A groove deeper than the rest appeared in her brow, large enough to lay a pencil into. 'The seaside? I haven't been to the seaside.'

Andy helped Maral Bernhard on with her fur coat and strapped her into his car and put her up for the night in his flat. And in the morning walked her to a café in Thackeray Street, where she ate a full breakfast, saying not a word as she gulped down a pint of fresh orange juice, next assaulting a croissant, then two soft-poached eggs.

Later that morning, he drove her back to Clarendon Crescent so that she might pack a suitcase. It joined his own on the rear seat, and the holdhall in which he had tucked *Missing Montaigne*, plus the diary given to him by his sister and Rian. As he was loading the car, at the last minute, on impulse, he grabbed it.

A large white removal van arrived as he pulled away. In his boot: those seven bottles of Pétrus 1982, plus the crate of rare Sassicaia Tuscan red that he had sat on and another crate of Colares that he had discovered in the hall. He was going to inherit half of this wine anyway. He was only taking what was coming to him.

They headed out along Hammersmith Grove, past his old office, to Cornwall. Maral Bernhard wrapped in her Siberian polecat – or maybe it was camel or caribou, it had a colour unlike any animal he knew, it was like the dust of the blown earth – and staring at the countryside, not saying a word, even as they passed Stonehenge. The only thing she said upon reaching St Buryan five hours later: 'You know, mister, you are a very, very bad driver.'

He had booked them into a B & B. From his bay window upstairs he had a view of a slate-roofed farmhouse less than half a mile away across a ploughed field.

The owner was all he would have guessed from her telephone manner: a bustling ex-librarian and Radio 4 addict with hair dyed the shade of her lemon marmalade.

She took them for grandmother and grandson. It was too complicated to disabuse her. As well, it felt right. The two of them strangely, inevitably, linked by Christopher Madigan's inheritance.

6

SEPTEMBER 23. ASHFIELD GUEST House, St Buryan.

4.30 p.m. Am writing this to keep myself occupied while Mrs Nettlefold makes tea.

We've done little, these past two days. I've been bogged down in Furnivall, making notes, going around in circles for a way to salvage his manuscript. Maral Bernhard is tuned out, too busy recuperating to say anything. Right now she's sitting beside me in the conservatory – a green blanket over her lap, staring at the hedgerows, arms folded in anticipation of the tea trolley and Mrs N.'s home-made flapjacks, stored in a tin with a joyful Prince Charles and Lady Di on the lid.

She's still mistrustful, unrelaxed. Yesterday Mrs N. asked her: 'And how do you like your tea?'

'Tea?' in a brusque voice that made the biscuit tin jump up in fright. 'It tastes like tomcat piss.'

'No, dear, I mean how do you *take* it?' and poured an imaginary pot in the air.

Twice, I've caught her frowning at me, muttering under her breath, as though she can't work out who I am. I've been careful not to probe. One time I did raise the subject of Christopher Madigan, she called me a bloody fool and burrowed deeper into her moody silence. 'There's no need to be so unpleasant,' I said. Haven't yet asked about Jeanine.

September 24.

Today, the sun came out. She raised her face into it, like a crumpled old map, and inhaled. 'Soon as the sun shines, it's a different place,' to no one in particular.

This afternoon, I helped her into the car and we went for a walk above Lamorna. She let me hold her arm and we climbed in silence. The breeze dropped as we reached the edge of the cliff and she stood very still, feeling the sun warm on her skin and losing that boss-eyed look she has. 'So this is the seaside . . .' and closed her eyes. In that moment, her wrinkles were rays and I caught the flash of a vivacious, open-faced woman.

'How old are you, if you don't mind my asking?'

'I'll be sixty-five in a minute. Next question.'

We turned to go, and for the first time it occurred to me that what we were looking at was Stuart Furnivall's landscape, and that he was the reason I chose this part of Cornwall – an opportunity to make it up to him in however small a way. To walk his cliffs, smell the salt air, watch the boats thumping through the swell to Newlyn, their holds slithery with the Dover sole that we have for our dinner.

Mrs N. continues to refer to my grandmother.

Spent the evening on my own trying to get to grips with Furnivall's manuscript.

September 25.

This morning I left MB asleep in the conservatory and followed Mrs N.'s directions, past a row of farm buildings, to a 1970s brick cottage set back on its own with a view of the sea. Mrs N. says that she knew Furnivall by sight and reputation only. She well remembers his curly-haired figure plunging along the paths, lost in gorse and thought, but never had occasion to stop and speak with him. I hadn't anticipated the emotion I would feel standing before his house. I was taking it all in – orange leaves in the trees, a ring of standing stones, the thud of sea against cliff – when a strong-faced woman came out of a low door, straightened to her full height and glared at me. 'If you're hoping to see Tricia, her dad's had a fall and she's had to go to Zenna, but looking as you left no number we couldn't call back.' I told her I wasn't hoping to see Tricia. 'Then who do you want?' she said sourly. I explained that I knew the person who lived here before. 'Well, he doesn't live here now.'

Drove back to Mrs N.'s where I found MB in an agitated state. She wanted to know where I'd been, who I'd seen. I blurted out about Stuart Furnivall, his importance in my life and how I had failed him in the one thing that he asked me to do. Failed myself, too. This seemed to pacify her. She looked at me and listened, suspicion and curiosity sparring in her eyes, saying nothing except 'So you *are* Andrew Larkham . . .' She said it two or three times. Who did she think I was?

September 26.

MB didn't appear for breakfast. At ten o'clock I went upstairs and found her in her room sitting at a dressing table. On it, various items she'd unpacked. A short stick about a foot long; a fragment of what looked like brick; plus a stack of photographs.

She held up a small black-and-white photograph and sniffed. 'He was so alone in his coffin. He wasn't wearing the yellow jersey I knitted him. I told him he must wear it when he got up and went to the lavatory at night.'

I stepped closer. On the brink of seeing him for the first time.

A young man astride a motorbike: light-framed, lean, about eighteen. His face beneath the dark eyebrows watchful and smiling, with the clean features of a marathon runner.

'Madigan?' my pulse quickening.

'Probably the best-looking man I ever saw.'

Next to this photograph, one of a much older man dressed in a cardigan and suit. His father?

'That's before. That's after,' she said.

'After what?'

'After Jeanine was taken away.'

I could see the tension in her hands. I was tense, too. I wanted her to tell me everything. But I had a feeling like vertigo to say something provocative.

'Taken away? I thought he threw her out.'

'Why do you say that?' a high-voltage charge in her eye.

'I was told he did a lot worse. He more or less killed her mother. That's what Jeanine said.'

'He didn't!' She was angry. 'It's wicked tommyrot, what she told you.'

Vamplew admired Madigan, and David has found out much in his favour. But standing in MB's room, I felt an urge that I couldn't resist to view him from Jeanine's standpoint.

'From what Jeanine told me, he sounds ghastly.'

'No! He was a good man. A wonderful man.'

I looked again at the two photographs and battled to square those contrasting faces with Jeanine's tyrant.

'His bread had no salt, that's all,' she said. 'That's all.'

'What do you mean?'

'His good acts weren't known. You've been told bad things.' She was quietly crying. 'I am to blame. You mustn't listen to his daughter. It was something I did wrong.'

September 27.

Some post came from London while I was eating breakfast – including two packages from David. Tore them open at once – a jumble of newspaper articles, transcriptions of interviews, photocopies of correspondence, addresses.

My excitement soon dissipated. It's the raw material of David's e-mails and makes no sense in its unedited state. Stuff from Turkey, Armenia, Syria, Australia . . . Notes of a telephone conversation with a Henry Pyke in Perth ('Madigan's father-in-law', David has scrawled across the top). An uninformative communication from Crispian Bennett ('Madigan's lawyer in London, 1968–2004'). A brief interview with a Mr Purves of Ducker & Son, 6 The Turl, Oxford. Another, with a Pamela Chenevix of 9 Holland Park, about a photograph Madigan took of her daughter. A retired eye-surgeon in Mooloolaba recalling an operation on Chris Makertich *c.*1959/1960. An Armenian government report into a cyanide spill from the Aurora Copper mine. And so on. Pages of it. Some names I recognised from David's e-mails; other names mean nothing.

I'd started to read a 1962 article in the *West Australian* about a spectacular discovery of iron ore when Mrs N. came into the breakfast room, concern on her face: 'Did I hear your grandmother groaning in the night?'

I went upstairs and knocked. No answer. I pressed an ear to the door. Asleep.

About tea-time, I knocked again and found her up and dressed.

She was holding the stick, which I saw was a dried branch. She waved it in the air, the way you'd imitate a magician casting a spell or a priest holding an imaginary crosier, then put it down.

'People never fight evil,' she muttered. 'Do you believe in the Devil, Mr Larkham?'

'What, red with horns?'

'No, in human form.'

'In a manner of speaking,' I said carefully. What trap was this?

She went on looking at me, and then with a smile so small you needed a magnifying glass to see it: 'You will have to take my word for it when I say I thought the Devil had come to his funeral.'

It took me a moment to realise what she was saying. 'You thought *I* was the Devil?'

'I did.'

While I absorbed this, she picked up another photograph and showed it to me. It was of Madigan as a young man, taken five years or so after the one of him on the motorbike. But in his misassembled features quite different, as though a forest fire had swept through him. He wore a black patch over his left eye and stood in a desert landscape with a mountain in the background.

I took the photograph from her, looked at it. 'Australia?'

She nodded.

'He was Armenian, wasn't he?'

'Yes, but his grandfather was Turkish,' and focussed on her hands resting together between her legs. 'Although,' she said quickly, 'I don't know anything about him, and neither did he.'

I looked at his face. 'Did he live in Turkey ever?'

'Never.' She cracked forward and said: 'He was born in Syria, grew up in Australia and had a British passport.'

'And a British name. Why?'

She did not answer.

I said: 'Was he ashamed of the one he was born with?'

She shook her head. 'No, it's not that simple.'

'Was he trying to hide from someone?'

'Only from himself.'

'What had he done wrong?'

She looked up at me sharply. 'Nothing! First thing to understand – he's Armenian. Anybody ever tell you about Armenians, Mr Larkham? No, I see that doesn't mean anything to you. But that's the answer. I don't know much about the seaside. On the other hand, I know something of what it is to be Armenian.'

Her chair protested as she sat back.

'If I begin to tell you about Krikor,' her leathery folds disappearing, 'I don't know when I will stop.'

I dug out one of Madigan's bottles. 'Start at the beginning, why not?'

'But which beginning?'

'Where did you meet him?'

Her hands went up to her face. She shook her head. Puffing up her cheeks. 'In Vienna. I met him in Vienna.'

September 28.

She slept all morning and came down for lunch. Even in a few days she has changed from the spiritless woman of a week ago. Her eyes clearer, browner. Her voice stronger, less choppy. She doesn't sound so foreign – or is that because I've penetrated her accent? She uses a precise, almost clerical English, which she speaks with perfect knowledge, although it can make her sound as though she's living in another era. I'm ashamed that I saw her as a cantankerous battleaxe. She's extremely together. Flashes of tenderness, too – except towards Mrs N.

After lunch, we went into the conservatory and she had a nap until the door opened hesitantly, as if a baby were pulling it and Mrs N. came in with the tea trolley.

Mrs N.: 'I've made some more flapjacks for you-hu.'

130

MB assessed her dourly. 'My good woman,' putting on her vicar-in-the-pulpit voice. 'I cannot tell you how indifferent I am to flapjacks.'

As soon as Mrs N. withdrew, she hauled herself up and took one and started to nibble. Then she said: 'Here, take this blanket. I hate its touch on my skin.'

So as not to offend her by not doing what she asked, I folded it away. She shook her head and I was afraid that she might have regretted talking to me yesterday.

'You've got a —' I touched my nose.

She wiped away the flapjack crumb and smiled. Her smile made her eyes small. But that smile she had, it was hard to earn, and once it had parted her lips, it remained on her face.

'Where did I get to last night?'

I reminded her.

Her tight voice all at once filled like a top-gallant and she was off. I hung onto it. She talked until dinner. Drank half a bottle of Sammarco 1997 from the other crate. (Mrs N. tried to palm us off with her late husband's Valpolicella, but MB dismissed it out of hand.) 'Wine invents nothing,' she said at one point. 'Everything I'm telling you is true.'

September 30.

Something is happening. I've abandoned Stuart Furnivall's text and have thrown myself into writing down what MB has decided to tell me about Christopher Madigan.

October 1.

Her cheeks have a new tone. Her fur coat, too, is sleeker, gleamier. There's something sun-streaked about it, alive.

October 2.

This afternoon she spoke for the first time about Jeanine. She described how she used to read to J. as a child. For no particular reason, I had an image of myself in the back of a large car looking at the blue tissue paper from which my father unwrapped a crushed, dried white snowdrop.

Talked all afternoon and evening.

October 3–14. Ditto.

MAKERTICH

I

LAST SATURDAY IN SEPTEMBER, light beginning to fail, Andy sat in one of two matching green armchairs in Maral Bernhard's room, an open bottle of Castello dei Rampolla on the table between them.

'You wish to know about Christopher Madigan,' she said. She was wearing a mauve and white summer dress with three large buttons at the back. 'Before I go further, I must tell you about someone who was the most important person in his life.'

'Jeanine?'

'Mr Larkham, *please*. His grandmother.'

Andy had to quell his frustration. He was not interested in hearing about a long-dead old woman. But to be lumbered with the story of Madigan's grandmother was a price he would have to pay. And the wine was good.

'She came from the Armenian village of Marash in Anatolia,' Maral was saying. 'And how did people in those days deal with what happened to Armenians in Turkey? The way people deal today with Chechnya or Rwanda – by not thinking about it. What everyone forgets is that the Turks used the First World War as an excuse to do some ethnic cleansing on a massive scale.' Her eyes, sensing his awkwardness, rested on him. 'Or do you know all this?'

'Not really,' Andy admitted.

'I grew up with it, but people who hear it for the first time are enraged. It was unexpected, completely. The Armenians – some of whom supported the Young Turks, by the way – were second-class citizens, but they held these powerful positions; they were the doctors, teachers, lawyers, musicians, intellectuals, and it was a shock when the Turks seized the opportunity during those months while the world's attention was on Gallipoli. It was done so furtively. The Young Turks didn't want Armenians to exist. To understand how they almost succeeded in exterminating them in their homeland, look at Hitler's justification for getting rid of the Jews – "Who now remembers the Armenians?" And he was talking about the foremost believers in Christianity . . .'

She had to stop and fortify herself. 'It's what I've heard pretty much from any Armenian I've ever met. The men were taken away, butchered. The women were raped. They were told they had to be transferred, then they were marched into the wilderness with no food and water, and left there in the scorching sun; either that or shoved off a cliff into the Euphrates. Most died. I'm talking about a quarter of our population. A million and a half men, women and children, Mr Larkham.'

She licked her lips. 'It's numbers of people, but then it dawns on you what else was lost. A relationship to this earth; centuries of culture, links, history – Armenia appeared on maps two thousand years before Turkey. But the Turks didn't even give Armenians time to pack their bags. They had nothing, absolutely nothing, just the sandals on their feet. Otherwise, like Krikor's grandmother, all they had left were stories and memories.'

Her family had lived on the same mountain for four hundred years, but in the winter of 1915 the Turks hounded her people across the Syrian desert and she settled in Aleppo, where, twenty-three years later, he was born.

'Armenians are always asking where someone is from. I was Ismirtsi – from Ismir. Krikor was Halebtsi – from Aleppo.'

His name at that period was not Christopher Madigan but Krikor Makertich.

Right from his birth, Makertich and his grandmother had a close relationship. 'He could tell her what he dreamed about, what made him nervous.' Things that he couldn't tell his parents because they were busy; his mother working in a tailor's shop and his father as a welder in a soap factory – 'that is, when he wasn't at the gambling table'.

Makertich grew up playing with his grandmother's cigarette butts. He listened to her singing the liturgy while washing up. *Der voghormia – Lord, mercify me.* He hid in her wardrobe.

'She kept her few good clothes wrapped up, a spare hat, a jersey. She was so careful with them, as if she was prepared to move again.'

His happiest moments were spent perched on the antimacassared arm of his grandmother's chair, listening to her resurrect her life when she was his age. Mists, apricot trees, goats' teeth on the bark, and in the lakeside sand the turtles' eggs that gave her hair its gloss. She was an emancipated woman who had studied in Paris and spoke to Makertich as though to an adult. Years before he understood their meaning, she would sit in the low front room, a Gitane worming into ash between long fingers, and in her gravelly voice that detested all dishonesty read him passages from her favourite authors – Dumas,

Shakespeare, Hugo – so that he came to associate the act of reading with the reek of tobacco.

'Her family had been financiers to the Ottoman Empire.' Before that, they were masons and tillers. They had an uncanny knack of making more money than their Turkish neighbours. Vastly outnumbered, they had to fit in and adapt, to negotiate and compromise. Keeping their heads down, noses clean, getting on with others. 'All of them were People of the Book.'

She saw it as her duty to teach him the unique alphabet that Saint Mesrob had devised in the fifth century for the purpose of translating the Gospels.

Though religious, Makertich's grandmother never lost the bohemian stripe that she had picked up from her time as a student on the Left Bank. She was unselfconscious about parading through the house in a slip or saying what was on her mind. She continually chastised his mother – 'What have you got in those breasts, water?' – and his father – 'No, I will not lend you any more money!'

Only in repose did the muscles and nerves around her eyes betray her continuous battle not to evoke certain scenes. Prime among these was the murder of her husband.

In the winter of 1915 a 'butcher battalion' composed of released convicts arrived at the farm. Nazareth Makertich was separated from his young wife of two months and taken behind the stables, along with the able-bodied men on his estate. Not yet pregnant with Krikor's father, she remembered to her last shallow breath the soft clubbing noise – 'the Turks didn't want to waste ammunition' – and, later, the bleeding body of her husband lying in a twisted, cruciform shape, the bayonets pegged into the snow through his palms.

She never married again.

'She was like me – an Armenian,' Maral said. 'Brought up to be faithful, totally, to one person. It was the same with Krikor. That, and never to tell a lie or seek revenge.'

Makertich did once ask his grandmother about her journey across the Syrian Desert. He remembered her sudden narrowing, the way she held him by the shoulders. Her parched lined face was a page of the Bible over bone. 'Krikor, look me in the eye,' and when he did: 'You can't understand the need to describe what I went through when there's no proof left, no witnesses. You can't tell people how it was. Impossible.' By and large, she had not told anyone. Easier to eradicate her memories than to enter the lunacy of verification.

'You find that a lot,' Maral said. 'People can't speak about it. They want to disappear so that they never have the knock on the door. My grandmother escaped from Ismir with my mother. Her husband was taken away. Soldiers came knocking at the door and I don't really know what happened.'

Alone to Makertich during her final illness did his grandmother at last talk about the events of 1915.

'She always had refused to be "a snivelling woman in perpetual mourning". But now she wanted to explain. She had this guilt that she hadn't fought back, that it had happened. At the same time, she had this passion to pass it on. It was clear that what she had wished her whole life was for the one thing – just for the Turks to say sorry, to admit what they had done.'

In the course of her rambling confession, she let fall certain images – the mirror in her donkey's feed-basket, reflecting a file of filthy, half-dressed men and women stumbling behind her to the pitiless horizon; the soles of her sandals sticky with blood; the puddle she tried to drink from, before the Turkish zaptieh sent her sprawling – and then, shifting his gaze from her face that she had smeared with mud to her young breasts moving freely within their blouse, advanced with a rigid expression towards where she lay in the dirt.

'When she found out she was pregnant – like all the women she was with, she thought she had stopped her periods because of shock – she immediately wanted an abortion, but her brother disapproved strongly.'

Pointedly, she entrusted to her grandson rather than to her son two mementos from that period: a bullet-hard pellet of bread baked from mud, manure and grass; and the silver bracelet from the monastery at Varak that she had received at her baptism and stitched into the donkey's basket.

'I'm giving you a history lesson,' Maral said, 'because this is where this man comes from.'

2

To begin with, Andy had sat and listened.

Sometimes the radio was on downstairs, and music or conversation could be heard between what she was saying; sometimes she lifted her hand in an animated way and the shadow of what he was convinced was a man would lean across the table.

Then, when he had said goodnight, he walked fast to his room and covered page after page of the notebook in which he had written down ideas for *Missing Montaigne*.

Maral Bernhard had lived with Christopher Madigan twenty-nine years. She knew his life by heart. Once she had made the decision to speak about him, the pressure of the memories building up inside forced her to talk with scarcely enough time to catch her breath.

And yet the frustrating thing was that the Madigan who stepped forward in her presence shrank the instant Andy left her side. When Andy attempted to record from memory what she had told him, even though virtually no time had elapsed, he felt as if he were jotting down a vital telephone number using a biro that didn't work. There were details he missed, phrases and inflexions he forgot. He was merely nibbling, as it were, at the rind of the man.

His impatience drove him on the fourth evening to transcribe Maral's recollections in front of her, as she was speaking.

'Hey, mister, what's that you're writing?'

'What you've just said.'

She flinched, and he filled her glass.

'Go on,' his pen poised.

Much later, he remembered another line from Montaigne: 'An open way of talking opens the way for more talk, drawing it out like wine and love.'

As Maral began to speak of Makertich, Andy found that he could visualise him.

3

THE SECOND WORLD WAR had been over for four years when his grandmother died. Makertich was eleven.

His throat closed up on him. He had practically no feelings. But her death was less traumatic for his parents: they could now be like everyone else. They decided to leave Aleppo.

England, their first choice, refusing to accept them, the following spring they sailed on a converted refrigeration ship to Western Australia, where they found lodgings in a market-garden district of Perth. The wooden bungalow in Furneaux Park had a creek at the back leading into a river, and a yard large enough to keep four ponies. It was the last remnant of pride to which Makertich's father clutched: on the family estate in Anatolia, on the grassy hilltops, his ancestors had bred horses prized by the Persians.

Perth in summer was hotter than Aleppo. The place became a tinderbox. His father stepped around the yard on tiptoe, as if his life were a rotten staircase that threatened to give way at any moment.

Makertich, being a child, picked up English much faster than his parents. After three years at the local school he was accepted as a pupil at Perth Modern, directly opposite the hospital where his mother worked as a cleaner. A little black head among a sea of blond.

Lessons over, he watched the boys and girls climb into their parents' Holdens or the bus, which headed off in the other direction, and then he walked for an hour (his parents could not afford a bicycle), down Roberts Road, down Hay Street, a street that ran forever, until he came to the 1890s bungalows which had housed the generation of his classmates' grandparents, before they got lucky.

'That's the thing about Perth,' his English teacher, Miss Stapenell, told her pupils. 'A little bit of knowledge and y'all might find a gold mine.'

Makertich's father never found gold, but he did, towards the end of the family's second year in Australia, strike peanuts. Once a week after school, Makertich walked with him down an alleyway to a basement like the mouth of a cave, dark and hot and smelling of the peanuts that arrived from Kingaroy in jute sugar-bags and were roasted in an oven beneath the street. They hauled the bags home on a billycart and opened them on the back veranda, emptying out the contents with beer glasses. His father, cigarette between lips – rolled from 'Champion Ruby ready-rubbed, fine-cut tobacco', as he made Makertich repeat on his errands to Mrs Gover at the Country Store – claimed the larger glass, Makertich the smaller, and together they dug into the sacks and filled up white paper bags with salted or roasted peanuts. A rhythm swept them along. Father sitting beside son, scooping the peanuts into the paper bag, folding the bag over to make piggy ears and stacking it in a cane basket. Then his father would go to the pub over the road, where the publican allowed him to walk around with his basket on his arm selling Uncle Dick's Fresh Roasted Peanuts, 'two bob for a middie, a shilling for a lady's waist'.

Soon Uncle Dick, as he styled himself, was vending peanuts in every pub and motel in the district. He spent most of what he received on the horses – not those in his backyard, but at the racetrack in Belmont Park.

'He was by all accounts a clever man,' Maral said, 'but his soul did not yield to Australia.' He liked being sociable, and yet at home he sank into a self-pitying moroseness, hardly speaking except to revive his dead mother's memories of the estate seized by the Turks, the summer house in Heliopolis, the Prince Henry Vauxhall – none of which, as his wife (a distant cousin) was quick to point out, he had ever seen.

'Shut up about that now,' she snapped. 'You're in Australia! In a house infested with termites and stinking of gas. In the peanut business.'

Maral said: 'I know what she went through. My own father was no different. All that hating – it's done secretly, as if to admit to such robust hatred is to admit what victims Armenians are. It's a ferocious but invisible cancer.'

Sick of scrubbing toilets to support her husband's gambling habit, Makertich's mother set up a booth, selling vegetables at weekends. The vegetables came from Lenny Sing, a Chinaman up the road; his allotment. She stored the money in a cut-down kerosene can with a wire handle, and kept a collapsible bed for her son under the counter, where he reclined among the onions and read.

'He said he only had to smell spring onions and it took him back under the counter.'

Makertich flourished at Perth Modern. He was an agile athlete with a quick, wiry frame and the charisma of a natural leader. As well, he had the beguiling quality of the exile from a country that does not exist. An intense open face, dark brows and eyelashes, and a watchful tilt to the eye which made you want to confide in him, it did not matter if you were student or teacher. About himself, he revealed little.

His olive skin caused scant comment; he called himself Chris and most people took him for an Italian. His history had taught him not to divulge where he came from; the bayonettings in the snowdrifts.

In his last year he fell in love with another student called Cheryl Pyke. Scrolls of light blonde hair to her shoulder, tall, supple and a lazy laugh. The moment they came together was when the maths teacher asked Cheryl a difficult question in their algebra class. Her face tightened as the teacher turned his back, chalk poised. She sat in silence, flustered and anxious, as he waited. Until young Chris Makertich, sitting a desk away, scribbled out the answer and slid it across.

Before long, Makertich was tutoring Cheryl with her maths and science homework; helping her with her English essays – her spelling was almost as atrocious as her algebra – and introducing her to his favourite authors. Only in the art room could she flourish without his assistance.

Not long after the incident in class, Cheryl invited him home to a barbecue. Her father was flying down from Marble Bar – where he was the resident manager of a newly reopened gold mine – to make his monthly report to the head office in Perth. She was eager for him to meet her new friend.

Cheryl had been weak on details when describing Chris to her mother, and Drusilla Pyke, upon being introduced to him in the English-modelled garden of which she was so proud, gave the young man a circumspect welcome. Henry Pyke's liking, however, was instantaneous. It made it easy for him to counter his wife's disapproval of the Italian-looking teenager with the movie-star smile.

That Christmas, Pyke offered Makertich holiday work at his open-cut mine. Though only seventeen, he was given the duties of an adult – dipping the tanks, measuring the solutions, driving hauler trucks.

For six weeks, Makertich worked in eight-hour shifts. Covered in red dust, he did not know white any more; white ceased to exist. The fine dust would fall out of books and envelopes years later, a reminder of being in the mine. 'When my shift is over, I shower, eat, drink, play pool, sleep, shake off the grog, get up and do it all over again,' he wrote to Cheryl, 'and never stop thinking of you.'

Most weekends, he got to spend time with her father.

'I taught him the rudiments of geology and the lithology of mineral formations,' Pyke said, speaking in a slow voice from his yacht in Fremantle, 'and how to peg a claim, so that no smartass prospector or mining company didn't overturn him on a technicality. He owed a lot to me. Without me he wouldn't have known shit from clay.'

One afternoon they scrambled up a steep bank of rocks to a stunted flat-topped tree.

'An iron tree,' Pyke said, with his fingers tracing its roots to where they writhed into a lump of solid low-grade hematite. He struck off a fragment and inspected it. 'If you were a prospector and you found one of these trees, you'd peg to the north of it,' and then, almost as an after-thought, 'except that you wouldn't be prospecting for iron.'

'Why not?'

Pyke explained that in 1938 the Federal Government had banned the exportation of iron ore. 'The day they lift the embargo, you can take a surveyor's pick and come out here. Until that moment, the ore's valueless.'

Pyke's mentality was gold. Every last skerrick of gold-bearing land had been picked over, but the iron under his nose signified nothing.

He threw the fleck of hematite at the horizon. 'Old Ziegler,' speaking of his geologist, 'reckons this is the oldest country in the world.'

'Who's allowed to peg out here?' Makertich, gazing around, wanted to know.

'With the right piece of paper, any Tom, Dick or Harriet.' He had no idea about Aborigines.

Makertich shaded his eye. In flashes far away to their left an exqui-site lightning storm was raging. 'How much of this has been pegged?'

'This land?' Pyke squinted down over the red expanse that mimicked the ravines in his face. 'A little bit around the mine, but once you go out there not one lousy rock of it.'

'How much are you allowed to claim?' He was remembering Aleppo. The importance of iron. His father welding scraps of metal. Smelting began in Syria, he was thinking.

'You can peg all you like,' Pyke said. He polished his palms on his trousers. 'The hard part is to find something worth peggin' that's not one hundred per cent dirt.'

He began descending the slope to the Land Rover, but Makertich was looking over the red earth at the electric blue flashes. Like the tip of blue flame into which his father used to focus all his concentration.

Weekends during term-time, Pyke employed Makertich to mow the lawn at his waterfront house in Perth – and in the summer holidays, to truck ore to the mills at his mine in Marble Bar. Makertich had proved popular with other truckies – 'Armenians are good at fixing cars.' Not that he ever disclosed that he was Armenian. Only to Cheryl.

She was not beautiful – she had her father's nose and her mother's hard jaw and over-wide mouth – but Makertich thought her desirable in her very clean shirt stamped with yellow sea horses.

After dancing with her all night at a New Year's Eve ball, the first time he had done such a thing, the two of them ended up on Cottlesloe beach, and he told her about his grandmother, his childhood home in Aleppo; but edited out details of the journey to Australia, the internment camp in Hay Street, what his parents did for a living. Cheryl urged him to speak to her in Armenian, and in his own language he told her that he loved her. Then asked her not to speak to anyone about where he came from. It didn't matter anyway, it was history. A day might come when he would write about it, but right now he was an Aussie – 'Thru and thru.'

'I won't breathe a word,' Cheryl promised, not really understanding the secret, but enjoying its intimacy, stroking the side of his face and the fading imprint of her earring, from where he had hugged her to him. And Makertich, who loved her, who was incapable of breaking a promise, another trait that he had inherited from his grandmother, believed her.

'Cheryl and Krikor, how far did it go?' said Maral. 'Left alone, it probably would have fizzled out.'

They were teenagers who loved each other in the feverish way you do when you are eighteen. The way Cheryl kissed him, she had been brought into the world to do nothing else. Her kisses kept him scootering around to the Pyke house in Peppermint Grove, his Agfa Box in a brown leather case dangling on a stiff strap from his neck.

When not mowing the lawn or driving hauler-trucks, he would take Cheryl to the beach and photograph her swimming or sunning herself, sometimes topless, but never naked, as longingly he would have liked. In the long intense year of their courtship, they never made love. 'This was the Fifties, remember.'

In their final year at Perth Modern, three drawings by Cheryl were selected for the school art exhibition. Only Drusilla Pyke seemed to notice that the most striking study, of a crabapple tree on her front lawn, looked as though copied from a photograph. Her first premonition that her daughter was reaching the dangerous age when every path to her heart might require the deployment of a well-trained guard dog.

Cheryl's father was happy to have Chris working for them as a driver-cum-lawn-mower, and treated him as a member of the family. Drusilla Pyke, however, could be breathtakingly rude.

'Do have that one,' pointing to the rottenest banana and never looking him in the eye.

She was imperious when alone with him. She washed her hands after shaking his, soaping off the dried earth and grass. She came outside to speak with him, rather than invite him into the house, and melted away at mealtimes on the weekends of her husband's visits.

'You can see where this story's leading. When Krikor threatened actually to become a member of the family all hell broke loose.'

Drusilla Pyke was promenading along the Swan River with her golfing partner, Heather Anderson, when she recognised her daughter on the bank, swimming costume unfastened, and an all-too-familiar tanned young man on his knees snapping away. She seethed inside. Already, she had been alerted to their possible intimacy by a school essay into which Cheryl had poured out her eighteen-year-old heart: Drusilla Pyke read it and was appalled. Miss Stapenell might have believed this essay to be the hand of Cheryl Pyke. Cheryl's mother most emphatically did not. Her daughter needed assistance even to fill out her membership card for Lake Karrinyup Country Golf Club. An enthusiastic member, Drusilla Pyke had plans for Cheryl to marry into her own kind, preferably Heather Anderson's nephew, a rich grazier in the Pilbara. Her only child was not going to fall into the swamp of poverty all at once opened up by a struggling immigrant would-be photographer with romantic ideas.

For this is what Drusilla Pyke had discovered their part-time gardener to be, explaining why it was that Chris appeared to have no parents, why he never discussed himself, why he had not once invited Cheryl over the railway line to his ripple-iron bungalow in the doggier part of Furneaux Park. Drusilla Pyke had done her research. She obtained an address and drove past an emaciated figure standing behind a crude vegetable stall on the south side of Hay Street. She had stopped the car and bought some spring onions. And beamed at the unsmiling woman who counted out her change. Black hair swept back in a bun, fake leather slippers, a cotton over-dress printed with a floral pattern like a cleaner would wear.

'Oh, don't worry about that. Tell me, where are you from?'

'I am Australian,' Makertich's mother said stubbornly. She had the brown eyes of her son, but leeched of their original colour.

Drusilla Pyke held her smile. 'You don't *sound* Australian.'

And that night stormed into her daughter's bedroom, where Cheryl, in the porous way of a Fifties Australian teenager, told her everything, even the Armenian word for love.

Drusilla Pyke was firm. 'He might be clever, darling, but dogs are clever too,' softly closing the door.

Next Saturday evening, Makertich parked his Vespa in Peppermint

Grove, having arranged to take Cheryl to the Swanbourne drive-in. He unstrapped his helmet and knocked on the door and entered. No one around. He walked out onto the back deck. A hot night, windows open. And was about to call out 'Cheryl?' when he heard voices arguing in the kitchen. Through the fly-screen, Cheryl's father: 'It's not that serious. They're just kids.'

Makertich, hitching a ride back from Marble Bar in Pyke's Auster, had landed in Perth the previous afternoon. It had taken since then to rid his ears of the drilling of pneumatic jackhammers, the clanking chains of the separation plant. Seconds passed before he realised that Pyke was talking about him.

After a raw silence, Pyke went on: 'She's not pregnant is she?'

'And don't think I'm going to give her the opportunity.' Then Drusilla Pyke was saying in a distressed way: 'I would be fine with an Italian. Even a Jew.'

'You say that . . .'

In the smell of spring onions, Drusilla Pyke had discovered everything she needed to know.

Most Perth mothers might have considered Armenians merely 'weird' and bracketed them with Greeks and Italians. But Drusilla Pyke's grandfather had died at Gallipoli. In her narrow although hazy cosmogony, Armenians – not that she herself had a clue where they came from, only what they smelled of: onions – were natural victims, like the Hungarians and Aborigines. And carrying God knows what recessive diseases in addition to genes that promised to make her grandchildren swarthy. And short.

Plus, she had done some digging into the character of Chris's father. The discovery that he was none other than 'Uncle Dick, the peanut vendor' and a regular at the tote, where he owed money, made the decision easy.

When Chris appeared at the entrance to the kitchen asking for Cheryl, Drusilla Pyke said in a voice of icy finality, not looking at him, but fixing her eyes on the crash helmet that he held to his chest: 'I'm sorry, Chris. Cheryl won't be seeing you tonight.' And after thrusting into his arms some handwritten pages – 'Here, I believe this is yours' – directed him out of the house.

She closed the fly-screen behind him, meeting his eyes through the mesh. 'Goodbye.'

For several days he lost his mind. He stumbled to a gap in the sea-wall, out of the wind, where he knew that she would not look for him, but hoped that she might. How many hours he sat on the beach, waiting to feel her hand on his shoulder, he never counted, but one morning he woke and rubbed the sand from his red eyes and after a while he stood up and left.

At some point in his delirium he understood that the locks had been changed.

'He had been an idiot to speak about his grandmother. To speak in Armenian. Henceforth, he would need to keep to himself.'

He did not go back to Marble Bar that holiday.

4

'AND NOW HIS PARENTS.'

In January, a bush fire swept through Furneaux Park.

It was a hot north-wind day, the sort of day that makes it impossible to breathe outside. Makertich was repairing his Vespa when his mother ran out to say that there was a fire over Shenton Way. He could tell that the blaze was enormous by the speed with which it whirled, unchecked, across the horizon. Ominous puffs of smoke appeared above the roof of the pub, growing larger and larger until thick pieces of ash were floating through the air and landing in black carpets on the grass around them.

His mother started to throw things into the car, yelling for Makertich to go and wake his father.

He ran to the backyard where his father lay on his stomach, half asleep in swimming trunks, sun-baking on the lawn, the radio playing beside him, listening to the Perth Cup.

'Dad, Dad, you've got to get up!' shaking him. 'Mum's waiting for you in the car.'

'The horses . . .' he said groggily.

'I'll round them up.'

His mother was shouting their names.

Makertich said: 'I'll join you at the river.'

The air was suddenly so dry. He felt that if he rubbed his fingers together they would spark.

He dashed across the grass, and froze. There, in the very next paddock, was a wall of flame roaring down on him at the most incredible speed. The smoke was thick and he could hardly see to catch the ponies. He started off leading a couple, but they reared and plunged with terror and he had to let them go, opening the gates for all four to escape.

The sun was obscured by the smoke. He could make out a copper glow, but nothing more. He ran along the creek and arrived at the river, choking and gasping. His parents' car was not there. He was frantic. He knew that the car – which his mother had bought off Lenny Sing, with money set aside from her stall – was a bad starter. After a few minutes, he heard tooting and through a band of rolling yellow fog he saw the Morris Oxford overtake him, his parents' shapes inside. He shouted out and even managed to touch the hot bumper, but the car failed to stop – they had not recognised him.

The last thing he saw before the smoke closed in were the shadowy forms of riders trying in vain to round up a stampeding herd of cattle. Then with a roar and a hiss the fire reached the river. Sparks showered around him, sizzling as they touched the water. To keep his clothes from catching alight, he waded into the middle, submerging himself.

A pathetic sight met his eyes when he surfaced. The publican's car had been driven into the river as far as it would go. Round about it crouched the publican and his wife and two daughters with a whippet pup, clinging together. And then, in what seemed an age, the smoke cleared – the fire had passed on.

Makertich staggered to the shore. The horizon lit up by the burning flax stacks as the flames swept invincibly onwards. He searched the faces on the bank, many with wet handkerchieves tied around their noses, but failed to spot his parents.

He discovered their Morris Oxford abandoned in the river. The river water, usually so clear and sparkling, was black with ash. A tractor took an hour to haul the vehicle out.

Makertich left the car by the side of the road, dripping onto the scorched grass. His parents must have hitched a ride home. He walked back wearily in the gathering dusk. The stones felt hot under his boots. He trod over the blackened ground, past the vanished allotment. His way lighted by the glare of the still-burning trees and telegraph poles, and hundreds of sheep lying in smoking piles.

In Furneaux Park, scenes of desolation. The population evacuated. Maddened cattle ran bellowing into the road or stood in quivering shock with blood dripping off their peeled flanks. Men searched for their families. Women huddled in frightened bunches, sitting on piles of possessions outside the smoking remains of their homes. His parents' next-door neighbour, a widow, sat speechlessly in her husband's air-force coat, a sewing machine and a birdcage beside her, while her two small children, very pale but calm, tried to comfort her. She escaped the fire when she lay in a ditch and it had passed over her. Of her bungalow, there was no trace.

Makertich saw with amazement and relief that his own home was untouched. The fire had come up against the creek and been deflected round the back, leaving it standing.

His parents were not inside.

He stood in the main room calling for them. The rotten-egg smell of gas and everything black. His Vespa. His father's rocking chair. The framed picture of Mount Ararat that had belonged to his grandmother. Among very few items not singed were the contents of his plan-chest. Quickly checking his photographs, he pocketed the silver bracelet and the lump of solidified bread that he had kept in the bottom drawer, and then he went outside. He was desperate to find his parents, but did not know how. There was no electric light, no telephone. He had been complacent and now he started to panic.

Lenny Sing pulled up. He looked awful, dirt and sweat pouring down his face.

'They went running after you,' he said shakily. He stared at his feet. Only his feet. They dragged him away from Makertich, towards a wooden-armed settee that someone had carried into the street. He lowered himself on it, covering his eyes.

Makertich sat down beside him and took Lenny's hand away from his face.

'Where are they?'

His parents had driven into the river, Lenny said. Not seeing Makertich anywhere, they had assumed that he was trying to catch the ponies.

'I hear your dad.'

And saw Makertich's father, arms in the air, waving over his car roof, shouting to Lenny, asking if he had seen his son.

'He wanted to find you. Your mum, too.'

Lenny watched as Uncle Dick squeezed himself out of the driver's window and next lifted out his wife and carried her in his arms through the strong current towards the bank. Not till the end of his days, Lenny's widow confirmed, would Lenny be able to expunge the sight of Makertich's parents, water and steam coming off their clothes, stumbling across the paddock towards the oncoming fire, calling for Krikor.

After a few days of roaring winds, the black ash was blown away, leaving the bare, scorched earth. The story persisted of a suspicious rag found at the source of the blaze, though no one had seen it. Soon the paddocks and streets took on a rusty brown appearance. The trees were particularly eerie, naked and charred and making a wailing noise as the wind blew through them.

5

ANDY WALKED INTO THE dining room the following evening. Maral was already seated at the table.

She looked up at him, her eyes odd and juddery. 'Go on, sit down,' in a flat voice. 'All this talk and I have not said a word about Don Flexmore.'

It was three years since the fire. Makertich had left Perth and gone to live near Sydney, a houseboat on the Hawkesbury – as far from Peppermint Grove as he could travel and be on the same continent.

The houseboat, a converted Danish cutter, was tethered to a grass bank north of Richmond. From the deck, he could see a scraggy orchard from which the ferryman who lived on the next bend pressed a throat-burning cider. A galah liked to cling to the bow-rail for breadcrumbs, the first thing Makertich looked for when he pushed open the scullery door. He would feed the bird and then continue down a gangplank and through the apple trees to the ferry. It was a fifteen-minute walk from the opposite bank to his shop on Bligh Street.

In Richmond, he had set up a photography studio that threatened to overwhelm him. It was 1959 and rumours of a new Banking Act had made life precarious for small businesses. All that stood between Makertich and insolvency was the insurance money owed on his parents' house. The pay-out was imminent, but legal wrangles had dragged the process out. To help with the rent, he stuck a notice in the window of his studio advertising a bed in his spare cabin.

The long-faced young man who stepped off the rickety dock several days later said that his name was Don Flexmore. He was of average height, slim, with yellowish hair that covered his ears and black eyelashes. They were the blackest eyelashes that Makertich had seen and had the effect of making the eyes that looked out at him appear even bluer.

'Haven't we met?' Flexmore said, with a boyish laugh.

'Don't think so.'

'I dunno why, I feel we have.' He had just returned from New Zealand. 'If you're ever in Auckland, let me know. I can get you a room in the best hotel.'

Makertich said that he would bear it in mind.

Flexmore's easy manner was almost a relief. He strode up the gang-plank with the confident prance of a pony and explained that he needed a place to stay between lodgings. When Makertich showed him the cabin, Flexmore squeezed the sagging mattress and threw his knapsack onto it. 'This'll do nicely.'

The knapsack had a coat hanger poking from the top.

Flexmore undid the strap and pulled out a navy-blue suit, in the same motion spilling onto the floor a paperback.

Makertich picked it up. *Dianetics: The Modern Science of Mental Health*, by L. Ron Hubbard.

'You should read it,' Flexmore said, taking it from him.

Makertich continued with his tour of the houseboat, Flexmore asking questions.

'What's in there?' of a closed door.

'My cabin.'

'Why live on a boat?'

'Only place I could find.' Not saying that he had deliberately sought out this boat. That ever since a boy he had hankered to live on an ark.

'What's on those trees?' peering out of a porthole.

The branches listened.

'Apples.'

Flexmore nodded. He looked as though he wanted to bound up the bank and introduce himself.

They went into the scullery and Makertich boiled some tea.

'Where you from, Chris?' taking off his linen jacket.

'Perth.'

He looked at him. 'I was there a while back. Before that, I mean.'

'Syria.'

'And before that?' He was looking at his thick black hair.

'Turkey,' after a while.

Flexmore smiled. 'Putting a bit of fungicide on the family roots, eh?' He lifted his shirt and started gyrating. 'Your mother one of them belly dancers?'

'My parents are dead.'

Flexmore stopped. 'Oh, sorry,' pulling down his shirt. And later, contemplating Makertich over his tea: 'Sometimes there can be nothing better than for a child to lose their father.' He took a loud sip. 'You know when I first saw you, I thought you were an Abo.'

At first, they got along. Makertich was relieved not to be thinking about himself. On his own too long, he was susceptible to Flexmore's addictive energy, his childlike need to impress.

From initial exchanges, Makertich formed the impression of a loner like himself who had lived until the age of seventeen with his widowed mother in Gundagai.

'Do you know Gundagai, Chris?' watching him spread the Vegemite.

'No,' meeting his gaze. Not for the first time did the blue of those eyes remind Makertich of the tongues of the lizards that crept about under the trees.

'They say in Gundagai everyone has the right to shoot one man.' He laughed quite easily.

The story of Flexmore's life emerged gradually. He had failed to join the police force and so worked for a while as a nightwatchman, before attending acting school in Tasmania. He loved to impersonate the posh-voiced English announcers on the ABC. Gregory Peck and Buddy Holly were also prominent in his repertoire. On his first night, he stood up and thumped the sides of the boat, singing in a surprisingly good voice 'Oh Boy'. He was mad for Buddy Holly; otherwise, he joked, the only music he liked was when people had to be spaded into the ground.

Suddenly bored of singing, he rolled a cigarette and lit the end with a match, inhaling. He watched the match blacken until it reached his fingers, and then he shook it like a thermometer and stretched back on the faded red cushions, expelling a sweet-scented smoke. What Makertich smelled was not his grandmother's French tobacco or his father's Champion Ruby; it was marijuana – the first time he had heard the word. Flexmore bought it from a Chinese herb doctor in Richmond and wanted Makertich to smoke it with him, but Makertich refused.

What he liked most about his new lodger was that he was an ardent washer-upper. Next morning, Makertich came into the scullery to find Flexmore on his hands and knees, scrubbing. 'These baseboards have never been cleaned, Chris.' Disorder, he confessed, made him itchy. 'You need a room-mate like me.'

Makertich, amused, asked whether he had seen the Vegemite.

Flexmore said: 'Check the cupboard above the sink. Third shelf up on the left between the half-filled Milo and Worcestershire Sauce – and a bloody strange place to put it, too.'

And registering Makertich's surprise: 'I have a photographic memory.'

It was a photographic memory of a particular and astonishing kind. Flexmore could draw on a strip of paper all the boats on the Hawkesbury after staring at the river for a few seconds. Or the configuration of the stars on a particular night. Or the basketwork of shadows cast by the trees on the bank. But it was a memory like a deformity in which certain elements were missing.

The following Sunday – an exceptionally hot afternoon – they were out on deck. It was already Flexmore's habit, while Makertich fished for yabbies, to lie with his legs stretched out, smoking one of his sweet-smelling cigarettes and listlessly rereading *Dianetics*.

Suddenly, he looked up from his book.

Makertich, standing at the rail, had also heard the grating sound. For several days after their conversation, he would remember the water around the boat, how it lapped with orange-bellied flies with wings the size of Cheryl's earrings.

'Cicadas,' he said. 'This hot weather must have brought them out.'

And with a spasm of generosity repeated what his neighbour Barry Cotton had told him: How, after the young cicadas dropped to the ground, they burrowed into the soil and fed on the sap of the tree roots, and there they stayed, shedding their skin as they grew larger and larger, five years, seven years, always primal numbers, anything up to nineteen years, silent, motionless, until their final moult, which took place at night. Then, a combination of their biological clock and what they were able to perceive from down there caused them to wriggle their way forth above the ground into a nuptial flight during which they turned into adult cicadas, living just a few days until they had found a mate.

'You sound like my bloody biology teacher.'

Makertich was not through. 'And once they've mated, one more thing – that's to lay their eggs, after which they're good for nothing but blue-tongue tucker and flotsam.'

'Well, they sure kick up a serious noise,' Flexmore said, relaxing enough to pick his nose. 'As one would after nineteen years keeping mum.'

'I reckon that's fair impossible for you.'

Flexmore smiled at the ribbing.

Makertich reeled in the crayfish trap that he had bent out of a milk-powder tin. 'Barry says the species that calls around the Hawkesbury is one of the loudest insects in the world.'

Flexmore contemplated the apple trees, relishing this sprig of good feeling between them. He was thinking something over. 'What about you, Chris? Yeah, I reckon you could. I reckon you could keep mum for longer than that.'

He waited for Makertich to respond. And when he did not: 'Well, I'm going to tell you something I've told no one before,' and lowered his voice, even though the river was deserted and the nearest person who could overhear was Barry, who anyway was probably already three-quarters pissed on cider. 'I mean that, Chris, no one. Not a soul.'

The cicadas were making their tinnitus noise.

Still, Makertich reeled in their dinner. He would cook them just enough to turn the colour and he never tired of the taste.

'I ask you not to repeat what I'm about to tell you,' said Flexmore putting down his book, and in an excited voice started to unravel a strategy he had for 'a real-estate related business' that he was involved in.

Gundagai was too small for the scope of Flexmore's ambition. Ditto Australia. Hubbard was right. 'If you want to make money, start a religion. Or plant a tree.'

Conventional wisdom was a foolish way to invest. His scheme was to plant eucalypts everywhere. The trees grew to a cultivable height in five years and lived for as long as four hundred. He was in the process of setting up plantations on the properties of rich folk in New Zealand, Uruguay and Britain. He intended to sell 'shares' in these plantations to other people. Let nature do the work.

'Well, what do you think?' Flexmore said.

Makertich could feel the lizards shifting behind the eyes, pushing their heads through and looking around.

He gave it some thought. 'It might work.'

Flexmore watched him haul up the trap and roll it on the deck and thrust his hand in. 'The thing is, Chris, I'm in a bit of a bind. I can't make the first move.'

Makertich stood up, a dripping, writhing yabbie in each hand.

'I wonder if you might be interested in helping me out,' in a reasonable voice.

The night before, Makertich had divulged to him that he was waiting for a payout on his parents' house. He had received a letter from the insurance company. It promised a resolution within days.

Flexmore removed the remains of the cigarette from his lips and dropped it on the deck.

'You'll get it back with plenty of interest.' He had a dark blue mark on his left shoulder that he scratched. 'It's only to tide me over, mate.'

Makertich reminded him that he needed the money to stop his photography business going bust. But there might be some left over, he thought.

Flexmore had the expression of someone who was looking at him from another angle.

'Is that a pledge?'

'Sure. Why not?'

For the next few days, Flexmore came and went; never up when Makertich departed for work and returning late at night, more often than not with an unsteady gleam in his eye, and invariably as Makertich was about to turn in. Whenever they bumped into each other, he was eager to strike up a conversation.

One night, Makertich lay on his bed and Flexmore stumbled in without knocking, banging himself on the low doorframe. He looked around, rubbing his head, bewildered.

'You take these?'

'I did.'

'Thought you had,' and peered thoughtfully at the photos that Makertich had tacked to the walls of his cabin, even to the ceiling.

Makertich watched his eyes slither from image to image.

'Not my type,' Flexmore said eventually, but went on looking at the blonde woman, all these pictures of her, a gleam of curiosity in his flicking eyes. 'Ain't seen you with a camera.'

'I don't bring my work home.'

'When was the last time you saw this sheila?'

'Three years ago.'

The fidelity of Makertich's allegiance was mystifying.

'You got it bad, mate,' his smile bent and wrinkled like the joint he produced from his back pocket.

Flexmore lit his joint and took a drag and brought his face up close to a photograph of Cheryl taken on the bank of the Swan.

'Look at those breasts!' his tongue sticking out of the side of his mouth and his eyes darker than black ice. 'That's someone who's not going to break her nose if she falls over, though she might hurt the back of her head if she bounces back.'

Makertich said nothing. The thought of Cheryl still rotted his sleep. Flexmore must have suspected that this was the reason for his behaviour. This fair-headed girl, this dangerous horse of Makertich's memory, whose lazy smile and shapely body covered his sad cabin like a shrine.

'If you ask me, Don was simply jealous,' Maral said. Jealous of something he could not feel and would never be able to feel. Even though he kept on growing for four hundred years. 'He had a bloodhound's smell for a man's weakness.'

Makertich once compared him to one of those willy-willies he had seen in the desert; a meandering whirlwind that gathered up tins and rattled them together, gathered up dust and paper and ribbons and chicken coops and roof tops, and from which there was no escape when it tilted towards you, no escape at all.

'Your eyes are the two largest nerves in your body,' Makertich would tell Maral.

The night he lost his eye was April 24, 1959. He and Flexmore were in a bar, drinking. He had come into town to light a candle in St Andrew's Church and afterwards to meet a girl. He had mentioned where he was going to Flexmore and Flexmore had showed up, but not the girl.

'Let's get out of here,' Makertich said.

They went to a restaurant across the street to get something to eat and Flexmore talked about a girl he had loved and left who had gone to live on the Huon.

'She's in a bit of a dilemma. She wishes she was back with me, but I'll never change.'

'What was wrong with her?'

Flexmore shrugged. 'She's a bit dizzy or whatever. Don't know about you, I can't stand dizzy women.'

They left. Makertich did not have to pay the bill, because Mike the owner of the restaurant owed him for some crayfish. They walked down the street to the Fovant Hotel and Makertich ordered a Scotch. It was not a drinking binge, but he had been drinking. Two beers and a Scotch. On the anniversary of his grandmother's death, and a lot else besides.

'Are we celebrating something?' Flexmore's lips outlined a sly smile. 'Not once in three weeks have I seen you touch alcohol.'

'Maybe it's my birthday,' with an unstable look.

Flexmore finished his drink and ordered another from the waiter – 'and this time make it bigger, mate. Last one was so small it had to be helped out of the glass.' He winked at Makertich and burped. 'Happy birthday, roomie. I'm going to the toilet.'

But Makertich had nothing to celebrate, and when Flexmore returned he told him about the letter received that morning from the insurance company.

Flexmore's jaunty smile left his face. He gave a depthless laugh.

'What do you mean "invalid", mate?' His mouth called him 'mate' while his eyes spoke the truth. They had the expression of a wild dog.

'They say the fire was an Act of God. They're not paying up.'

His words caused an odd facial movement in Flexmore. His eyes turned hard and directionless at once. He ran his hand down from the corner of his mouth and said in a voice of such loathing that Makertich was brought up short: 'I don't give three slaps for any insurance company.'

Whoever invented insurance companies could go to Hell hard. They should be drawn and quartered. The point was, this completely screwed his agreement. He had signed himself up on Makertich's pledge.

Makertich kept as wordless as he had on the back porch when the dejected slump of his father's shoulders betrayed his losses at the tote.

Damn you, he said, but to himself.

'You've conned me, Chris,' and Makertich heard his father's contemptuous laugh, full of impotent knowingness. 'You've fucking conned me.'

This Makertich could not let pass. He went as red as when his mother slapped him in the face after he refused to fetch his father his slippers. 'What about me? What about my business? How do you imagine I feel?'

But Flexmore paid no more attention to what he had said than if it came from the overhead lightbulb. He pushed himself up from the table with the ease of an angry man, and when he failed to come back Makertich realised that he must have left. He paid for their drinks and walked outside to where Flexmore stood arguing with a girl. The waiter came out with some other guys and gave Flexmore a push. Flexmore had been drinking more than Makertich, and started making a scene.

Any other evening, Makertich would have walked to the ferry. But with Flexmore getting rowdy, he flagged down a cab and Flexmore jumped in. Makertich gave directions and the cabby drove over the bridge, but Flexmore was singing loudly 'When I think of a million dollars . . . tears come to my eyes.' The cabby had had enough and pulled over.

Makertich paid and they climbed out.

A foggy night. No leaves on the trees, and all the branches and grass covered in a light skiff of rain. Makertich started to walk down the bank and Flexmore elbowed past. The grass was slippery and they both started to slide, and Flexmore grabbed Makertich by the shoulder to keep himself up. Makertich took two strides, but with Flexmore grabbing his shoulder he fell. He put his hand out and the branch of an apple tree that was pruned at an angle went straight into his eye.

Makertich felt the impact like a knife going in. The tree limb was captured in the socket. He recoiled, and the limb pulled out, splitting the globe and tearing the retina.

He was on the ground, clutching his head.

Flexmore freaked out. 'Holy fuck! Your eye's hanging out on your chest! I'll take you to the houseboat.'

'No!' Makertich said in a lashing voice. 'Flag down a car,' and tried to look around for Flexmore, to see where he was in the dark, but all he saw was blackness.

*

There was something unfathomably cruel and absolute about an eye gouged out. Whenever Makertich heard that someone had been tortured in this way, he would cover his face with both hands.

Although, once he had his glass eye put in people did not always notice.

'Which one is it?' Maral had asked. This after six days in his service.

'My left,' and took off his dark glasses and for the first time she saw: a large, brown handsome eye, but unmoving; and a sharper, smaller, quicker one. Cloudier, too – and never without a ring of tiredness. As though it had been pressed up hard against a telescope.

At the hospital, they frocked him up and sedated him. He felt the needle going in and was worried about moving his head. But they could not save his eye. The cells failed and died out and the cornea filled with water.

Out of his good eye, everything appeared to him in a blurred vision, and then the freezing wore off and a purplish light shone through and he started to see again in focus.

There was no grey-pink bird to greet him on the morning he came home. At the scullery door, he smelled something sweet drifting up from below deck.

He opened the door to his cabin and saw Flexmore lying on his bed, blond hair slicked down with lubricant, and half-naked beside him the girl Makertich had arranged to meet in the bar. She was lying with her bare legs up and through a garland of smoke Flexmore was quoting from some handwritten pages.

'Hey, Chris. Didn't hear you come in,' and tossed aside what he was reading. His cigarette had gone out and he struck a match and relit it. His fascination with the flame seemed unnatural. He went on in a contemplative voice. 'I was just saying it's a good point, about love and justice both being blind.'

Makertich stared at him. 'What are you reading?'

Flexmore picked it up. 'I found it on your bed. *The Boundaries of Love*. By Cheryl Pyke.' And winked.

'I think it's time,' Makertich said, with a sense of almost liking him better by admitting how much he hated him, 'for you to leave.'

Flexmore took another drag. He raised his blue gaze to the face of the blonde girl tacked to the ceiling: 'I'll fucking well leave when I please.' A day later, he was gone. When Makertich woke up and went into the scullery, he found a half-drunk mug of Milo still warm, but Flexmore was gone. He owed five weeks' rent.

Two days later, a policeman stepped on board. It was then that Makertich learned about his lodger's doctrine of scavenging and deceit. Before absconding, Flexmore had taken possession of a small shop in Richmond, renting storage spaces, as a front for his fraudulent business, and employing a strand of copper wire that he earthed into the public telephone box – 'into the button for your money back' – to make un-limited free long-distance calls. He would keep the money from the 'shares' that he sold in his phantom eucalypt plantations and investors would wind up with nothing.

'He's nothing but a big prick in a small brothel,' said the policeman, who had heard that Flexmore had been expelled from two schools for violence towards other pupils. 'Just as well you didn't lend him money.'

6

FOR THE NEXT TWO years, Makertich wore an eyepatch that he acquired from a costume store in Richmond. He felt unattractive and self-conscious. He felt like a clown in China, where a clown is a symbol of death. He felt that no woman would look at him again and he would never know what it was to have a child.

He told Maral: 'With one eye, your depth of perception is destroyed. You lose thirty per cent peripheral vision and you're further away from things than you think you are. But what you see means so much more to you. Now, when I look at things I really drink them in. Whether with two good eyes I would have noticed what I saw out of that plane – well, that's an open question.'

He lasted another five months on the houseboat. He was ugly and skint. Ostracism came in small steps. The bank seized his camera shop, he could not find work. In September, the houseboat's owner served notice and Makertich left the Hawkesbury.

On buses, people were wary of his eyepatch and refused to sit beside him. Running out of money, he resorted to hitchhiking. Mid-October saw him hiking west in a loose southward curve. He thumbed his way to Canberra, down through Melbourne and Adelaide, and up from Albany to Perth. At some point on the journey, he fastened on Cheryl's father as his improbable saviour and his path straightened. When he reached Perth, his plan was to fly to Marble Bar and ask Henry Pyke for his job back.

One clear November morning, he took off from Jandakot airfield in a single-engined Auster. The pilot was a gossipy Finn who remembered flying him back from Marble Bar at the end of one holiday season, together with Mr Pyke. Today, he carried an important package for the old fella. The murmur in Perth was that the Federal Government might be about to overturn the ban on exporting iron ore.

Makertich was his only passenger. He sat reflecting on what the pilot had said as they rose above the tin rooves.

How quickly the houses receded into wheat-farming land and then into scrubby sheep stations, becoming less and less fertile, until

Makertich was looking down on red dirt, and in the red expanse white pock marks around the collar of some old mine shaft.

The plane flew north, following the Great Northern Highway, over deep narrow gorges and conical hills and salt pans, then over country that was rugged and flat. Afterwards, he came to feel that the landscape had moulded him in its shape, making him intractable, impenetrable, contradictory.

There was no indication that they were heading into a thunderstorm until they passed Tuckanarra. The sky ahead was dotted with cumulus, a mob of grey clouds that filled the horizon from one limit to the other. The pilot was keen on reaching Marble Bar and decided to take the risk. He flew on, expecting the cloud level to lift, but every minute it grew thicker and darker and lower, until the peaks of the mountains disappeared into it.

One moment they were flying on the edge of cloud and then they were inside it and coming to realise that they were caught in a Charlie Bravo: a thunderstorm. What they had been looking at was all that year's rain gathering itself to be dumped on that sun-baked wasteland in the space of ten hours.

All of a sudden, the little plane was bumping about.

The pilot looked at his artificial horizon, watching his speed. His face still relatively calm. They should not really be in here, but here they were and he needed to do a one-eighty to get out pronto.

He tried to turn the plane around, but it resisted violently. Straight-middle one second, the next thrashing to one side.

'This is bad news,' he shouted, fighting to gain altitude. He tapped his trembling gauge. The Charlie Bravo was moving and the wind was blowing them west through the Hamersley Ranges, and he could not see a thing.

'What about climbing above it?' Makertich yelled.

'In this Auster? Not a chance.'

'Can you go through it?'

The pilot peered ahead. 'Too thick.' And too wide to fly around. 'We have to get down or we're dead meat.'

He gripped the stick to stop it vibrating and forced the plane lower. The rain hitting the windshield in stair rods.

'Shit!' he exclaimed, when they burst out of the cloud. He was hoping for a claypan free of scrub, a station track, any place to land that was flat. But they were flying over gorge country.

They dipped lower, following an ever-narrowing ravine. The pilot too busy concentrating on avoiding the river gums to see what Makertich noticed out of his single photographer's eye. Left and right, not far from the wing tips, sheer sides of mountain glistened red in the rain.

162

Makertich knew immediately what he was looking at. He tapped the pilot's shoulder: 'Where are we?'

At the mine, all Pyke's men were axle-deep in mud. No one able to go anywhere and rivers of fox-brown water running down into the pit. All day, Pyke had tried to deflect the water by grading a barrier and organising loaders to dump dirt. The rain had stopped by the time he strode back into his office, where there sat a young man wearing an eyepatch.

'This is for you,' and handed over the envelope that the pilot had given him.

Pyke's greeting was strained. His hard green eyes responding coldly. But he relaxed when Makertich explained his mission. Out of guilt, he overruled his foreman and hired Makertich as a haul-pack driver. A one-eyed, impoverished Armenian posed little threat to Cheryl. On the sole occasion when Makertich enquired after her, Pyke said that she was good and was engaged to be married next January.

'He's a Pom. But we're not holding it against him.'

Pyke had less than a year to run before his retirement. Once he had finished paying for his daughter's wedding, he planned to invest the rest of his superannuation in a forty-eight-foot crayfishboat called the *Daphne*.

It took Makertich a fortnight to gather his gear. He borrowed a sextant from a Polish surveyor whose distributor he had fixed, and spent a weekend learning to use it. The garage hand in Marble Bar lent him the Land Rover. He would have all his security on board, including the tarpaulin from the top of Pyke's piano under which to cower from the sun. He hoped to get as close as he could in the vehicle, even if it was unlikely that he would get all the way.

At first opportunity, he packed a compass, a map, a pick, a measuring chain, a bundle of star-posts, four coir mats to put under the tyres, and a fortnight's food and water, and drove out along an old exploration track. The sun beat down through the windscreen and the washed-out track stretched before him like a rib of the earth's bones.

He slept that evening on the roof of the Land Rover, a night of stillness and moon, and was on his way before the sun came up.

It was past midday when he came to a homestead: compressed earth walls because of the white ants, a big veranda, a few tame goats. Fed from an elevated tank, a hose dripped water onto the ripple-iron roof.

The foreman was away and an Aboriginal girl boiled him a mug of tea.

He drank it, watching the water splash from the roof onto the veranda.

The girl did not ask where he was going, nor did he tell her. He knew that he should not be on his own, but he was not risking another betrayal. He left her with a time estimate, enabling a rescue if he was late.

He drove north-west on the old station road across a plateau. The tyres scrunched over mulga and porcupine grass, and a wavery heat distorted the horizon. When he ran out of trails he followed the flat country. Progress was slow, rocks everywhere, and he worried about breaking the axle. After two hours, he almost got bogged in a wide river bed. He stepped out to test the ground and knew that if he drove on the Land Rover risked sinking up to its steering-wheel in mud.

To orient himself, he climbed the highest scree slope, several times losing his footing. He thought that he could see it from the top, but was not sure. There were different outcrops, and they did not have the same shape from the ground as from the air. He made his calculations. His best guess – he was less than twenty-five miles away.

He returned to the Land Rover, culling into a pack all that he needed to carry – water, tarpaulin, food for seven days. He marked on his map the spot where he had parked. Then he slid the ribbed key from the ignition, popped a dried apricot into his mouth and started walking.

A snake undulated into a crack. It was stiflingly hot. The view barren and eye-aching. Bushes with glossy leaves like small beetles. Mountains red and dusty with the texture of dirty suede.

In himself, a similar desiccation was going on. But if ever he considered giving up, he had only to think of his grandmother, stumbling on pebble-hardened feet beside a donkey.

For a day, he watched his shadow shrink towards him and disappear behind him. On the second morning, he turned south. And on the next, found his mountain.

He kept the location a secret until he had blanket-pegged the area. Exactly as Pyke had taught him, he marked out his claim in 300-acre lots, each the shape of a parallelogram and indicated at the boundary edge by a three-cornered datum post, which he photographed, and – when he had run out of star posts – by a cairn of stones four feet high and a shallow trench six feet long. He wrote down the coordinates using his sextant, knowing that when he made an application for the lease with the local registrar he would have to define where it was.

'When you go up against the big companies, they'll find any loophole,' Pyke had told him.

His rights of occupancy established, he requested a meeting with Pyke's geologist, a Berliner called Zeigler.

Zeigler was a grey-eyed cynic and one of those Marble Bar characters who were always there 'for just one more year'. He was not swayed by this young man, whose heart so evidently was in his story, and tried to fob him off with geological reports.

True, the samples of hematite and magnetite that Makertich produced from his specimen bag yielded a grade higher by 2 per cent than the ore fed into the Kaiser Steel furnaces in Fontana and the Buss Nissho-Iwai Company in Japan. Even so, what the fellow asserted was not credible. But Ziegler's scepticism turned to excitement and next into marvelling when, at Pyke's intervention, he flew with Makertich to the mountain that Makertich had decided to call Ararat. Makertich stood back and watched him weld a piece of iron to the rock. Following an extensive survey and percussive drilling, Zeigler was able to confirm that the lease pegged out by Makertich constituted one of the largest deposits of iron ore in the continent's history.

Through his father, Makertich understood iron and had seized his chance. Speculative eyes were trained on uranium, bauxite and titanium. Iron ore was never much prized, unless sited close to coal deposits. Plus, its export from Australia had been banned for twenty-two years. But Japanese mills were clamouring for steel. The documents that the pilot had delivered to Pyke were from the Ministry for National Development, outlining the Federal Government's plan to lift the embargo.

Makertich still had hurdles to cross. The State Government refused to confirm his rights. That a twenty-three-year-old truck-driver could be the legal holder to 578,000 hectares of temporary reserves. But he was as obdurate as his ore. In December 1962, Makertich's rights were granted, and six months later he sold out to Rio Tinto for an undisclosed sum. The Marash lease was smaller than Lang Hancock's in the Pilbara, but the royalty that Makertich was able to negotiate on every ton of iron-ore mined from it, fractionally larger. Makertich had refound in himself his mercantile blood. He revealed to a correspondent from the *West Australian* that he had named the lease after his grandmother's town in Armenia.

'Armenia?'

'Do you even know where Armenia is?' in a voice of steel that startled his interrogator.

'I wouldn't say America and I won't say Africa. Maybe somewhere in Europe?'

In the course of the first and last interview he ever gave, Makertich explained that the iron industry began in Armenia with the Hittites, and he shared with the journalist his grandmother's conviction that the Man in the Iron Mask had been Armenian. More than that he was not prepared to say.

7

SIX WEEKS AFTER HIS interview appeared in the *West Australian*, Krikor Makertich vanished.

He did not wish to be defined by his chance discovery. He left his adopted country and went to live in London under the name of Christopher Madigan. There, like his grandmother in Aleppo, he would learn to fit in as securely as the glass eye that replaced his patch. He would become – on the surface – an Englishman, with a feeling for oak trees and the jewel-like sweetness of the English spring.

Maral said: 'He never had it in for the English. Some people do, not Krikor.'

He bought a house in Holland Park that had belonged to a Scottish artist. He converted the brick tower into a darkroom, cocooning himself in his photography, and shed his Australian accent, as a decade before he had mislaid his Syrian one. He was massively secret. 'A spouting whale gets caught,' he told Maral.

His wealth was an abstraction. It did not become, as for so many, an obsession. And though he caught the millionaire's disease to endow schools and hospitals, he would always think of himself as a young man on a Vespa, turning the corner into Peppermint Grove.

'He fitted in so well that there was no room left for himself, the person he was,' Maral said. 'Let alone anyone else.'

Witnesses other than his housekeeper gave away little. He surrounded himself with an entourage of lawyers, accountants and bankers that he kept separate from each other and who safeguarded his anonymity. Two or three mornings a week, he walked through the park to the family office in Duke Street where a team of five portfolio managers looked after his assets. Headed by a former chief investment officer of Morgan Grenfell, they invested the royalties that Makertich continued to receive from Rio Tinto and from his other mining investments. The bulk of the profits he put into a children's charitable foundation, although no one who had dealings with him would have known of his philanthropic activities or that Christopher Madigan was Armenian or of the story behind his astronomical wealth. He had chosen London because it was discreet. Because London of all cities is a place where you can hide your name, background, fortune, lover. At least, for longer than in most places.

'He told me that he decided on London because his parents had wanted to go there first. Or was it because Cheryl had chosen an Englishman to marry over Krikor? Did that have something to do with it?'

8

NINE YEARS WENT BY. Despite his trials and tribulations, he was still a young man. The mothers who slowed their prams when they saw him on his morning stroll through Holland Park paused to admire a good-looking bachelor in his early thirties, wearing sunglasses and smart polished shoes, his dark hair thinning, although not his eyebrows, which had grown thicker.

One mother in the group was bold enough to strike up a conversation, and upon discovering that he was a photographer approached him later with an embarrassed request. Did he do children's portraits?

'To be honest, I haven't.'

'Can we afford you?'

He smiled. 'You can if you make a donation.'

She was delighted with the portraits that he took of her daughter and developed himself – hanging up the sheets like plates in a dishwasher, his face bathed in a green light, and writing the name of the girl in the margin beneath – but she never was able to summon the courage to ask him about himself. He showed little interest in flirting. He was like his handwriting: controlled, neat, slanted. At the same time, there was something roomy about him, generous, a sweetness.

The young mothers, in short, did not know what to make of him. He never asked any of them back to his house. Those who invited him to their homes gave up after the third attempt.

None believed he was homosexual, although one or two were reminded of the handsome, persecuted features of Dirk Bogarde in *Victim*. Word got round that he was a widower. Exactly how rich, hard to say, although one young mother fancied that she saw him step out of a Bristol. In fact, the car belonged to his lawyer. Madigan himself drove a Golf, and that only on rare occasions. Most of the time, he preferred to walk.

'Meeting him in the Turl you would have thought him well-to-do, not flashy,' his cobbler said, a slim old man with the face of a greyhound. 'You would never have known his wealth, only by his wine – he always sent a crate of twenty-year-old claret at Christmas. And his footwear,' bringing out a ledger and leafing through it until he came to two drawings. 'First time he walked in, he wore moccasins. He sat down and told me: "I've been here, there and everywhere, and everyone looks and says nothing we can do." I could see as I measured them that his feet were wrecked. Arches dropped, heels misshapen, bunions, blisters – all sorts of nonsense. He said he had ruined them on an expedition through the Australian desert – for minerals, could it have been? But I made a beech last and lined the shoes with horse-skin, so that his feet could shunt up and down without getting calluses. After that, he ordered two pairs a year. There you are. Heavy gorse brogues – because he was a walker. Size nine-and-a-half.'

One lunchtime, he walked into a pub in North Kensington and was served by a woman in her early thirties: buxom, short fair hair, opal earrings. She handed him his change and out of habit he counted it, and when he raised his head to thank her she was staring.

'Chris?'

For a while he stood there, not saying anything, as someone took cigarettes out of the machine, and the drawer opening and closing was the noise of a screen door shutting on a hot night in Peppermint Grove, and the face of the mother behind the screen merged into that of the woman who went on staring at him over the beer taps.

'Cheryl?'

'That's right.'

'Cheryl . . .'

What were the chances? His last action on leaving his makeshift ark on the Hawkesbury was to scrunch up her image and cram it into a milk-tin, along with each and every photograph that he had taken of her, and throw the whole lot overboard for the yabbies to nibble at.

Her face was thinner, more elongated. Her gaze cloudier. Her smile less lazy than slack. She was different. Both were different. They should have left it at that.

She was still looking at him. 'Your eye.'

'I lost it. And you?'

She gave a little laugh. 'My heart, you could say,' and he noticed that the corners of her mouth did not seem to get the joke.

They talked for ten minutes. He learned that she was taking a night course in etching – 'Plants and trees, mainly'; her visa was about to expire; she was no longer in touch with her parents; and was not married. Never had been. Nothing she said made him suspect that she had lost her heart – and her father his money – to anyone other than a neat, impeccable Anglo-German businessman.

Makertich would visit her in the pub. It was hard to have a conversation with people interrupting all the time to buy matches and crisps. One night he stood there like a steaming horse and asked her to marry him.

'In a way, one shouldn't reproach her,' Maral said. 'She was just a girl he thought he still loved.'

He had appeared before Cheryl at an Anzac Day parade: a man in a well-cut midnight-blue suit and with a refined Pom accent, who introduced himself as Carl-Andrew, a businessman with an ancestry that began with King John and enough stripes on his tie to umpire a Test match at Lords. She was clutching a copy of *Scarlet and Black*. He told her that writing and reading books were not his thing, what was important was how you read people, and if she wanted to know the dishonest truth, books were tosh anyway, and enthused about his two nieces, how good he was with children and his strong belief in community. She liked Carl-Andrew immediately, his patrician energy. He seduced her within a fortnight. 'I don't think I've seen upstairs.' Which meant that he would start to tear off her blouse as soon as they stepped into her bedroom. 'My parents have gone to the Seacrest for lunch.' Which meant that she would let him. The strange thing was that when Drusilla Pyke found them in bed together, her twenty-two-year-old daughter and Carl-Andrew, she did not seem to mind. 'Oh, sorry, darling, I thought you were calling for me,' and gently closed the door.

No sooner had Cheryl accepted his marriage proposal than her parents fell under his charm too. How they approved, Drusilla Pyke especially. His Oxford education and refined manner – 'He was at Magdalen; his mother a Bodley, of the family who donated the money for the famous library,' she ululated to Mrs Anderson in the club-room of the Karrinyup. And went on to describe his lathe-turned face, his blond hair and black eyelashes, his all-consuming smile that crinkled his eyes at the corners and made you believe in him, made you fall for his confidences and wild schemes, so that his ideas appeared not only tame, but somehow extraordinarily sensible when you compared them to your own, to what you had in mind for yourself, which, once you began to consider it through Carl-Andrew's ever-so-blue eyes with their pinpoint pupils, stank worse, frankly, than a dead fish. So that Drusilla Pyke was persuaded to cancel every plan she had put in motion for Cheryl to marry Mrs Anderson's nephew – an honest, hard-working grazier called Hands – and was quite over the moon at the prospect of seeing her daughter united with the Hon. Carl-Andrew Purcell (MA, Oxon; MBA, MIT). So that instead of buying the boat that had transported his dreams for nigh on three decades, Henry Pyke was persuaded to sink all his super, every last cent of it – bar, naturally, the amount set aside for his daughter's wedding – into a 2,000-acre eucalypt plantation in Uruguay. Then five weeks before the wedding, Carl-Andrew invites Cheryl and her parents to lunch at The European Club and over a glass of Penfold's Grange, the same glass with which he would toast all their futures, tells them that he is going on one of his trips, to oversee the planting of Henry Pyke's 'bluechip investment' – that is what he calls it – in a place named Solis; it will only take a week, ten days maximum, after which no man on earth could be more impatient than Carl-Andrew to walk Cheryl up the aisle of St Mary's in her long white gown of embroidered satin that Drusilla Pyke has had designed by Jean-Jean, the best dressmaker in Perth. And is never seen again.

When several months had passed, her mother reached for her address book to invite Heather Anderson's nephew for dinner. Cheryl organised her escape the following day.

By the time – the early Seventies – she met him in the pub in North Kensington, Cheryl had stopped thinking of Makertich. What he had meant to her had grown very remote. The same could not be said of Makertich. He was still defined by what he had lost. Cheryl was the girl he had loved most in his life. She was life before it changed for him. He did not see the lumpier, disappointed Cheryl, on the verge of losing her figure. It was irrational, the happiness he felt on meeting her again. When he should have entertained doubt, he had no reservations. He had captured so well her image that he insisted on preserving what no longer existed.

They married six weeks later in a civil ceremony. His Armenianness not an issue. Nor Drusilla Pyke. His comfortable circumstances allowing Cheryl to forget whoever he had been in Perth and whatever it was about him that her mother had objected to. She liked the name Cheryl Madigan and had C. M. embroidered on her cuffs and pillowcases: the initials, as she pointed out, might refer to either one of them.

Five years on, following two miscarriages, she gave birth to an eight-pound baby girl. They called her Jeanine, after an aunt of her mother, at which point she did tell her parents about Makertich.

'Her mother comes over, couldn't stay away, all forgotten now that Krikor is rich and her daughter soiled goods.'

But the agility of Drusilla Pyke to celebrate what had been an obstacle did not impress Makertich. He remained aloof – and Drusilla Pyke afraid of her new son-in-law, because she had wronged him. She stayed until Christmas, helping Cheryl out with the baby.

'This is where I come into the story,' Maral said.

SO DEEP RAN MAKERTICH'S desire for privacy that he refused to employ live-in staff. But one evening, to avoid his mother-in-law, he flew to Vienna for a meeting of the Austrian branch of his Foundation. On the corner near his hotel he saw mounds of horse shit. He saw open carriages and coachmen in bowler hats. Then, walking through an arcade near the palace of the Habsburgs, he almost tripped over a sticklike young woman who lay sprawled on her side. Her legs stretched out on the pavement and her abnormally round, cupped eyes looked up at Makertich from an upside-down face wrapped in a dirty headscarf, but without false or dramatic expression and, remarkable to say in that city of fur coats and opulence, without hope. She muttered something to cause him to stop, turn around, bend down. Some words of his grandmother streamed back, and when he uttered them she nodded and sat up. She had the shyness of a tall woman without actually being so, but presently was able to make herself understood.

She was a refugee from the overcrowded Traiskirchen camp. There had been an outbreak of meningitis. Her baby girl had died.

He asked the woman her name. When she told him, he closed his eyes. Then helped her to her feet and escorted her back to the Sacher, where he ran her a bath, and after she had slept for two days and washed her hair and filled herself with noodle soup and schnitzel, they went out into Stephensplatz and along Vorgartenstrasse, where she chose a wardrobe of inexpensive but sensible clothes, including a dress of blue organza, two white shirts, five pairs of underwear and five of stockings, and a long thick possum overcoat that he insisted on buying her.

After what she had gone through, nothing would matter again. But it was pleasant to stand with the coat on, observing him. One of his eyes seemed ringed with her own tiredness.

'He helped me, but it was not a big rescue. More to help his daughter. I was a poor, defenceless refugee, but I was from his homeland. He had a sudden mad moment in which he envisaged I would take care of his child in a wonderful way, because I was Armenian and I had references to that culture and my own baby girl had died. It was a silly, romantic impulse. It did not last long. And here's the odd thing. I was his link to Armenia, but once he took me to live with him in London we never once discussed Armenia, not for years we didn't. Anyone coming into his house would not have known, listening to him, that he was anything other than an Englishman. Anyone would have thought, looking at his oak furniture and his oil paintings and his decanters of claret, this is an English gentleman's home from tower to wine cellar.'

From Australia he had brought with him a few objects – an Aboriginal axe head; a lump of iron ore, molten shaped – 'like Henry Moore on a good day' in the opinion of his lawyer – and put them on a high display shelf in the hall. But not one thing from Armenia.

'He refused to let an oriental rug through the front door. No horn music. No novels by William Saroyan. No paintings by Arshile Gorky. No kitsch tapestries of Ararat. All banned. He said that Armenia was like any other badly remembered dream pieced together at breakfast. The fact is, he was at war with his Armenian blood. Anyone whose name ended in –ian, he avoided. And he never spoke a word of Armenian, except that one time to me. But that doesn't mean he wasn't thinking in it.

'Anyway, my arrival in London. Cheryl did not understand what this strange woman suddenly was doing in her house. She had this stubborn habit of mispronouncing my name. I soon stopped correcting her. Maybe she was right to be like that. I made mistakes. I could be difficult. I was a nonentity who had not read books. Not that Cheryl was a reader. I did not even speak English – so for six months Krikor sent me to the Bell's Language School in Fitzroy Square. Then after class I would go to a film or drink with another student in a pub.'

MAKERTICH PUSHED THE PRAM through the park, showing off his daughter to the young mothers. Cheryl, walking beside him in white socks, plimsolls and knee-length khaki shorts, likewise seemed content. The weak English sunshine made it too cold for swimming, even in August, but when Makertich put his arm around his wife's waist and slipped his hand up under her Pringle jersey, he could persuade himself that his fingers touched the bare back of the eighteen-year-old who had posed for him beside the Swan River. Right up until Jeanine was five or six, he was able to shake his head in happy disbelief at the long arm of coincidence that had bowled her mother back to him.

Unsparing when it came to business, at home Makertich denied Cheryl nothing. She was the person for whom he had composed his essays, with whom he shared initials, pillowcases, a daughter. Everything that was his was hers.

So that his wife might continue with her art, he bought Cheryl a studio in a mews off Oxford Gardens. One summer, in the same week as Jeanine's third birthday, a gallery in Portobello held an exhibition of Cheryl's tree etchings. 'She went round telling everyone how her show had been a sell-out. She never discovered the truth. Krikor had purchased the lot.'

He allowed Cheryl complete freedom. She was able to go where she liked, spend what she liked. Because of what she called her dyscalculia, he had a lawyer deal with her affairs, notably her work for the Cicada Foundation, the children's charity that he set up not long after he arrived in London, and of which he continued to be the anonymous benefactor. He appointed Cheryl a trustee on the audit committee, responsible for the mailing lists, with a signing authority of £100,000.

His generosity extended 9,000 miles to the family in Perth who had rejected him all those years ago. Among the photographs pinned to the cork-board in Jeanine's bedroom was a Polaroid of her grandparents on board the *Daphne*.

*

Jeanine had turned five when Maral started to notice a distractedness in Cheryl, a look of absence in her eyes.

A devoted mother at the outset, Cheryl took to asking Maral to drop off Jeanine at her primary school in Bassett Road. She asked Maral to collect Jeanine from school as well, although her studio was around the corner. She wore more make-up. Sometimes she came home from her studio with dark circles under her red eyes that her face-cream could not hide.

Makertich noticed, too. Or perhaps his lawyers alerted him. Money was going missing from his Foundation. In small but steady amounts. A consultant hired by Cheryl to help her with the mailing lists had submitted invoices from an offshore company in Jersey that specialised in buying property. Not in London, but in the oddest parts of the world. To begin with, Makertich chose not to question Cheryl. If his wife's consultant decided to invest in a Moroccan tower block, that was his business. But the amounts grew larger, until it reached a stage when too much money was leaving his Foundation for Makertich to ignore.

The first time he broached the subject with Cheryl, he kept his concern vague. His wife had to be approached obliquely; if head on, she adopted the superior detachment of her mother. He stroked her arm and said, 'Are you in something over your head?' and she gave a brittle laugh. 'What are you talking about?' And when he asked, 'What have you got yourself mixed up with? Why are you behaving like this? Are you being blackmailed?' she could not or would not tell him.

Maral said: 'I've wanted to say this to Jeanine for a long time, but I'll say it to you. Her father had married a woman – Jeanine's mother, I'm talking about – who was obsessed by someone else. It happens. After Carl-Andrew abandoned her at the altar, she never quite recovered. So when, in another country ten years later, she unexpectedly meets up again with her first boyfriend, Krikor, and he brings back memories, not of himself necessarily, but of an uncomplicated time before everything went sour for her, she is surprised and I dare say flattered, to discover that in all these years, ever since her mother threw Krikor out of their house, he has not forgotten her, but still loves her. And believing that she will never have this other man, whom even now she cannot get out of her mind like an itch permanently out of reach, she agrees to marry Krikor.

'Is his marriage what he hoped and expected? It can't have been. He was not that foolish, to think they could continue from where they had left off. But he could not stop feeling that she was the one. He had met no one else and was unable to form any kind of relationship. She was the swan – although from Krikor I learned that swans in Australia are black. What he was not able to see until it was too late was that no amount of money could have regained her, what she had been to him. Someone else, a worldlier man, would have understood that, but he was innocent despite his wealth. He was that guileless.

'Was Cheryl happy? Well, she didn't love him, I could see that. But it certainly wasn't my place to say anything. Even if she was happy, it's not allowed.'

'Not allowed?' Andy said.

'I'm sorry if I'm not making sense. It's the wine. I must be tighter than I thought. Let's go back a few steps . . . before the disappearing money and the dark circles under her eyes. One day, Cheryl's old lover tracks her down. He has discovered who Cheryl is married to. And not only that, but where she lives. He even knows the time when she'll be there alone.'

Makertich was one morning meeting his lawyer and Maral taking Jeanine to ballet when, as his wife would afterwards confess to him, the doorbell rang.

Standing on the front step, in a slightly larger suit but the same stripes on his tie as when she last saw him in The European Club in Perth, and humming 'all of my life, all of my kissing' –

'Carl-Andrew . . .'

'I'm back,' his tongue sticking out of the side of his mouth and his blue eyes smiling at Cheryl as if he had stepped off the plane from Montevideo and had only stopped by to reassure her that he was – even now – on his way to St Mary's and none of the intervening twenty-one years had occurred.

She started to shake, wanting to hug him so much. 'Where have you been?'

'Singing the Lord's song in a strange land,' he deadpanned, and held out his arms.

'She wants him. She can't help herself. I don't know what he has over her, this good-for-nothing, this abominable, mendacious man. She's so pathetically pleased to see him that she's ready to make any sacrifice – same for his damned eucalypt plantations. She believes in his trees even more than he seems to.'

He touched her face and pulled his finger down her cheek, and it felt to Cheryl as if he was unpeeling her.

'He asked if she could lend him £5,000 and that would be the finish of it, but it was only the start of it, and pretty soon she's siphoning off more and more. What did it matter to her husband? Krikor was not going to say anything. She knew he would honour the cheques. He was such an honourable man, he would be bound to ascribe it to her dyscalculia, until it's impossible for Krikor to keep silent, absolutely downright impossible.'

One night he walked into their bedroom, where Cheryl was brushing her hair, and sat beside her and watched her in the mirror, and then he put down his glass of wine and said, 'Who or what is Xemu Holdings?' She lowered her brush and blinked, as if she had a hair in her eye and they started talking together, and he was saying: 'If you won't tell me, tomorrow I will instruct my lawyers to investigate,' and she was blurting out: 'It's a company I've been putting money into.'

'Owned by?'

Cheryl looked back at him in the mirror, his smaller eye a rabbit hole down which she saw a classroom in Perth, a teacher waiting for her answer and Krikor's outstretched hand clutching a scrap of paper, urging her to take it, go on, take it.

She looked away. 'It's owned by the person I told you about.' Then, with an atrophying smile: 'The man I was going to marry.'

'Carl-Andrew Purcell?'

She nodded.

He did not say anything. He was not ready to face her. He had a presentiment that if he asked another question his marriage was over. That the period of horrible grace in which he had thought himself happy was a sham. He could sense it in the way that barking dogs in Marash sensed an earth tremor before it happened, alerting his grandmother to race out of the house before the ceiling crashed down, and his heart started howling in anticipation of the rupture, and a moment like darkness came over him.

He tried to put his hand on her shoulder, but she flinched, and he saw that she thought he was about to hit her. He stood up, spilling his wine, and kissed the top of her head. Her hair impregnated with the wrong smell.

She was mopping up his wine with a tissue.

'Did you two have a fight?' when he saw the bruises on her wrist, each the size of a grape.

She pulled down her sleeve with its monograms on it. 'I thought you said people who ask questions are enemies.'

Makertich had a crisis. Two weeks went by. He did not refer to their conversation. He had clung to his wife's assurances with the obstinacy of his father, who had kept alive in Perth the notion that their family were horse-breeders. But the situation, it was not tenable. A catastrophe was imminent.

The crunch came when his lawyer, Crispian Bennett, mentioned in passing that he had been chatting to a colleague about this latest venture.

'I can remember precisely what I told him,' Bennett said, a snipe-faced man in his seventies with a small mouth. 'I would be extremely surprised if the soil there could support such quantities of the type of timber as the prospectus promised, and when he asked what the bloody hell was I talking about, out it came, how the Cicada Foundation had invested £2 million in a business in Northern Ireland that involved the planting of 200,000 eucalypts.'

Makertich was tenacious with figures. He had known what it was to lose everything – the bailiffs in Richmond had seized even the leather case of his Agfa Box. But right up until the moment when he heard his lawyer utter the words 'eucalypt plantation' he had not put two and two together. Like a cancer that you think has gone away, Don Flexmore had come back into his life.

That was when he realised that he had lost his eye, and Cheryl her heart, to the same person. Only then did it blaze into his head where on a previous occasion he had smelled that smoky-sweet aroma in his wife's hair, and that Don was none other than Carl-Andrew, who had left Cheryl waiting in her white wedding dress, clutching her father's arm on Collins Street, at the entrance to St Mary's (in which every living soul of importance in Perth was congregated, not to say twisted around in their seats), watching each vehicle that motored towards them, a milk-truck, a Ford Zephyr that shot past at 70 mph pursued by a police car, even an old man on a bicycle (who raised his arm to call out something as he rode by, momentarily lost balance, and pedalled on), waiting, waiting, waiting for a blond-headed bridegroom with blue eyes and dark eyelashes to take off his milkman's cap or bicycle clips and turn around and say, 'Hi, it's me.'

When he returned home that night Makertich opened a bottle of Colares and walked in slow steps up the stairs to confront his wife.

'Mary, is that you?' hearing him enter, not lifting her eyes from her magazine.

He put down his glass and felt the sorrow mounting in his heart. 'It's him, isn't it?'

'Who?' looking up from the pages of *Celebrity*.

'Don, Carl-Andrew . . .' And saw a face coming in and out of marijuana smoke. Saying: 'If you want to make money start a religion. Or plant a tree.'

She lowered her head. In her expression, the utter fizzle of her attempt at secrecy. 'People *do* change.'

'Once a liar, always a liar.'

'*You* don't know him, Chris. You think you do, but you don't.'

'Did he tell you?' pointing to his eye.

'About the apple tree? It wasn't his fault, he said.'

Her face was very tight, her knees were shaking, her arm was heart-breakingly limp. But he looked at her with detachment, the carcass of his adolescent hopes, and thought again how much she resembled her mother, the hair flatter, the nose larger, the mouth always too wide.

She tossed her magazine aside and took a tissue and blew her nose. 'You haven't asked.'

'Do I need to?' He had never felt so far away from her, not even on the Hawkesbury. In that mirror.

Her face said it was over, what they had.

'I'm sorry, Chris. I know you think he's a shit, and maybe he is a shit, you're worth twenty of him, but what can I say that's not going to sound corny, he suits me.'

He could talk to her reflection in the mirror. In this other dimension. 'All right, you love him, I see that. I won't stand in your way.'

'He didn't try to hold on to her,' Maral said. 'He wanted her out of his life. Out of his daughter's life, too. At the same time, for Jeanine's sake, he didn't want it to get ugly. He offered to set Cheryl up hand-somely in a big house in St John's Wood, where Don had a hankering to be, with enough money to live with him, and she agreed.'

'But there's one condition,' he said.

Her body tensed. He had had second thoughts. He was about to take it away, what he had promised.

'You can have Don, but I keep Jeanine. You won't see her. Do you understand?'

She hesitated. Then, in a church whisper: 'Yes.'

But he needed to be certain. 'Once you leave this house, you do not visit Jeanine again. If you or that man come within one hair's breadth of my daughter . . .'

Her smile took time to form and then she was weeping.

'What do we tell her?'

'We tell her you've gone back to Perth,' he said.

'And Cheryl goes along with it. She wanted with all her heart to be with Don.'

11

CHERYL LEFT THE HOUSE the next morning and from that day on Makertich was no longer in love.

'The break-up doesn't seem painful. No doubt, in time, he would have forgotten her and she would have been scattered to the four winds of long ago – if it hadn't been for Jeanine.

'You can't believe that someone so intelligent, with his means, could be so stupid about not letting Cheryl see her daughter. When you think of the problems that stemmed from it . . . At the point where he agreed to pay for everything on condition that he and Jeanine could be left alone, he was rushing blindly into the eye of the storm. But he could not forgive Cheryl. He could not see that though she was a careless mother, this was her daughter too. Of course, it was more than that. He was desperate to protect his little girl. He did not want that man near her.'

But the first days were difficult.

'The tug of a child towards parents who separate is a loathsome thing. From the moment Jeanine opened her eyes, these two people were there. She was loyal to both. It was an assault on that loyalty when her mother left. Children are conservative in their emotions.'

'When's Mummy coming back from Australia?' she would constantly ask him.

'Not yet.'

Waiting for the day when her mother would reappear, Jeanine busied herself. She read. She practised her dance steps. If the weather was fine, she sat on the lawn and sketched the copper beech as her mother had taught.

'She was quiet, not good with other children, and sometimes very grumpy. I'd say: "What's the matter?" and she couldn't tell me. I'd touch her, and she'd say: "Go away," and I was not able to comfort her.'

She felt divided, powerless. She resented that her mother had changed her world.

'But what could she do – cut herself in half? She asked if her mother had gone to be with God. A bit like "Where do I come from?" I can't remember what I said.'

As the days passed into months and the months passed into a year and still no word came from Australia, Jeanine turned to Maral.

'I walk her to school, I dress her, I knit jerseys and scarves, I pin up the photographs that her father takes of her, I read her to sleep with the books that he gives me to read when he's not there – his work for his Foundation often calls him away. I tell stories of mountains and high plateaux and men on winged horses. I have to be her mother. And no one is more pleased when she is back to her old self. She stops wetting her bed. She has a friend to stay overnight. She is like any girl.'

The return of his daughter to something approximating happiness brought Makertich back from the brink of collapse, on which he had teetered following Cheryl's departure. All his love concentrated on Jeanine.

'That girl was his joy. She was his reason for living. Without her, I do not know what he would have done. You should have seen their faces when they were together. Whatever she says now, she adored him. She may try to tell you otherwise, but I was there and I saw it.'

Their happiness lasted the best part of three years. In all that time, Jeanine's parents did not speak once; nor did Cheryl make contact with her daughter.

12

'THIS PERIOD WAS A bright spot in our lives. We thought there was no reason it could not last. But you always hope you'll have more time, more courage.'

Like all things violent it began with a peaceful act.

On the morning of Jeanine's tenth birthday, Maral sat upstairs with Jeanine while she wrote her holiday diary, prodding her to recollect what she had done the day before – on this occasion, a visit to the orthodontist to have a plate fitted for her front teeth, which were too far forward – and suggesting various illustrations that she might draw to accompany her account, after which, depending on the weather, they would walk to Holland Park.

At eleven o'clock, they prepared to go out, Maral having relented, agreeing that Jeanine might remove her tooth plate for the duration of her birthday party – 'but this applies only for today' – when an urgent rapping sounded from downstairs.

The noise interrupted Maral on the landing as she tried to scrub a white deposit from Jeanine's coat. It could not be Makertich knocking like that – he had driven off half an hour before to collect his daughter's birthday present, plus some extra balloons.

'Wait here.'

Maral came down the staircase and peered out through the hall door that was made of coloured glass and saw through it a woman's outline.

'I open the door and the hair rises on my neck.'

Opal earrings in the shape of dolphins dangled from her red earlobes.

It shocked Maral to see the change. The expression so pitiful. The face of a mad, unhappy person who had lost everything.

'Mrs Madigan!'

That stricken look in her eye. Maral might have been looking at herself in Vienna. Her own little girl was three months old when she became infected, and Maral made a pact that she would exchange her life for her daughter's if she could be shown how – 'I said please God, transfer her sickness to me' – and her daughter revived for a few days, but then went downhill, a diminishing, gasping bundle of reddening flesh until she was just a cough in a shawl, and then she died. Seta, her name would have been.

'Could I see her?'

'Mrs Madigan, you know it's not allowed.'

'Only a glimpse, that's all I want.'

'You're risking everything . . .'

'I haven't seen her *for four years*.'

'I really don't think you should be here,' Maral said dismally.

'What harm could it do – my own daughter?'

'I was trying to do the right thing. How I wished Krikor would come home. Then she grabbed my arm and looked me in the eye and said: "Mary" – she always called me Mary, not Maral which is what he called me, which was his grandmother's name – "let me see her. Please. Then I'll go."'

'Maral, who are you talking to?' And before Maral could prevent it, Jeanine was coming down the stairs dressed in her green coat, fiddling with its collar from which Maral had been removing the pigeonshit.

'There you are!' and with a laugh Cheryl reached out her arms. 'I worried that I wasn't going to recognise you. Happy birthday!'

Jeanine watched the beringed hands stretch towards her, the fingers that buttoned up her coat, pausing over the damp collar, turning it down and then up again, tousling her hair and smoothing it, unfastening the buttons, one hand sabotaging what the other had done, as if five hands were touching her.

'And Jeanine gives me this uncertain, shy look, because she doesn't recognise the hulking woman who falls to her knees and kisses her frightened face all over, causing her to squirm away.'

'Your hair, it's darker – shorter. What a pretty comb. Oh, honey, you're beautiful, so beautiful!' talking to her in this hysterical way. 'What were you doing, my darling?'

Jeanine looked down, away from this fraught, importunate stranger. She mumbled, trying to make her let go of her arm: 'Maral was helping me with my homework.'

'Mary was helping you with your homework. How wonderful! You know that Daddy used to help me with mine? And what was your homework, my precious?'

'I was writing my holiday diary.'

'And now you've written it what are you going to do?'

'We were getting ready for a walk,' Maral said, determined to put a stop to this nonsense.

'Could I come with you? I won't be in the way. I know it's not allowed, but for half an hour. To Holland Park. On her birthday. Thirty minutes.' And touched a square watch-face on her wrist, and plucked at her dolphins.

'How do I know what she's going through? Because I recognise a mother's instinct. I want to beg her to leave, but I have this irrational need to help her. And like an idiot I say yes.

'Jeanine had no idea what was going on. I explain to her: "Your mother would like to come for a walk with us." And she looks up and only then does she recognise who it is.'

'You're back from Australia . . .'

Cheryl's hands fell silent, expressing what her face could not.

'As soon as I see Jeanine's face, I regret what I've done, but there's no turning back.'

'Let me get rid of this,' and Maral put down the cloth she was holding and went to fetch her coat.

'Not a word to your father,' Cheryl was saying, smiling.

'Anyway, it's only for half an hour, I tell myself. What would I not have given to be reunited with Seta for half an hour! And I'll be there to protect her. I tell myself.'

Outside, the sun was shining on the railings as if trying to be summer. Maral locked the door behind them and pocketed the key and the three of them – Jeanine walking in small steps between Maral and her mother – turn up the street and into Holland Park, where Maral sat on a bench and watched two kids throwing an orange frisbee, while Cheryl and Jeanine sat on another bench and talked.

'I imagine that Jeanine is telling her about her birthday party, the friends she's invited, their names, her new plate to reposition her teeth. Then the two of them stand up and come over. Cheryl is holding her hand.'

'She wants to go to the loo. Her stomach's a bit upset. Don't worry, I can take her.'

Maral resumed her place. She did not feel like moving. At one end of the playground was a public convenience, a small brick shed with a green asphalt roof. She watched Cheryl lead Jeanine into it – in full view of Maral, so that she was not concerned – and went on looking at a boy playing frisbee with his younger sister. The age that Seta would be now. She would have sat there for the rest of the morning, looking at the girl catching and throwing the frisbee, for the rest of her days, until the end of the world.

After a while, she checked her watch.

'This is taking a long time, and I think: *Funny, she didn't have an upset stomach earlier*, and then I decide not to wait for her to come out and I go in, and there's no one in there, and I call out Jeanine and no one answers and that's when I see the window is open and I realise that Jeanine will not be there for her party.'

At one o'clock, Makertich heard a key turn in the lock. He stopped stroking the cream-bellied kitten, frowned. 'Where is my daughter?'

The rest of that day was terrible.

Much later, the doorbell rang and they had a surge of hope, but it was Phoebe's mother dropping off Phoebe early for the birthday party, which in all the tumult they had forgotten to cancel. And when the telephone rang, it was a policewoman to say that Mr Madigan's daughter had been located, was with her mother all afternoon, perfectly safe.

That night was the only time she saw Makertich drunk.

'Where's that bottle of Colares?' and he poured some for himself and then as an afterthought for Maral — 'though I didn't deserve it'.

1 3

DON FLEXMORE HAD WALKED out on Cheryl five months earlier, but for most of that time she was too proud to accept it. She believed that he would come back. He had squeezed her till there was nothing more to squeeze, and vanished again without a sigh, faithless to a proverb.

'He left her without even enough to pay the telephone bill.'

Upon their divorce Makertich had settled on Cheryl the six-bedroomed house in St John's Wood. Plus a substantial lump sum, which ensured that she would be able to live well for all her days to come.

'We, as his lawyers, were hardly involved,' Bennett said. 'His idea of the right thing grieved us. We disagreed with the deal and wanted to protect him. But would he take our advice?'

Maral said: 'At first, Cheryl didn't mind not seeing her daughter. She had Don. This passion she has for someone so rotten, you must feel sorry for her.'

But Cheryl was useful and interesting to Don only when she was with Makertich: inside the honeypot and spooning it out. The last thing Don wanted was for Cheryl to leave 11 Clarendon Crescent. To be living with her was not in his scheme. Until one morning in their fourth year together, she overheard him in his dressing-room singing 'The Carnival is Over' in a melodious voice, and then silence, and minutes later out of the window there he was, swinging a canvas suitcase into the back of a cab, and when she raced outside and demanded to know where he was going, he looked at her with eyes that could be so beautiful, but which came staring from the face of a dingo, and said: 'There's a top block of land I have to check out in Jarvis Bay. Don't worry, baby. I'll be back in a week, ten days max.'

She took it badly, and not only because she could not stand to be on her own, the Seekers' words reverberating in her head, the words like flies that dashed against the window and buzzed around and died, and all the while imagining Don and those holes he was digging for his eucalypts, that he had dug her into. Because her own true love had left her with a habit worse than missing him.

A space, a loneliness, yawned open. Unfillable, not even with row

186

upon row of blue gums and scribbly gums and manna gums, forests of them, covering mountain slopes and deserts, until one morning she woke up and through the dark spidery scaffold of branches she heard on the radio what day it was, August 13, and climbed out of bed to put her face on and go and find her daughter to wish her happy birthday. But once she had lifted Jeanine through the window of that public convenience in Holland Park, her determination was maniacal to go on clinging to the girl with every muscle in her body, like the trunk of a tree that if she wrapped her arms around would lead her back up into sunlight.

I4

SMALL HAND NO LONGER IN his: Makertich's desire to have Jeanine returned was more than matched by Cheryl's savage resolve to keep her.

'Cheryl hired the services of a solicitor called Skilling who knew about matrimonial law.'

Skilling, acting quickly, acquired an ex parte application that allowed Cheryl to keep custody. Makertich was cautioned that if ever he took back his daughter a tipstaff would come on the judge's order and return Jeanine instantly to her mother.

Over crisps the following evening – leftovers from the birthday party – Makertich and his lawyer discussed the matter.

'To my client's disgust, I advised a cautious approach,' Bennett said. 'It sounds odd to say this, in these days of over-parenting and Fathers for Justice, but you have to remember at that time the father had fewer rights.'

'Skilling is lethal,' Bennett warned Makertich. His fingers on the hand-cut glass were thick and white. 'I knew him at Cambridge. He makes the point that you – without a legal leg to stand on – forbade a mother from gaining access to her daughter. And that's the *amuse-bouche*. His line of argument: at the time the mother was under a lot of pressure, she regrets it now, but it was monstrous of the father to have made not seeing the child a condition of providing reasonable financial relief. It was not in the interests of the child, and however badly the mother behaved in succumbing to the lure of this buck, she regrets it and she would like to see her daughter again. It grieves me to say this, Christopher, but the judge will find in her favour. Which is why I have come here tonight to give you this advice as your lawyer, but I hope also as your friend: don't sue for custody. Go for shared access.'

'Krikor never forgave Mr Bennett for that. All these expensive men to advise him and he could not get his daughter back. The final straw when he discovered that a man in Bennett's own firm, David Blaxworth, the same person whom Krikor had paid to deal with Cheryl's affairs, had recommended Skilling to her! Not to mention that Krikor would be footing the bill for the case against him. He never discussed it with me.

188

It was too painful. To be paying for the lawyer who was denying him access to his own child!'

As well as hoping to change the subject, while letting Makertich brew on it, Bennett had brought along a file on Don Flexmore. It added little to what previous investigations had uncovered. Don Flexmore was a fictitious name, as was Carl-Andrew Purcell. He had been born Craig Edge, the son of a telephone engineer from Darwin who left home when he was a child. His 'nieces' were daughters from a previous marriage. He was bisexual and a suspected rapist, with a liking for heterosexual young men. As James Thetan, he had briefly worked for a Dutch investment bank, until he was sacked following accusations of bid-rigging. And then he had disappeared, a habit in which he excelled. Xemu Holdings no longer traded. 'He's probably assumed another name in pursuit of another victim,' Bennett said. 'We're talking about one of the biggest rogues God put breath into without bringing him to account.'

But Jeanine was Makertich's priority, not Don. That he followed his lawyer's advice was neither from weakness nor out of fear of the Press. It was because he dreaded the impact on Jeanine's well-being of a violent and protracted tug of war.

'Bluntly put,' Bennett said, accepting another glass of Chambolle Musigny, 'the law is so framed so that no power can wrest Jeanine from Cheryl if it isn't Cheryl's wish to let her go.'

15

JEANINE MISSED HER FATHER. She could not sleep and would not eat. She wanted cinnamon toast like Maral made; her home-knitted cardigans. She pleaded with her mother: 'Let me go home.'

Cheryl was obliged to deliver Jeanine to Makertich at 5 p.m. the following Friday, but from the outset she ignored the family court's decree that the father had the right to shared access.

Makertich telephoned her the first time she failed to arrive.

'I'm afraid the child won't come,' Cheryl said.

'Let her speak to me.'

'She doesn't want to.'

Makertich applied to the judge.

'How old is your daughter?'

'Ten.'

The judge was sorry, he could not force Jeanine to speak to her father. Still less could he order her to stay with Makertich.

His impotence exasperated Makertich. 'Then why don't you ask her yourself?'

She was too young to be asked to express a view. She was not a reliable witness, he was told.

Maral said: 'At that age, the assumption was that the mother was the more appropriate parent. But it became apparent that Cheryl was not telling the truth.

'One afternoon, Jeanine rang – speaking from a call box. "I want to come and live with you." Her mother had had to go off somewhere . . . and then the coins ran out. It was a big decision for a child to make, and she had made it herself. I couldn't get hold of Krikor, so I grabbed the car keys, but I'm not a confident driver and I was in Swiss Cottage before I realised my mistake. If I had not lost my way – if I had arrived sooner in Tallis Drive – who knows how things might have turned out?

'She was sitting on the front step, bag packed, this little figure, with a Mexican hat and a koala bear. She leaped to her feet when she saw who it was, and was already at the gate when a car pulls up and Cheryl leaps out, eyes wild, and seizes Jeanine and yells at me. All I can do is stand in the street and watch her pushing Jeanine inside. I was struck by how lonely and destroyed she looked, with the only thing to plug her loneliness being her daughter.

'And that night she rang Krikor, Jeanine standing next to her in the call box, saying that she was going to take Jeanine away . . . unless . . . unless she had his word he would not try anything like that again.'

'But, Cheryl, it was she who asked to come home,' Makertich said.

'Then I will take her away and you will never see her again.'

'All right, all right,' Makertich said. 'I give my word.'

'On your grandmother's memory,' for she was crafty enough to know what would bind him.

'On my grandmother's memory,' through his teeth. His grandmother who had set store by keeping a promise. 'But what are you going to tell her?'

When she did not answer, he pictured her standing in the kiosk, looking down at their daughter.

Then in a voice of unnatural calm: 'I'll let her know what you've decided. She'll be disappointed, but I do think she ought to be told.'

'Told what?' Jeanine said, staring up at her mother, wiping her eye, fully aware that the conversation was about her.

'Your father has decided to leave us. He is going back to Australia.'

16

RAIN, AT FIRST A few untrustworthy spots, and then the leaves all dripping. From her window upstairs, the view was brown and grey, autumnal and chill. She heard the woman calling. 'Jeanine . . . ? Jeanine . . . ? Jeanine, what are you doing?' It didn't seem like a question.

Her body still stiff from standing there, she turned and went downstairs.

Cheryl stood on the landing, looking up.

'I've made you some egg noodles.'

'I don't like eggs.'

'They don't taste like eggs, but they've got eggs in them. They taste nice,' and reached out to take her hand.

Now that Cheryl had rediscovered her daughter, she had rediscovered her dreadfully. She promised Jeanine that she would not let her go again. Only when she suspected the immensity of Jeanine's longing to be with her father did her anger and pain flare up.

Despite all the harm his wife had done to him, Makertich had never allowed Cheryl to be bad-mouthed in front of Jeanine. This is not how Cheryl behaved. Almost from the instant that she bundled Jeanine back into the house and slammed the door on Maral, she worked hard to fell the image of Makertich that existed in Jeanine's head.

How flammable Cheryl had been when she and Chris Makertich kissed on Cottesloe Beach. The sea breeze swelling her Thompson's ball gown and jingling her earrings. Warmer than the sand, the memory of their intoxicating dance at the Golf Club, still dancing on a white shiny table when the sun came up – 'Armenians are good dancers, too.' Her heart had burned down since then. Deserted by Don Flexmore and yet unable to blame him, she fixed on the easiest target.

In doing so, she twisted things in her head. Remembered them in different colours. All that Flexmore had done to her she piled instead on to Jeanine's father. But she had not blotted Flexmore out. In her warped alchemy – and in the greatest insult of all to her husband's life – she turned him into Makertich.

'He never loved you.'

192

'Daddy?' in a small voice.

'You don't remember this. I had to take care of you.'

Jeanine, though young, had pleasant memories, wonderful memories. 'No, no, that's not right.' She remembered how scary her mother had been when she came to collect her from Clarendon Crescent; how she herself had resisted climbing out of the toilet window; how she had wept and wept, wanting to go back for her birthday party.

'The birthday party was a set-up,' Cheryl said. 'There was never going to be a birthday party.'

'But he was getting me a present . . . I saw him drive off.'

'He was driving to the airport,' Cheryl sighed. 'He was leaving you. Us. "I will go to where you will never find me."'

'That's not true!' She did not believe what her mother was saying. She ran upstairs and crawled into bed and covered her face with a pillow. It would be a long time before she did not cry herself to sleep, although when she was older she would cry in someone else's house, so as not to cry at home.

But like a mutton-bird chick, Cheryl was harvesting her daughter before she had learned to fly.

Jeanine's memories of her father began to totter and creak under Cheryl's barrage. She could not work out why someone so evil should have aroused in her such warm feelings, and why, if her father really was so mean, she and Cheryl continued to lead a good life in a comfortable house. But as she listened to her mother's plausible, soft voice, so, inevitably, bit by bit, did Jeanine conspire in rubbing out the tender image that she had preserved of Makertich and replacing it with her mother's treacherous version, until what she retained was not the portrait of a kind man who would have protected her and done anything to keep her from harm, but an ogre from a children's book, a one-eyed monster who had abandoned her in the dark forest and deliberately put the widest ocean in the world between them.

During all this time the name Carl-Andrew was never uttered. Jeanine would not have known who Carl-Andrew (or Don Flexmore for that matter) was, what he looked like, or have had the slightest suspicion of the part that he had played in her parents' lives. Cheryl's refusal to mention him was a dam she had erected against her grief.

'Don't ask me why she didn't tell Jeanine about him. Maybe she was ashamed. Maybe she was disgusted by the rotten crayfish stink she knew she would have to smell if she dredged him up. Maybe her pain had radically altered her, and the drugs she had ingested, because she was quite ill by then – with liver damage. Or maybe there was another reason.

Maybe she was, even now, diseased with hope that by not mentioning him, like the promise you make to yourself when you are a child – as I once made – he might come back. After all, had he not come back before? Maybe it was a mixture of all these things.'

17

THE HOUSE FELT EMPTY. Just the two of them – and a kitten that pissed everywhere. She heard him shout in the night.

'Nothing can convey the misery I saw in his face. They become ghosts, those to whom it has happened. They exist in a different dimension. I'm talking about losing a child.'

Jeanine, her absence, infused every aspect of their daily life.

'I had cut her hair two days before and he upturned the dustbin and went through the garbage until he found a few strands that he kept in a frame by his bed.' Her clothes he sent on to Cheryl; plus her tooth plate. And recalled and dwelled upon the tightening pressure of her hand as they walked past Holland House.

He missed her with a physical pain. Sometimes it was obvious that he was thinking about her and tears would be running down his cheek, into the beard he had started to grow.

'I'm not blaming you, Maral,' his yellow cardigan pinched up at the back where the hook had left its impression: he was guilty, too.

But Maral blamed herself. 'Day and night, I carried around these feelings of remorse. I didn't sleep. My muscles hurt. Because of me he had been robbed of a daughter – no one could have known better what that felt like. I hated myself for the pain I had caused.'

'It *was* my fault,' she told him. 'If I hadn't insisted that Jeanine go with her mother when she had no wish to . . .'

'Please don't exaggerate. Cheryl would have found a way. No, it was wrong what I did. I should never have forbidden her access to Jeanine. I see that now. I see that.'

He would sink into a deep silence. Simmering in his own thoughts, his head going around in circles, trying to avoid the mines that the situation had laid. An orange felt pen at the back of a drawer. The shape of Jeanine's satchel.

Once, walking through Holland Park, he ran up to a girl and called her name and when she turned around he had to apologise.

The silence broken by the sound of wine replenishing his glass.

'Or he would change the subject. He'd say: "They say on the radio it's going to get warmer." I'd say: "That would be good." And he'd look at the carpet and say: "Is that a new stain?" And I'd say: "It's the cat." And he'd say: "That cat," shaking his head.

'If it had a name I don't remember, but one day the cat wasn't there any more. I didn't know if he'd got rid of it or if it had gone away of its own accord. I didn't ask. It wasn't as though the cat was sick of being fondled or anything.'

Overnight, happiness had slunk from the house.

'Sad. It was so sad. Sometimes all I could think of to do was to make him another cup of tea and take it along. Things weren't good.'

18

HE MARKS THE DAYS. He counts them like beads.

Three months go by and Makertich can tolerate it no longer. In the hiatus of his sheer desperation he writes her a letter. Cheryl, who has subtracted his daughter from the world. Asking that Jeanine spend half-term with him.

Cheryl sends back a curt note: Jeanine's state of mind is too delicate. Anyway, the girl is under the impression that her father has departed for Australia.

He writes again. If not half-term, a morning, an afternoon. They could tell her he had come back on business . . . No reply.

Then Cheryl's lawyer produces a letter. Skilling claims that his client's daughter has written it of her own volition:

Daddy, I don't want to go to your house again. I want to stay with Mummy.

19

'It was hard to differentiate one day from another. If I describe a day, it will give you an idea of how we spent our time.

'The house smelled like us, like two middle-aged Armenians who had put away their country and talked to each other in a different language.

'I prepared him breakfast – tea, two slices of toast, marmalade, a bowl of muesli and in winter porridge. I would leave it on the landing outside his door. In the evening he ate early, at seven. I would cook him his meal – he liked watercress soup, roast beef and rhubarb crumble – and bring it to him in the dining room.'

He looked out of the windows of that autumn, that winter. His still eye like the eyes of paintings in the hall, like the eyes of a stuffed creature.

'I don't know how many months went by like this. Neither of us slept.'

Before, Makertich had been private. His reclusive persona a suit and tie that he put on to conceal his passionate nature. Now, he withdrew altogether. He went underground and thrust his feelings down into his core. Submerged into a waiting game.

'He kept his promise to Cheryl and did not contact Jeanine, not once in eleven years. It wasn't simply that he had given his word: he was too afraid of Cheryl taking Jeanine off as she threatened. Rather than his daughter disappear forever, preferable in his mind was that Jeanine should regard him as the one who had gone away. Cheryl understood that much about him. Even if he didn't get to see Jeanine, it was better to know that she was well and being looked after, in a fixed address in St John's Wood, where he was able to send funds. Better that than never to be knowing where she was. And Don would be out of her life. That was one consolation.

'But for now, the best thing he could do was to affirm Jeanine's relationship with her mother.'

Cheryl having spent her divorce settlement, he arranged for his lawyers to wire her a monthly allowance, ample for mother and daughter to live on well. 'And whenever Cheryl had to go into a clinic he paid her medical expenses. She never wanted for anything.'

Spring came. He watched it arrive with a fixed expression. In the garden, the sparrows sang. Purple-black buds sprouted on the copper beech, the crocuses bloomed, the needle on the face of the sundial cast a stronger shadow. Only, he could not associate himself with what was taking place outside his window. The world carrying on as though nothing had happened to Jeanine.

It was detestable, but he saw no option other than to sit it out until her twenty-first birthday, when she came into the trust fund that he had set up for her. Administered by Bennett, its terms dictated that upon Jeanine's coming of age she was to receive £5,000,000.

Maral said: 'Krikor fastened on the hope that if he left Jeanine alone she would return to him of her own accord.'

Exactly as a cicada buries itself for years in the ground, he would not give up; he would keep faith; he would endure until she came home. His obstinacy kept him going.

20

JULY AND THE TEMPERATURE had risen.

It was not all misery. He had some small enjoyments. He owned a quarter share of a racehorse and would go to Epsom and watch it run, and afterwards sit around discussing form with the trainer. Or fling a coat over his shoulder and walk to his club in St James or to a wine-tasting. Or to dinner with one of his girlfriends.

The summer after Cheryl took Jeanine away, he began a relationship with a Swiss diplomat's wife. Early one morning a high-breasted woman stepped out of his bedroom, just a towel on, and looked at Maral, who stood there, holding the breakfast tray, in the awkward radiant silence of a mistress at a funeral, and when she went back into the room Maral heard her talking in a low voice, 'You never told me she was attractive,' and the rest was lost in play.

'Then he met someone else in a travel bookshop. That didn't last long, either. They were casual affairs. He said he didn't have it in him to fall in love again. He was over fifty.'

Only on one occasion was he dancing by himself to a song on the radio – Charles Aznavour singing 'À T'regarder' – and he saw Maral enter the drawing room and he came up and put his arm on her shoulder and another around her waist, and he looked at her as if he was about to say something, and stopped and shook his head.

'He said I was free to go. Go where? I should have left him. I wish I had. Because it was depressing to be in that house, and by then I was almost forty-five. But I felt sorry for him. Responsible, too.'

She was serving dinner soon after when he said: 'Where did you get that cardigan?'

'I knitted it.'

'Perhaps you could knit me one?'

He asked her to pull up a chair and sit beside him.

'If you're going to stay, we ought to learn more about each other.'

Up until then he had kept a formal distance from her; they were strangers who had no knowledge of one another's lives.

Maral said: 'In a way, we did not have to talk for him to know my history. But now he wanted to find out more.'

Urged on by him, she revealed that when he first met her in Vienna, a woman of thirty-three, she was returning from the Cemetery of the Nameless, where she had buried her child. She was delirious, a taxi-driver gave her a lift, she walked to the city centre, not wanting to go back to the Traiskirchen camp, the doctor's warning in her head: 'They'll deport you.'

'Where to?'

'Your country of origin.'

And her giggle: 'It's not there any more.'

She told Makertich of her immediate thought when she saw him walk towards her in the Schweizerhof arcade: he had come to seize her – until she saw his upside-down face.

'Help me,' she said. So weak that she spoke in Armenian. '*Okne inzi.*'

A few nights after getting Maral to speak about herself, it became Makertich's turn. 'He didn't look as though he wanted to talk, but as he went on he grew more emotional, savouring his wine. He had not known about wine in Australia. He had discovered it in London. Wine was all he trusted – and me, I suppose. That was what he said. But he must have trusted me, otherwise he would not have told me about his grandmother and about what happened in Australia.'

Two or three evenings a week they ate together, and over the meal that she had prepared – and a bottle that he fetched from the cellar – they talked.

'We talked about a lot of things. I had plenty of opportunity to watch him. I didn't find him intimidating; more timid than intimidating. He could have had a lot of friends. He was funny and clever.'

She told him about her upbringing in Ceuta, where her grandfather peeled potatoes in the bus depot; her passage to Gibraltar, smuggled in the bottom of a sardine boat; her years in Paguera, Mallorca, where she cleaned for an eccentric deaf widow, and in Austria, as a waitress in the Café Western, where she met the musician with the brandy-swollen eyes, the folk part of an itinerant folk-rock duo from Ottakring – who would never be aware that he had had a daughter. In return, Makertich wound her back to the souk in Aleppo, the courtyards like Oxford colleges; the voyage out on the converted refrigeration ship, and the displacement camp where his family were interned, on a hill next to public gardens, an ex-compound for Italian POWs, two rooms for forty people, so that there was always a great deal of noise; and his first lessons in English, from a Latvian doctor, a gentle man who was President of the Pacifist Club, and how everyone teased him at his first school in Perth – so that he became a gang leader, a kicker and spitter, fighting and meeting at a certain rendezvous to argue things out – but not at the next school.

'That's how I learned about Cheryl and black swans. And about the gold mine and the houseboat and Don Flexmore.'

The image of Flexmore persisted, like the outline of a crayfish in muddy water. He tried to stop his thoughts of him, but his memory was not obedient.

Any mention of him, and sadness cut into his face.

'He never stopped trying to work out why fate had arranged this revenge by a man who didn't have the muscle that most of us are damned with, that makes us behave well. It was incomprehensible to him and frustrating. But good men never learn to figure out bad ones. They don't understand evil and never will.'

One November evening, Maral brought up Flexmore's name and it dislodged something in Makertich and carried him, struggling and resisting, to a low-ceilinged room in Aleppo and the awful coliseum of his boyhood. To the moment when he became aware that his father's gambling had passed out of control.

In a slow but unstoppable pageant his childhood in Aleppo with his grandmother and parents came tottering past.

He was nine years old. He was pouring a glass of water in the kitchen, when his grandmother's voice blazed from the next room. Her defensive fury so raw and fierce that Makertich, overhearing it, felt that he was committing a transgression. But he stood there, gripping the jug that he slowly lowered and held to his ribs, listening.

'I won't let you sell this, Nazareth. Look, see how old it is. How old do you think?'

His father mumbled a reply.

'No, you fool – centuries earlier!'

His father began to say something, but she interjected. She had never sounded so coruscating. 'This is only a band of silver to you, something to pay off a debt – No, listen to me!' flaring up like the head of a matchstick. 'You do not have any idea why I wear it, do you? All you know is Aleppo. You do not know where we come from. You do not know about our desert fathers, our Church. Yes, *our* Church, Nazareth. Your father may have been a Turk, but you, my son – look at me, damn you! – are Armenian – that is how I brought you up. And for us Armenians, to worship is as natural as gambling is for you. I wear this bracelet to guard the mystery that you are in such a hurry to have explained. I wear it to guard against people like you asking: "What is the Trinity, what is the relationship between Father and Son? What is going on here?" *You must not try to explain it, Nazareth.* This mystery you can't abide is the very essence of us. This bracelet that you were about to pawn is my taproot into the faith we have lost.' A pause and the sound of a cigarette being lit. Then, in a steadier voice: 'You ask me what He is. I can only say what He is not. He is not a burning bush. Not an angel. Not a Father Christmas for grown-ups. Let me spell it out. What is at the jagged end of definition when you have finished trying to define everything is the outline of a mysterious space. He is the shape of that hole, Nazareth, and each one of us is proof of His presence – even your own father.'

Makertich overheard his grandmother inhaling on her Gitane, reflecting. 'Maybe this empty space lies at the heart of Satan too.'

2 1

'DID *YOU* UNDERSTAND DON Flexmore?' Andy asked Maral after dinner one evening.

Her mouth drew into a taut line of concentration and she thought. She was not in any degree intellectual. But her answer when it came, in her flat, dry Bell's School accent, surprised him.

'Do you know the saying *perfect love casteth out fear*? I know that Krikor's grandmother believed this. Well, shouldn't the opposite also be true? *Fear casteth out love*. If you ask me, that explains Don Flexmore.'

'Why fear?'

Her head bent forward and there was an expression ferocious and painful both, on her face. 'Fear is terribly controlling, Mr Larkham, and very closely related to selfishness. You have only to look at addiction. I don't know your experience of addiction, but if you're addicted to drink or drugs or power – it makes you utterly selfish. The father of my child was like this. Nothing else matters apart from you, apart from getting your fix. You cut out other people and focus on your need only, so that it becomes more important to your life than any other person, until one day you look around and all you have left in your life is despair. And that was Don Flexmore. He never stopped behaving like a newborn baby who needed the breast, who carried on being the sun, the moon and the stars of his own world. There can be something very appealing about a need that admits no reason, and also something very frightening. But it's not appealing as you grow older and despair creeps in. Despair is where you come to when fear has run its course, when you're routed. And now I'm sounding like a nun.'

'No, no, go on.'

She shook her head emphatically. 'You mustn't imagine I'm religious. A lot of this comes from the books that Krikor gave me to read and from what we talked about. As far as I understand it, and even now I'm not sure that I have got this right, the so-called glory and agony of God's love is that we are free to reject it. God – I'm talking here, you understand, about the God that Krikor's grandmother believed in – gives us the freedom to retreat from all that is beautiful. He gives us the potential to feed on addiction. The problem is, God is hampered by the fact that he is truth. He can't use the powers available to the Devil. He can't deceive.

'The Devil, on the other hand, is a comedian whose stock-in-trade is deception. He makes things appear as they aren't. If love is about shedding power, deception is about stealing it. The Devil's agenda is to destroy love, to take people away from God, to sow doubt and despair. What he's peddling is very similar to truth and hovers on the perimeter of what is good and godly. He tempts with a relationship that is precious to people, which can exist, for example, between an adolescent boy and an old man – and which, if it goes right, is marvellous. But if it feeds the needs of the adult and not the boy, then it's the opposite. When the Devil comes harnessing his talents, there's always a hair's breadth between what is positive and beautiful and what is pernicious and destructive. Once you cross that distance, you are on a road that has no end. Because evil is never sated. It gobbles up what you give it – as Krikor found out. When he denied who he was, he was colluding in deception.

'And now, I will have some more wine, please,' and pushed out her glass. She looked up. 'You're not writing this down?'

22

EARLY APRIL, THE SUN pressing through the branches, the roots protruding from the lawn like the bones on the back of his hand, Makertich sat in a chair under the copper beech, tartan blanket over knees, reading his newspaper. He looked up at her over it when she came outside to collect the tray.

'If you're going to insist on staying, hadn't we better find you something to do?'

He introduced her to aspects of his life of which, until then, she had remained ignorant. As part of her new duties, she visited bookshops, antiquarian dealers and libraries, to collect the books he had ordered.

She cut out newspaper articles that he circled with his pen, and pasted them into a marbleised green album.

'Up until then, I did not have much time for reading. My level was the children's stories I read aloud to Jeanine. But these books became my education. The articles, too. Krikor was very good at encouraging me to study whatever he had marked. And anything I did not understand he explained, in the same way I imagine as he had helped Cheryl. Like that, I learned a lot – well, except about horses. I'm not interested in horses.'

Most of her work continued to centre around 11 Clarendon Crescent. She had nothing to do with the Cicada Foundation or the family office in Duke Street.

'He never talked to me about his charity or his business or his mining investments. That's why this sticks in my mind.'

One December morning, Makertich ran into the kitchen.

'There's been an earthquake in Soviet Armenia!'

'He had seen the images – villages reduced to rubble, a teacher with his dead daughter slung over his shoulder. The ethnic fights affected him most. Boys clubbing old women. Young Azeris pouring teapots of petrol over girls, setting them alight. It was another smash to our culture, and he needed someone to tell it to.

'We looked on the map. Some of the worst damage was in Alexanderpol, which the Soviets had renamed Leninakan. Streets of half-blocks of flats, the temperature 20 degrees below with no electricity or gas, because the Azeris had turned off the supply. The strange thing was, the tenth-century churches had survived. They were built with two layers of walls, so that any tremor reinforced the strength of the foundations. But modern flats had collapsed, because they had skimped on the right cement.'

She asked him if he intended to go there.

'Can you imagine? To go back and feel some of that antagonism.' Anyway, he would be a liability. Rats everywhere, no clean water. He would only fall ill.

'But he wanted to help. He went and packed supplies in a giant hangar in Heathrow. There, he learned just how bad things were, much worse than he imagined, and he made an approach through his Foundation to charter a plane to fly in food and medication. Initially, the Communist authorities blocked him. Why would an Englishman do this? – because that's who they thought they were dealing with. The truth was, they didn't wish to rock the boat with the Soviets to whom they were fantastically grateful for saving them from the Turks. Thanks to Russia – their Uncle Kedi – those Armenians had never felt more secure, with one of the world's great armouries on their side – and in return they had this loyalty. But when rumours circulated revealing what a large amount Krikor was prepared to donate, a local bigwig got in touch: they would accept his offer of support on one condition – that he invest in a copper mine that the earthquake had closed down. And, of course, Krikor agreed. For him, the copper mine was a shortcut, the fastest way to reach those who had no shelter. The only reason he gave money to reopen it was so that he might feed people who were dying of starvation and cold, who didn't have a tent to sleep under.

'Soon afterwards, when Soviet Armenia became independent and the mine came up for tender, the same official approached Krikor to buy it outright. Krikor did not own it for long. It was one of several mines that he bought and sold. I'm telling you this because of what happened later, but don't get me started – here is not the place to go into it.

'What I want to say is that after the earthquake, I noticed more references to Armenia in the articles I cut out. It was obvious that the earthquake had opened up hidden feelings. But he did not talk to me about it. There were still some questions that as soon as you opened your mouth to ask them, you had to pull it shut.'

One of the articles that Maral read before pasting it into his album was a review of a biography of Byron, who had spent a period of weeks in Venice learning the Armenian language. Makertich had underlined the quotation: *My master the Padre Pasquale Aucher . . . assured me 'that the terrestrial Paradise had been certainly in Armenia' – I went seeking it – God knows where – did I find it? – Umph! – Now & then – for a minute or two.*

The quotation struck her as a curious one for him to be contemplating.

He stopped shouting at night. Jeanine's painful ghost receded. Everything carried on as before. The sun, the birds, the copper beech had nothing to do with him. They could not penetrate his mood, the envelope of restraint into which he had folded himself until the day when he could be with his daughter.

23

JEANINE PYKE WAS SIX weeks shy of her twenty-first birthday when she met him.

She was sitting at her desk on the fifth floor of a modern building off New Bond Street. It was her second year at Amazon Solutions, an environmental organisation of which she constituted half the staff. She was forwarding an e-mail to her boss, Henry Bale, who made up the other half.

Their two desks were situated on the landing in an exposed position between the loos and the lifts, and faced the spacious offices of a derivatives trader. Xavier Bidencope had been at school with Bale, and guiltily admiring of Bale's concerns for the environment had leased to him this dog-leg of vacant space from where to pursue his planet-saving strategies. Whenever Bale was away, Jeanine held the fort. Watching out for the barbarians.

On this sunny morning in July, around noon, a man about as old as her father would be stepped out of the large glass double doors opposite and stood waiting for a lift to take him down. Jeanine was suspicious of every person who made it to this floor, but something in his grim expression caught her eye. He had the crumbled, preoccupied face of someone bearing the cares of the world, condemned to hang, before he gave her a quick sideways glance and saw her examining him.

Then he smiled and sauntered over.

He was thickset, his hair blonder than his moustache, and dressed in an over-tight blue suit in a style now out of fashion.

'What's this company?' looking around at the photographs of whales and polar bears, and the poster of a line of Indians in a jungle, standing in a warlike posture with spears and their bodies painted in tribal designs.

She said: 'The philosophy of Amazon Solutions is to give an attributable value to the standing forest by paying for its ecosystem services.'

'How does it work?'

Her tone was cool, professional. 'Governments are too slow, philanthropists too few, so we're looking for private individuals who believe in the cause.'

'Go on.'

'The idea is that you're putting your money into a fund and a percentage of the profits trickle down to those who live in the forest. You're paying them not to cut down the trees and also paying for the service that the forest is delivering. We need to make the forest worth more standing than cleared.'

'You mean for palm oil, beef and soya?'

'Exactly. Which means the money goes to those who are the true guardians of the forest.'

He nodded, peering more closely at the Indians on the wall. 'The soldiers on the front line in the battle against climate change . . .'

She looked at him. 'That's right. At the moment we have a pilot scheme going in Guyana. For more information you can see our website.'

'What a coincidence,' he said, stretching the vowels for dramatic effect.

He was like a friend in a dream whom she did not know. In his tight suit and striped tie. His smile made her uncomfortable. He looked as if he wore mascara on his lashes. She wondered if his hair was dyed. Also, if he might be wearing blue contact lenses.

'You happen to be looking,' and performed a drum roll with his fingers, 'at an uncompromising eco-warrior.'

She had to restrain a laugh.

To bolster his point, he told her of the sharkfin bust he had been on in the Galápagos. And of the time when he had sailed with Greenpeace in New Zealand. 'If you're ever in Auckland, let me know, I can get you a room in the best hotel.'

'I don't stay in that kind of hotel,' she said with her usual taunting frankness. Still scornful of anyone who came in or out of Xavier's office, sharkfin bust or no.

He had hoped to impress, but he felt her irritation and it put him on his guard.

'Like your job?' glancing down at her. His eyes were the colour of carbon paper.

'It doesn't pay well, but I like it.'

But he had noticed something was wrong. He leaned over. 'Man trouble?'

'My mother just died.'

'I'm sorry.'

'Yes, she'd been ill for some time.'

'Were you close?'

'We had our moments.'

'Where are you from?' he asked.

'I was born in London, but my mother was from Australia.'

'Ah,' he said significantly, '*ça s'explique.*'

Two large brown eyes squinted up at him. 'What did you say?'

'In Australia,' he remarked in a solemn way, 'when the Kurnai of Victoria saw the Aurora Australis, they exchanged wives for the day and swung the severed hand of a dead man towards it, shouting: "Send it away! Don't let it burn us up!"'

'I didn't know that,' with an involuntary smile.

'You remind me of the Aurora Australis,' he said. 'I'm Kes, by the way. Kes Wakefield.'

'Jeanine.' She denied him her surname.

'Jeanine?' Something in him had stabilised. His blue eyes looked at her carefully. No longer reckless or smiling. 'Your mother wasn't from Perth?'

'She did come from Perth.'

'Peppermint Grove?'

'How did you know?'

The peculiar way his eyes delved into her – they did not seem made of what eyes normally are made of, but hard, chunky conglomerate; as they observed her, they excited fear, the sort of fear a kid goat feels when it steps to the back of a cave to lick salt and all at once the stone has claws, sabre-teeth, fur.

'Your mother wasn't Cheryl Pyke was she?'

'That's right . . .'

'Oh no!' and clapped a hand to his head. 'I was a friend of hers.'

'You weren't!'

'We were at Perth Modern together. I used to write her essays for her.'

'You're an Australian?'

Nothing so far in his accent had suggested that he was anything other than a public-school-educated Englishman of the type constantly to be seen emerging from the fifth-floor lift on the way to beg a financial crumb from Xavier.

'I'm sorry to hear she's carked it,' he said, momentarily lapsing into an Australian voice. 'She was a top woman, your mother. A crackerjack of a girl. But I hardly need tell *you* that.'

The dining room of the East India Club was on the ground floor of a Georgian building in St James's Square, next to the London Library.

While they waited to be seated, she took in the other diners. Her lips thin with disapproval.

'I hate these places,' as if she had thought up the phrase in the street outside and was going to deliver it anyway.

'Yes,' he said agreeably, 'they are rather ghastly. But ideal for eaves-dropping on the enemy.'

Her very word!

At that moment, a young waiter with an oriental face minced into the room.

'Sir Richard!' his face brightening. 'How are you?'

'All the better for seeing you, Sanjit,' and ordered two Bloody Marys, extra-spicy. 'Put it on someone else's bill,' he joked. Then piloted her to a table in the centre of the room.

'Sir Richard?' raising an eyebrow.

'It's a joke between us. Sanjit's from Brunei,' as if that explained it.

From the instant that she sat down, Kes Wakefield was charming and attentive, bombarding her with questions while dismantling a bread roll, and listening to her answers as he dipped the pellets into a saucer of olive oil and chewed on them.

'How old are you?'

'I'll be twenty-one next month.'

'You seem older,' assessing her full mouth, her large, fiery eyes.

Over a Bloody Mary, he extracted more. She had left St Paul's three years ago, had supported Greenpeace for a while, and was impassioned about saving the whales. On the point of training to be a reflexologist, she was distracted by a television documentary concerning a visit by the Princess of Wales to a minefield in Angola. She decided to go and work in Luanda for an Italian charity that looked after children who were mine-victims. 'My dream is simple,' she had told her mother, quoting the charity's mantra. 'If you help an adult, you help an individual. If you help a child, you help a nation.'

'How was Angola?' he asked.

'Upsetting.'

'I'll bet.'

Days after returning from Luanda, she met Henry Bale, a young man consumed by Al Gore's mission to alert every government on earth to the effects of greenhouse gases, and had gone to work for him as his secretary.

At this point, the young Malayan waiter interrupted them.

She said in a grown-up voice: 'I'll have the soup, then the vegetable curry with spinach.'

Wakefield ordered oysters and Aberdeen roast beef from the salver.

'Room 300?'

'You remember!'

She watched the waiter leave, a blush fluttering his cheeks, and then leaned forward and crossed her arms. 'Enough of me. Now you.'

While they waited for their first course, Wakefield revealed that he had been at Magdalen College, Oxford – 'Hence the tie' – two years ahead of Xavier Bidencope.

'What were you doing at Oxford?'

'Oh, you know, sabering the corks.'

'Aren't you much older than Xavier?'

'I was a postgraduate,' he said.

His mother was a Bodley, of the family who donated the money for the library. His father from a German émigré family to Australia. He had spent his formative years in Argentina – here his face clouded – during the Dirty War.

He looked at her, those blue eyes crinkled down at the corners, and she wondered if he was having her on. But over the next two hours she decided that what she had first taken to be ingratiating optimism was a defence mechanism. Disarmed by his account of his sister, who was caught by the police in Uruguay and tortured, Jeanine's suspicions started to recede.

'What did you do after you left South America?'

'Gosh, lots of things.'

He lectured on business in Iceland; was private secretary to the King of Tonga; smuggled Poles to the West in the Cold War and was a lover of General Jaruzelski's daughter.

It all sounded preposterous, but then again not.

Later, he married a Czech girl whom he tried to bring out of Czechoslovakia. It was 1983. He stood behind the German wire at Hof and watched her come towards him, his bride of three months, and then the Czech police opened fire and she fell to the ground before his eyes.

'To see someone you love die –' in a furred voice, 'it cuts something out of you that can never be replaced.'

He had never remarried. He travelled instead – on what he called his 'assignments' – driven by the passion that his cruelly murdered wife had stirred in him and which, though it could never replace her, was his means of commemorating the selfless ideology by which Zdenka had lived. It was owing to this passion that he currently owned land in Sierra Leone, Morocco, Brazil, Croatia, New Zealand, Jarvis Bay, British Columbia, Northern Ireland and Guinea-Bissau.

She asked what he did with this land.

He told her that he planted trees.

She looked at Wakefield in her serious way. 'We don't think much of afforestation.'

'Really?' His eyes were swimming-pool blue with pinprick pupils.

'We're not against planting, but we haven't got the time,' she said. 'It takes thirty years for a tree to mature enough to sequester carbon efficiently.'

'Don't worry, I've got shares in carbon capture and storage, too.'

She was still not impressed. 'What's the point when you already have the most sophisticated mechanism on earth which delivers it for free – which is the rainforest.'

At this Wakefield smiled. 'Ah, but let me explain to you about my latest project.'

He went into detail about a rainforest in Tasmania that he was involved in trying to protect, and she at last became interested. Of everything that Wakefield had so far told Jeanine, this information made an impression on her. At the words 'old-growth rainforest', the image that she had had of him completed a somersault in her head. He grew very real.

It was a sizeable tract of land south-east of Zeehan, comprising two river valleys dense with ancient eucalypts, some looking as old as the world. In an awed voice he described walking up beneath a canopy of electric-green ferns ('like the fan-vaulting of a cathedral') to the trunk of an immense Tasmanian swamp gum, the *Eucalyptus regnans*, the tallest flowering plant on earth. 'I stood at the base of that tree and I pressed my face against the bark and I said to myself: "This has been growing since the time of Abel Tasman, this has survived God knows how many fires and draughts and storms," and I looked up at the sky and I tell you, Jeanine, it was as though I was looking into it up the spine of an endangered whale. How anyone is able to fell such a tree and live with themselves, I do not know. It's no different to killing a whale. And now there's a massive pulp mill about to be built that will bring these trees crashing down – and for what? For loo-paper to wipe Japanese bottoms, that's what. Well, not if I can help it.'

She looked at him with the face of a child, her eyes big from the practice of suppression. 'It's funny, but my mother loved eucalypts.'

He smiled. 'Could it have been me who planted the idea?'

She half-listened. 'It's probably why I became interested in the Green movement.'

'You don't say . . .'

'Towards the end, eucalypts – they were all she wanted to draw. Etching after etching.'

'I'd like to see those,' he said. 'God, I miss your mother,' with vehemence.

She nodded.

'Tell me, how did she die?'

'All I was told is that she had a heart attack. An accidental mix of prescription drugs. She had a raft of pills to keep her up, down and sideways.'

'I'm sorry,' and covered her hand with his. She moved to withdraw it, but, affected by the emotion in his voice, allowed it to stay there.

'She was only fifty-nine, but her liver was shot to pieces,' Jeanine said. 'Whether she died accidentally or on purpose, who cares? She'd reached a stage when it made no difference.'

He gave her fingers a tender squeeze.

When she looked around for something to wipe her eyes with, he handed her his napkin.

'What about Carl-Andrew?' he asked. 'Did your mother mention him ever?'

'No,' dabbing her eye.

'Don Flexmore?'

'No.'

'James Thetan?'

She shook her head. 'Sorry.'

Luther Azavedo, Wesley Stibbe, Simon Horner, Bijou Mandrake?

'Bijou? What kind of name is that?'

Her frown returned him to the table. He brought his chair closer. 'It's just that we were all at school together.'

She looked at him. 'Did you write their essays too?'

'Some of them. Some of them.'

'What did Xavier say?'

'Xavier?' releasing her hand.

'You went to see him just now.'

'Oh, yes. I wanted to involve him in my project to save those giant eucalypts.'

'He wasn't interested?'

'He suddenly remembered he had to do something . . . Then you came into my little world.'

'Honestly! That's so typical of Xavier! And you were at Oxford with him!'

His eye mechanically tracked the waiter who was wheeling in the cheese trolley.

But she was pensive. 'Maybe I should invest in your project.'

'You?' swinging his head back.

When she spoke, her voice was patient and serious. In a little less than six weeks' time, she stood to receive a sizeable sum from her father's trust fund. She had planned to invest in Henry's pioneering 'forest bond', but . . .

Across the table an eyebrow lifted.

Spontaneously, she said: 'I'd have to see the existing legislation, who has the rights to the forest.'

'No problem there. It's the indigenous people.'

'But you don't have indigenous roots.'

'Oh, dear girl, but I do.'

'You?'

'My grandmother,' with an air of unimpeachable gravity, 'was part Aborigine.'

She gazed at him with brown eyes the colour of new-hoed soil, full of tenderness.

'Tell me,' Wakefield said over a slice of cheddar, 'about your father.'

'My father?' her frown returning.

'You haven't mentioned him.'

'Why should I? I never see him.'

He selected another Bath Oliver. 'When did you see him last?'

'He walked out on us when I was ten.'

'You haven't been in touch since?'

'He didn't want us to meet.'

'I'm so sorry.'

'My mother impressed on me that the last thing in the world my father would have welcomed was for his only child to contact him. I don't even know where he lives. Somewhere in Australia. He only dealt with us through lawyers.'

'Oh, no, I don't think he's in Australia.' Taking another piece of cheese. Pleased by what she had revealed. By the indication of a tendency – which seemed to have dictated her interests since leaving school – to idealise and forgive everyone save her father. 'You may find he's closer to home than that.'

'What, you know where he is?'

'I have an inkling, let's say.'

She looked sharply up.

His face assumed the cast of a father confessor figure. 'What if I told you he's right here?'

'In London?' gaping.

'I can give you his address in Holland Park if you like.'

'That's impossible,' shaking her head, not wanting to allow her thoughts to go any further.

'More cheese? You must taste this one.' With his knife, he levered on to her plate, from his, a yellow Lancashire cream cheese made, he told her, by Butler's. He relaxed back in his chair, stroking his moustache, his tie. 'Before doing anything precipitate, it's always wise to eat cheese.'

Coffee taken, chit signed, Wakefield showed her upstairs to the library and the room where, he said, the Prince Regent was sitting when news reached him of the victory at Waterloo.

Tall windows opened onto a small balcony and they stood for a moment in the sun.

'Smell that air? Smell the lead in it?' He inhaled and thumped his chest and coughed. 'That's why we need to save that forest. Think how much healthier it would be if this square was full of ancient swamp gums instead of those . . . those manky oaks.' The wine had made him expansive. 'Why, they'd be pumping quantities of fresh air into the lungs of every man, woman and child in England. Plus it would be good for my angina.'

'Are you ill?' she touched his arm.

He coughed again. 'I do have to look after myself. But I mustn't complain. It's not so bad for me as for some of your father's victims.'

'What are you talking about?'

He gripped the stuccoed edge of the balcony and looked out over St James's Square. 'I shouldn't be telling you this, seeing as you're his daughter. But it sticks in my gullet what he did to those poor Armenians.'

'Which Armenians?' the strain of their conversation showing.

He suggested that they go down into the square, where, seated on a bench inside a mock Doric temple, and surrounded by secretaries eating their sandwiches, he elaborated.

'One of my assignments was to work for a Canadian mining company that had dealings with your father.' He coughed. 'I was their environmental adviser.'

Angry, upset, confused, she waited for him to resume, which he did in a regretful voice.

'Some years ago now, this company bought one of your father's mines – in Armenia, it was. Dreadful affair,' and shook his head. 'Whenever we had to speak to him, he was in a hotel in Burma. Even Rio Tinto refused to do business with that regime . . . But it sounds very much as if he did to those Armenians what he did to your mother, what it frightened her that he would do to you – if only he had the chance.'

'Go on . . .'

She heard him out, her emotions overcome by this stranger who in the course of two and a half hours had confirmed every single thing that her mother had said about her father.

What surprised Jeanine was that she warmed to Wakefield even more. She talked more freely, encouraged by proof of his interests, their shared concerns. She felt that she could trust him; he would be as good as his word.

An hour later, when, on the corner of King Street, she waved goodbye to him with the sheet of East India Club stationary on which he had written her father's address, she couldn't help but see through his solid, broad frame to that other man, the ogre of her adolescent years, with eyes black and unreflecting, so that it seemed a single tiger snake had taken possession of his skull and lay behind their empty sockets.

She gave a final wave and with reluctance turned and walked up King Street. She had not spoken to Wakefield about her mother, what she was like as a girl, but that could wait.

24

THE DAY BEGAN COLD. In the afternoon it drizzled, and then the sun came out and for an hour it was unusually warm.

On the dot of six, a sober-dressed young woman squeaked open the metal gate and quickly climbed the steps. She kept her eyes down. Only when she raised them to the front door and saw the zodiac of stained glass, its blues and reds, did a memory shift.

This was the first time that Jeanine had returned to her childhood home. Out of some superstition, and in reaction to her mother's warnings, she had avoided this corner of London. The house held too many associations for her.

But now she made out, inlaid into the door, a herring-bone pattern of coloured glass. Memories sprang up to greet her like a kennelled dog. Maral's trembling hands. A child's green coat with an upturned collar – she felt its dampness rubbing the back of her neck and involuntarily hunched her shoulders. She reached out and pressed the instantly recognisable ding-dong of the doorbell.

Her eyes were open. She had rehearsed what she was going to say.

25

INSIDE THE HOUSE, MAKERTICH prepared to receive the daughter he had not seen for eleven years.

Handkerchief in mouth, he had paced his study, rereading Jeanine's letter. The note was brief, but, he was pleased to observe, in an intelligent hand.

'Look, Maral, isn't that written by a bright girl, wouldn't you say?'

'She doesn't say very much,' she said cautiously, failing to keep the concern from her voice.

'Nonsense!'

There was no limit to the qualities that Makertich was able to read into those two lines, re-examining the handwriting for signs of character, evidence of determination, humour, honesty – and excusing his daughter that her letter was so short. Disappointed by its brevity, he was also touched by it.

'There's too much to say.'

Jeanine had written to remind him that in a few days she would turn twenty-one and this was an opportune moment to discuss her inheritance. She proposed coming to the house at 6 p.m. the following Wednesday. No mention of her mother's death.

'She wants to see me. It's just as I hoped. I upheld Cheryl's request and now she's coming back.'

Maral was despatched to the florist in Elgin Crescent with a mission to fill the house with lilies, irises and roses. She hoovered Jeanine's room, laid clean sheets on her bed. And spent Tuesday and a large part of Wednesday preparing a meal appropriate for the prodigal daughter.

Makertich hoped to persuade Jeanine to stay for dinner. He had a superheated discussion with Maral about what to serve her. Aged nine, she had been partial to cinnamon toast, lemonade and beetroot.

'We can't give her beetroot! Go to Lidgate's and order filet mignon.'

'And if she's a vegetarian?'

'To Portobello and buy the freshest vegetables.'

'What about to drink?'

'Leave the wine to me.'

'What if she's teetotal?'

'Then you and I will drink it, woman!'

Maral's questions, apart from emphasising how rarely he entertained, revealed that he knew virtually nothing about his daughter. Ever since Cheryl took her away, he had received no news, no photograph, no school report. Not one scrap.

Wednesday arrived.

He spent part of the morning sitting on her bed, leafing through her drawings, her books. He reread her holiday diary and smiled at an illustration, more cartoon really, of a girl fitted with metal fangs. He stood and looked at the images pinned to the cork board on the wall opposite. Although he had long ago put away his camera, he continued to change lenses in his head. But when he tried to capture Jeanine at twenty-one, his imagination faltered: he could not reach beyond the girl of ten. Any older, and he started to see a person resembling Cheryl at the age of their first encounter in the back of a Perth classroom.

Next, he shaved off the beard that had obscured his face since that appalling day eleven years ago. He looked different at sixty to the person who had hurried up his front steps holding a kitten and a bag of party balloons. His exposed cheeks, tingling with Floris shaving cream, had narrowed and darkened – they were almost as dark as his father's. His mouth had tightened. His eyes had set deeper in their sockets, with quills springing from the corners. What a horrible face. Guarded, clenched, light-deprived. Only his hair remained black and shiny. The colour of a cicada.

With a finger, he tugged down the skin below his left eyelid.

Jeanine was five when she caught him inserting his glass eye. He had not told her about his previous life as Krikor Makertich, still less about his Armenian and Turkish blood – he had been waiting until her confirmation. Tonight, over dinner, he would tell all. Also to himself before the mirror he said other words that he looked forward to repeating to Jeanine. He told her how sorry he was to hear that her mother, the love of his life, had died. He told her how in his bleaker moments the prospect of this reunion with his daughter had acted as his principal motive for living. There was also her inheritance to discuss – not only her trust fund, but the responsibility of his estate. So many things to talk about.

He was nervous, and also jolly. Maral had not for many years seen him in such good humour. The rain stopped, the warm sun came slanting in through the windows. And still he could not decide what to wear.

'Which one, which one?' And instantly changing it.

'He was like an adolescent choosing the right shirt and jacket for a dance. My instinct warned him not to expect too much, but he glowered that I was being too Armenian.'

'Tell me, Maral, what do you think she will see?'

'She will see her father.'

The bell sounded as he patted his jacket, checking the pocket.

'Maral! She's here!'

26

THREE STEPS AT A TIME, he came down the staircase. But already Maral was opening the front door.

A confident young woman strode past her, into the hall, in the same moment as Makertich reached the bottom of the stairs.

The way he held on to the handrail – steadying himself against his irresistible compulsion to enfold her in his arms, and against a negative force, almost as powerful, that was set on repulsing him.

She glanced around at the paintings in the hall – two studies of Ned Kelly by Sidney Nolan, a gouache by Ian Fairweather and a portrait of William Dampier – before her eyes settled on Makertich.

He was staring at her in wonder.

His daughter.

She did not look filial. Her eyes emboldened in black eyeliner; her dark hair parted, and wearing a formal black coat that embodied her grief and anger.

He let go the handrail and flew across the hall towards her. 'My darling, my dearest.'

'It was painful to see. All that withheld love overspilling. It would have touched the most vicious heart.'

Ignoring his outstretched arms, Jeanine stepped to one side and said in a stinging voice: 'Please don't!'

He was not listening. 'Why don't we go upstairs –' where we will be more comfortable, he was about to say.

She cut him short. 'I won't stay. I'm here to deliver this message. I am disinheriting you. I don't want another penny from you.'

He stood still, open-mouthed.

Her look was piercing. 'I've been wanting to talk to you face to face. I still can't believe you were here all along. I can't believe you made no effort to get in touch.'

'It was your mother's wishes.'

'My mother's wishes,' her eyes despising him. 'You know what she used to say to me? "You watch it – or he'll ruin your life the way he ruined mine."'

'Believe me, Jeanine, I'm the first person who would have wanted it otherwise,' he said, feelingly.

But the anger in her voice was also genuine, nourished by all the sinister suspicions that fear and her mother and Kes had put into her head.

'You're a con man, Mr Makertich.'

'Jeanine, no!' Maral cried.

'Let me finish,' pushing Maral away and turning back to face him. 'Your money's tainted. You can't tread anywhere on this planet without leaving a trail of poison.'

'What are you talking about?' Impressed that his daughter had developed into this passionate woman, but horrified to have her scorn and hostility directed at him.

'You threw us out with no more consideration than you ejected those villagers.'

'What villagers?'

'You poisoned our lives just as you poisoned that lake.'

'What lake!'

'Did you or did you not own the Xemu open-cast copper mine on the edge of Lake Sevan?'

'Lake Sevan?' He lowered his forehead. 'I once owned a copper mine there, yes, but it had another name.'

'Oh, like you?' she laughed, and launched into the speech she had prepared.

'Hang on, hang on,' he said, once Jeanine had delivered her diatribe. 'Now I know what you're talking about. But all this must have happened after I sold the mine.'

'It's not what Kes says.'

'Kes? Kes who?'

'Kes Wakefield. I'm helping him to set up a business. The reason I've come here this evening is to let you know how I intend to distribute the money in my trust fund.'

'And what does he do, this Kes Wakefield?'

'He's an environmentalist like me. Dedicated to stopping priceless trees from being logged.'

'What kind of trees do you and Kes propose to save?'

'Eucalypts.'

His head took it in before his heart. He looked at her with a dull and strange detachment and apparent calm, and then his heart started beating wildly.

'This Kes – have you known him long?'

'I don't think it's any of your business.'

He was having difficulty breathing. 'When did you meet him? What does he look like?'

'It's a little rich, don't you think? Interest in my personal life after eleven years of complete indifference –'

'Don't you see! This wasn't an accident. He sought you out.'

'I don't know why I'm telling you this,' in the overly grown-up voice of someone trying to project a more knowledgeable self, 'but he's asked me to move in with him.'

'Jeanine, you must not!' his face now pale with horror.

'Maybe I will, maybe I won't. It's not for you to say.'

When he still had her in his sight, all was not lost. But she was preparing to leave.

'Wait!' He put his hand into his pocket and produced a small packet and stretched out his arm to her. 'I kept this for you . . . for your birthday.' And when she recoiled: 'It belonged to my grandmother.'

She wavered.

'Please – take it.'

She grabbed it and looked at him and said: 'I'm glad I came. It's good to lay ghosts to rest. For me, you are dead.'

He ran after her to say it was a lie, all lies, but she turned on her heel and slammed the door behind her.

Some time later Makertich's arm found Maral's shoulder. He stood there, leaning on her.

Sparrows chirping outside. The smell of fresh-cut lilies. And the soundless sobbing of a sixty-year-old man.

Maral said: 'I can't rub that scene from my mind.'

She would not let him go to bed until she had served the meal.

At the table, his tears continued to fall. Snuffed out, the lovelight in his eye. He felt he no longer existed – any more than the place laid for Jeanine that Maral had hurriedly removed. All he was left with, the shards of himself.

The next day she never saw him. He stayed in his tower.

In the middle of the night she heard strange sounds coming from Jeanine's bedroom, and went to investigate.

The door was open.

She stopped in the middle of the room, stood still. The drawings gone, the photographs gone. The walls glared back at her with an emptiness that was menacing.

'I thought for a second he had thrown open the window and snow had come in, even though it was summer, and then I saw that the whiteness on the carpet wasn't snow but pieces of paper. And then I heard this quiet despairing voice full of emotion and I saw him sitting on the edge of the bed, bent over, his face pallid as if he were out in the snow.

'I remember it with a shudder. This naturally kind, fair-minded man, who had seen the person he loved most reject him, was reading her holiday diary, and then he stopped, couldn't go on, and tore out the page, tearing it into small pieces, and then I realised what had become of his photographs of Jeanine – what had become of all her drawings, her books. He heard my gasp and looked around, and it was as though his eye had been flung into his face. He thought I had come to help him, but he said he didn't need help, it wasn't the first time he had had to do this, and went on tearing the pages.'

In the morning, through his half-open bedroom door as she went to collect his breakfast tray with its untouched newspaper, Maral overheard him on the telephone to Bennett. 'Listen closely now. I need you to do this expeditiously. I wish to postpone the date on which my daughter is due to come into her trust fund.'

'People did not want to be around him after that; they didn't want to be a part of his personality. After Jeanine's visit, it would have required all God's ingenuity to placate him.'

YOU'RE A CON MAN, Mr Makertich.

His daughter was right. His life was a lie. His identity a lost horse that had failed to come to his whistle – and why? Not out of any principled resolve to estrange himself, but because ever since boyhood he had lacked the courage to summon it.

He walked around the house picking up objects and putting them down. He was English on his passport, but England was not his country. He had no country. His country was a mountainous plateau in the middle of nowhere. A rocky promontory he had never visited and could never visit; a space vanished from the maps, carved up by Turks and Communists, about whose forgotten crimes no one cared.

Jeanine's rejection was a fist in his face. It made no sense. Like people who die without warning. It threw him back into a separate dimension parallel to the one in which he had lived. A dimension that he came to know as Armenia.

A few days after their meeting, Makertich found himself outside the Turkish baths in Queensgate, and entered. He returned home possessed by an overwhelming craving to play a recording of Armenian horn music to which previously he had felt indifferent, even antagonistic.

On Sunday morning, he walked to the little Armenian church in Iverna Gardens and sat in the back pew, listening to a white-bearded preacher giving a passionate sermon. Even as he struggled to make sense of what the man was saying, the following words dropped into his head: *How can you help pass on your identity to the next generation if you have disconnected yourself from your roots?* He slipped away before anyone could talk to him.

By spring, he had fought through his reticence. He joined a small crowd on 23 April for an afternoon vigil outside the Turkish Embassy, and the next day attended the commemorative requiem at St Sarkis.

'It would be too much to say that he was accepting himself. Rather, he was scrambling up the slopes of a place he'd shut out.'

He had nightly and vivid dreams of his grandmother, slowly moving about the low-ceilinged house in Aleppo, sideways like an old seal.

He saw a semi-naked woman with a French cigarette – he had puffed it once and it nauseated him. Her eyes squeezed to a sightless crack by the bight of her years on earth, her lined gaunt face saying to his ten-year-old self, but addressing her own demons as well: 'Armenians did nothing to the Turks. We believed in a different way in God, that's all. Yet the Turks destroyed us. Why were we so passive? Why this un-questioning obedience? Did our passivity arise from our faith? Or was it because we were so desperate to fit in? Find me the answer, Krikor, will you do that? But promise me this. I want an answer, not revenge. Seek revenge and you'll dig two graves.'

Fifty years on, he had no answer. His parents did not speak of the forces that drove his grandmother and countless innocent others from their homes, one hour to pack, the million and a half dead. 'We can never forget,' was all his mother said, this after yet another of his father's self-pitying lamentations. 'But you have to forget. The Turks won't admit what they did. And no one else gives a brass razoo. So unless you're going to turn this rage and hate into yourself like your poor father, you'd best ignore it. That's my advice.' From his mother, he had caught the bad habit of not asking.

But the unacknowledged story had swelled in his bloodstream like a gallstone. Dormant for so long, a need to learn about Armenia began to torment him.

He knew the alphabet from Aleppo, suddenly remembered it, and started reading. With the dedication of the autodidact, he discovered in Rue Monsieur le Prince in Paris a bookshop which specialised in Armenian authors, and ordered volumes by the shelfload. The Nolans in the hallway yielded to two paintings by Gorky; the Cromwellian oak chest in his bedroom to a stone cross from the time of St Thomas the Apostle; the biographies of English explorers sent by John Sandoe to a miniature Bible in the Armenian script.

He commissioned a tiler to put up, outside the front door, the name of his grandmother's village. He imported honey from Kebussije and took to drinking coffee with cardamom. The house filled with the smell of roasted vegetables. He stopped eating watercress soup and roast beef with horseradish, and requested that Maral feed him aubergines, dolmas and kofte, meals that she was encouraged to lash with paprika and cumin – because Armenia had been on the spice route. And plenty of spring onions.

'Before, he had been resolutely not interested in proclaiming his Armenian background. Now, it became a fox tearing at his stomach. He was coming to terms with what he had spent most of his life avoiding, but in the knowledge that it was too late.'

Early one morning Maral let in some Brazilian builders and led them up to the tower. The men removed the photographic equipment – the bottles of D-76 fluid, the developing tank – as well as each and every one of the framed etchings from Cheryl's exhibition, which, unbeknown to her, Makertich had stored here. His darkroom had lain unused since his wife's departure. He wanted the space for his Armenian books.

His good eye twisted inward. He turned his back on England and retreated like a desert father into his library. The thought of Armenia obsessed him. It was a simple word, but part of something supernaturally larger. The invisible trellis up which his spirit all this while had climbed. The first Christian country on earth. The country of Adam from whom all men sprang. The site of Paradise, but also of untold hideous massacres and environmental disasters.

'Whenever he went to the tower, I could see that he was disappearing into himself, into his own Armenia. His mind was like a stone that he was pushing uphill to get to the right place and always falling back. To the day he died, he did not have an answer for his grandmother. He didn't know why people behaved like the Turks or, in his own life, like Flexmore.'

Denounced by Jeanine, he refused to revisit their encounter. His daughter was welcome to Kes Wakefield. He knew that he was innocent of her charges.

Maral said: 'In Armenia, mines are always being sold. All Krikor did was sell a licence on a piece of paper. What he didn't realise was that Wakefield was one of the purchasers. After he became Don Flexmore, and before he was Kes Wakefield, he was Bijou Mandrake. There was a good reason he knew the details of the cyanide spill. *He* had presided over the disaster, not Krikor.'

Obedient to his grandmother's wishes, Makertich instructed his lawyers to desist in their pursuit of the man who had been the bane of his adult life. It was virtually his last demand of Crispian Bennett's firm. As for Jeanine, she was free to bleed her trust fund into lost causes, but only once he himself was dead. He would not contribute further to her addiction. About this, he remained adamant: while he had breath in his body, he was not going to leave his daughter one more thin penny.

'He sold his racehorse, wound down his Foundation and was never the same towards me. The relationship we'd had before, talking about ourselves, it was over. He got harder of hearing, which isolates you. He would sit there and smoke his cigarettes, and I would talk and talk and he wouldn't say anything, until finally he would look up and say: "Are you finished?"'

229

If they met on the stairs he glared at her moodily, looking out as if from behind a mirror, and continued walking. Either down to the cellar – he never lost his taste for wine – or up to the tower.

'Please don't ask me what he did there. There was a campaign chair on which he liked to stretch out; on the floor, a pile of battered paperbacks and a ream of paper. Sometimes I heard Komitas's liturgy playing or the sounds of a *duduk*. I like to think that he was nourished by that music in a way that he might not have predicted. Most of the time the room was silent. I would collect the glasses and empty the waste-paper bin, but never saw evidence he was writing anything – except the *Telegraph* crossword. Oh, and that essay which Mr Vamplew sent me. Mainly the bin was full of cigarette butts. He took up smoking in those last years – I would have to go to a tobacconist in St James's and buy him French cigarettes, which is what in the end killed him.'

The Pykes called, angling for an invitation to stay.

'He refused to see them. He wouldn't see anyone. He was extraordinarily absent. The outside world – those planes crashing in New York, the men blowing themselves up in the London Underground – it didn't concern him. Only the racing pages and the business section. That, and whatever he was doing in his library.'

Like this, seven slow years passed. He grew a bit more stocky, his nose broadened, but his mood stayed the same. He was alive, but only in the way that nails and hair grow after death.

'What I would like to believe . . . this resignation – I'm sorry, I'm slurring my thoughts.'

She sat forward and brought her hands to her face, her fingers curving round it, concentrating. And began again.

'Maybe this is what happens. His life has pretty much had it. He's not a fool. But he has a presentiment that someone in the future will redeem him.'

Because late one morning Makertich shuffled into the kitchen. He was wearing his favourite Hardy Amies suit, her yellow cardigan visible beneath it.

She waited for him to bark 'Maral, get me some coffee' or 'Please cut this out' – for she noticed that he was holding the *Daily Telegraph* and had double-circled an article, a legal report she discovered afterwards, about a charity for the blind.

To her surprise, he stuck a hand into his jacket and brought out two objects, laying them one after the other on the table.

'Look,' in a breathy voice, his black hair scarred with grey. 'What do you see?'

'A stick of wood and a piece of mud.'

'Look again.'

'And I saw a limb of the apple tree that had taken out his eye and a shrivelled pellet of the bread that his grandmother had survived on in the desert.'

'I'd like you to have these. Now get your coat, we're taking a drive.'

'Where to?'

'Ealing.'

'Are you sure you want me to come with you?'

'What?'

'I said, are you sure you want me to come with you?'

His brusque temper, finding nothing to fasten on, deepened on hearing her tone. She sounded so apologetic.

'I have to make my will,' he said in their language.

28

'MORE WINE?' ANDY ASKED.

'I've had too much,' Maral said. 'But I'll have some more. Why not? I got used to it on my own. What was I talking about?'

'His will.'

'There's little else to say. He died four months later. I found the card that Jeanine had written to him. I called the number that was on it and left a message with details of the funeral. Midway through the service, I heard the door open and when I looked around and saw the blue suit and blond hair I thought for a dreadful moment Don Flexmore had arrived.'

'But he was a man of seventy or more.'

'I didn't have my glasses on, Mr Larkham. Then Jeanine turned up and I tried to speak to her – but she didn't want to know. When you left together I was convinced that you must be connected with Don or Kes or whoever. And I thought so again when I met you in Mr Vamplew's office, and I went on thinking that until – well, until whenever it was that we came down here.'

'Were you surprised by the terms of the will?'

'I could not believe what I was hearing. Yet looking back, it made sense. Mr Vamplew told me that he thought it was Krikor's wish – how did he put it? – to leave his fortune to fortune. I agree.'

It had grown dark outside. Andy stood up and closed the curtains. A radio was on and there was the sound of the sea in the distance.

He turned and sat down, finishing his glass. 'I wish I'd met him,' he said.

'And you would have liked him, Mr Larkham. In some ways he was a very shy, tender man and in some ways a very frightened, broken man who died without admitting who he was. It was a sad end, to love no one like that, himself least of all. But I loved him. Something I will never forget is the peace I saw in his eye when he emerged from his meeting with Mr Vamplew. It was as if for a small moment he had got rid of all that troubled him. There was no pain hidden there. No pain whatever. He had a kind of calm in letting go of everything, and within that calm he had – one wouldn't call it hope, but a sense, even though it didn't matter any more, that it would come out all right. That his daughter would understand who he was.'

INHERITANCE

I

Dear Jeanine,

Forgive me for intruding on you like this – Maral gave me your address. My reason for getting in touch is that I misled you.

It was circumstantial that I ended up in this position. I didn't know your father. I stumbled into his funeral by mistake. Despite this, I have made it my business to find out who he was.

Through an unlikely set of events, I feel that I have come to know your father better even than my own. You were the trigger for this. It may sound far-fetched, but I believe that I have discovered a way to honour him, and for this reason I hope you will agree to meet me.

I understand if this doesn't appeal, but should it interest you to know more, I can explain over dinner at the Camões restaurant next Wednesday at 7.30 p.m. The above number will reach me.

Yours, Andy Larkham.

2

ANDY COULD NOT SHAKE off the suspicion that this was the table where Richard had pretended to be engrossed in his book. It was 7.30 in the evening, the week before Christmas, and he had never known the Camões so packed.

It reassured him to see how little had changed, aside from the restaurant's suddenly acquired popularity – and the Christmas tree in a terracotta pot at the centre of the room, a fir roughly of his height that flashed with emerald-and-red electric candles. Otherwise, the same paper tablecloth, the grubbiness of which always offended Sophie back in the pre-Cambrian era; the same photographs of Cintra; the same hoarse, aching voice of a mezzo-soprano singing fado.

Rui was still serving, refusing to take off his dejected face. He had given Andy a mournful glower when he came in, as though he did not recognise him; and then limped across the floor and scraped back a chair.

The majority of diners were local Portuguese and Spanish families, some with small children who peeped in Andy's direction, wondering what he was reading, before they returned to what they had been doing, which mainly was to doodle on the tablecloth, perfecting dragons and goggle-eyed insects that passed for portraits of their parents or, perhaps, Andy. A tall, blond-headed young man who kept looking at his watch and back to the pages that he had printed out that afternoon and out of habit started to correct.

He had arrived early. It was now 7.35.

Andy could not help wondering what Jeanine had made of his letter. He had – finally – told her the truth. But would it turn her away or would she accept his apology? About one thing he was clear: he did not want to come together again with a woman over a misunderstanding.

He looked at his watch. She had left a message on his machine to say that she would be here. Had she changed her mind?

But it was all right that she was late. There were olives left in the saucer and he had a glass of wine. And it was a while since he had had the chance to sift his thoughts, most of his waking hours for the past two and a half months being devoted to Madigan/Makertich. Most of his sleeping ones, too.

3

MONTAIGNE BELIEVED THAT THE greatest thing in the world was to know how to belong to oneself. Jeanine's father had learned this too late. So Andy came to understand during his days in Cornwall with Maral Bernhard.

At a pivotal moment, as Maral unfolded her stories, all Andy's frustrations about what to do with Furnivall's text transformed themselves into an overpowering wish to correct Jeanine's false impression of her father. Andy would always believe the turning point was the moment when he saw his teacher's cottage – where Furnivall had written his book. He liked to think that the solution which presented itself allowed him to step up to the mark and do good by both men. His wild scheme to enlist his teacher into restoring to Jeanine the person she had so misunderstood. And by showing Jeanine her father as he was to reveal the love that her father had felt for her.

Andy realised even before he left Cornwall that he was going to be working hard over the next weeks, submerging himself in Krikor Makertich. Now, with David's persistence and Maral's help, he had the opportunity to achieve something.

He drove Maral back to London after three weeks in St Buryan and reinstalled her in Clarendon Crescent. Separately, they had telephoned Vamplew and requested him to cancel the forthcoming sale of the house and its contents. The lawyer saw no reason why the two of them could not continue jointly to own the property. Andy's opinion of the house swiftly changed. In broad daylight with the shutters open and the lawn mown, 11 Clarendon Crescent was a lovely place. Much lovelier than his own.

It was the middle of October when he returned to pack up his Kensington flat: the Warhol, the Corbusier chair – they belonged to another person, a friend he had had for a while and tired of without even the need for an argument. He donated them to charity.

In a holdall on the next chair was the manuscript that he had been working on since.

He wrote it at Clarendon Crescent. He set up his desk in the tower and switched on the central heating and kept the windows open to blow away the stale tobacco smell. Maral was around to answer queries and make coffee. Initially, he worried that it would creep him out to be in Makertich's space, but the effect was the opposite. Idle and guilty for a year, Andy worked with a vitality that was new to him.

'Anything else we need to talk about?'

'Not for the moment,' Vamplew had said.

Even so, Andy could sense the lawyer lingering on the line. No longer sweeping Andy's concern into the dustpan of his absolute indifference.

He waited.

'It's nothing important, but I was wondering,' Vamplew said after a while, 'if you have seen his daughter again?'

'I'd love to read his book.'

'And read it you shall.'

One reason Andy had not turned up last time at the Camões was his impetuous promise to Jeanine. He had never stopped asking himself: *Why did I agree to let her see her father's autobiography?*

Had they met eighteen months ago, he would have had to confess that her father's life story – which in a further act of idiocy he claimed to have edited – did not exist, was a ruse to get her out of his flat before she started to suspect the extent of his ignorance. Then, he would have had nothing to show her save for a manuscript concerning a centuries-dead philosopher. All that had changed since he had whisked Maral off to Cornwall.

'Is that the end of the wine? A pity.'

It was their last morning at the B & B. Clouds resembling eagle tails floated over the treetops and in the field a young roe deer picked its way between the furrows towards Tregiffian.

He suggested a walk. They put on their coats and he drove her along the lane, past the Merry Maidens, to a farmyard where he left the car. A breeze blew up as they descended the deserted path to the sea.

They passed Furnivall's bungalow and when they reached the next clifftop Andy stopped and said outright: 'I would like to speak to Jeanine.'

Odd to see a blush on that wrinkled face and lending to her cheeks the aura of dried roses. The way Maral glanced at him, he could tell what she was thinking. He shrugged.

'So would I, Mr Larkham, so would I.' Maral's sigh came from the deepest part of her. 'She hears my voice, she puts down the phone. I write to her – letter after letter. She returns them unopened.'

'You haven't been able to tell her any of this?'

'Not one word.'

Maral rubbed below her eye with a speckled hand and turned away. 'When I was cleaning up Krikor's room, I found a photograph of her great-grandmother. The resemblance was uncanny. I sent it to Jeanine. Maybe it shocked her, because she won't talk to me. Last time we spoke, it was a week after her father's funeral. She rang to say that she had learned she was not going to inherit and who were you – the only thing she wanted to know. I told her that I'd mistaken you for Don Flexmore. She said: "Impossible." That was the end of our conversation.'

She promised to write down Jeanine's address.

They returned to the B & B and went upstairs to pack, but Andy could not get out of his mind the image of Jeanine's father, surrounded by ashtrays and whodunits, brooding. He pictured him in his tower, combing through his past, looking for the white ants. What was going on in his head? The only thing to show for his time up there – a short, bitter diatribe about love, its impossibility.

Other memories flapped at him. The heated look in her eyes. The first time he had touched a dead person. Gulls around a landfill site of his own garbage – screeching, pecking, clawing.

He had bought off Jeanine's threat to challenge her father's will with a pledge to tell her about Christopher Madigan. But why pretend to have known her father in the first place? Andy had no legal obligation to tell her anything. Out of what long-suppressed habit, then, had he sprung to his defence? It wasn't only the money.

A noise from the lane made him look outside. A flat-chested girl with a heavy lower lip walked by, humming.

His eyes followed her until she disappeared, but a sound remained in the air. He craned forward. Starlings meddling in hedgerows. Sparrows perched on the telegraph wires. Suddenly notes for an out-of-reach calypso that his father used to sing coming up the stairs.

It wasn't so simple picking away at the past. You try to unpeel it like one of Mrs Nettlefold's breakfast eggs and sometimes it's easy, but sometimes a memory or an image comes away with soft chunks clinging to it like flesh.

On the last morning of his childhood Andy went for a walk along the Nadder. He lay there in the summer sun in the grass beside the river, careful not to move. From time to time, a trout rose to the surface and sipped. He pushed himself to his feet and two large fish flared off.

The plane was due in at ten. 'I'll try and be with you by one,' his father had promised. In time for lunch.

His mother, a terrible cook, had prepared his father's favourite meal of lamb shanks. She had trimmed the roses and bunched the freshest-looking into a vase. But she was not pleased with her hair. It mimicked her swells of anger and hope. What was he coming back for? What was this 'something' he had to tell her, that was better said face to face? The paparazzi idea – stalking her, popping its flashes – that he wanted to consign to oblivion the past three years, begin again.

'He's only coming back because Lynn dumped him,' his sister said in a jabbing voice.

'He never said that he was going to stay,' defended his mother chirpily.

'Of course he doesn't want to stay,' at her most sarcastic. She stood on the landing in her old green sweater that she wore all the time, slopping about in it like a large bath. 'What he wants is for you to forgive him.'

'Well, I still think you should look nice for your father.' Meaning: *Go and put on that dress I bought you.*

Back from the river, hair brushed, teeth cleaned, hands washed, Andy waited for him to arrive. At the sound of a car engine, he flung open the door.

'Tell him to wipe his shoes,' called his mother, and went to take the lamb out of the oven.

He ran across the front lawn.

A thin man in a cloth cap was paying the driver. Then turned.

His revenant father.

George Larkham saw Andy and awkwardly raised his hand, and after straightening his cap, lifted a small suitcase and began walking towards him. The tie he had taken off made a lump in his pocket. He started to unbutton his jacket when he stumbled.

He swore. His face had gone pale. And his hand – his hand was clutching his side. Gasping in the air of a late summer morning. He looked at his feet as though surprised to find himself still upright. A yellow cedar swaying in a dazed, perplexed way.

'Dad!'

Andy raced over to where his father had crumpled to the lawn. He kneeled, bending over the grey corduroy face. There was a tired, hunted glaze in his eyes. They stared into space, reflecting a depth of anguish no one could have invented. His arms clawed the grass and there was a dribble at the corner of his mouth.

'Dad!' slapping him. He could smell something medicinal in his breath, and then he lost the scent.

'George?' His mother had stepped outside. 'George . . .' flying towards them, her oven gloves still on. A lone tundra swan. 'George!'

242

Upstairs in her room his sister was unaware. She was pushing her new dress up over her head and it had got stuck, her arms in the air, her face pressing, ghost-like, through the stretched cotton.

Down on the grass, Andy clutched his father's face in desperation. Everything irrelevant except the words that his father had come home to say. But no words came.

Andy turned from the window, grabbed his holdall and suitcase off the bed, carried them downstairs. Something in him rejected Krikor Makertich's bleak vacuum. He refused to believe that Jeanine's father had accomplished nothing other than to read shelf after shelf of books about Armenia, stare at the spaces between his toes and do the *Telegraph* crossword, all the while smoking Gitanes. Better to imagine that he was contemplating the mystery of life like a desert father – like Montaigne. And should he have reached the conclusion that love is a cheap illusion that doesn't pay, Andy wanted to prove him wrong with every particle in his body.

Maral waited for him downstairs. She stood in the conservatory, looking out of the window. 'One thing I never see any more: deer.'

He had already settled the bill with Mrs Nettlefold ('What's this?' 'Corkage.') and was piling their bags into the back seat when Furnivall's manuscript slipped from the holdall in which Andy had been lugging it around all these months. He stuffed the pages back in, his eyes falling on a sentence. *In every man is the history of all men . . .* Wait a moment, wait a moment. What if . . . ? And he was a boy again, leaning out of his father's helicopter. Filled with the same calm certainty as when he watched the grappler seize hold of a grey ghost, a parachuting sense of what was right. In that moment – he remembered it with pinpoint accuracy – it came to him what he must do, which was to follow the example of the young woman who had loved Montaigne: his adoptive daughter, Marie de Gournay. The driving theory behind Furnivall's book was that Marie had destroyed the missing Montaigne manuscript not long after her mentor's death, but only once she had extensively drawn on it to edit the posthumous – and significantly altered – version upon which everyone relied today.

By the time he reached London, Andy was resolved. He could not bring Krikor Makertich back to life, but he might go a small way to reuniting him with his daughter.

It took two intense months to blend *Missing Montaigne* into *The Trials of Christopher Madigan*. It was important that he honoured his teacher by putting the essence of his book, its philosophical core, into his 'self-portrait'. No less important was to find a way to respect what Maral had told him.

Andy would never have pretended that her words, which he had written down, were precisely the same, or in the same order, as in the narrative that he stitched together from a range of sources and using the unexercised muscles of the editor he had hoped to be. There were also thoughts that entered his head as he wrote. To paraphrase Montaigne, he stole from this flower and that, but always with the aim of turning his 'pilfering' into a honey that was Makertich's own – even though in order to do this he had to look into himself. Because, as David had pointed out, this was also about Andy. Only in writing this story would he set himself free. Montaigne again: 'If I must serve as an instrument of deception, let it at least not be at the expense of my conscience.'

To begin with, he was beset by doubts. Wasn't he making a forgery of another man's life and character? No. He was revealing to Jeanine the truth of her father in a way that he could not hope to do on his own, but perhaps in combination with Furnivall.

His task was to develop what his teacher had written and adapt it towards a goal after Furnivall's own humanist heart. In the end, all he was doing was using a little imagination, plus connective tissue. Only the imagination knew how to turn a manuscript about Montaigne's missing essays into the autobiography of an anonymous Armenian.

But he had no doubt, as fumblingly he discovered the process of his storytelling, that the man whose distinctive shadow he had sensed during his conversations with his fellow Attender was, out of all competing versions, the authentic one.

4

ANDY PLACED TO ONE side the page he had corrected and checked his watch: 8.00. He looked up. But did not see Jeanine, and then he did see her. Standing at the entrance – talking to Rui, who was taking her coat. She wore a leaf-green dress with a yellow scarf around her neck.

His mouth went dry. He wanted to stand up and leave. It would still be snowing outside, and under the trees it would be dark and he could hide in the street. He wanted to run along the icy pavement. Past Sophie's maisonette. Past his old flat. To Shaftesbury. Where he would not be overcome by this panic that was engulfing him. He knew that his mother would accept him as he was, at this moment, and stood abruptly to his feet, spilling pages everywhere – which he stooped to retrieve from the floor, hastily pushing them back into the holdall – then turned, in time to see her weaving towards him. Brown eyes, jet black hair, pale.

'Hi,' hesitantly extending her hand.

'Hi,' grabbing it.

He was relieved that his hand did not tremble. On hers was a silver bracelet.

She sat down, resting a black-bead handbag on her lap.

'So,' sounding nervous, her dark, tense eyes examining him from the boundless distance of the other side of the table, 'we've made it at last.'

He sat on his hands. But did not hear his own voice, did not feel that he was sitting at the table. He felt adrift. Nothing he said taking flight. His words inert as the olive pits waiting to be tidied away by Rui. And Jeanine behaved no differently. The lavender sprig in the glass flute a microphone that made them both dry up; whatever words they uttered, stilted and self-conscious.

Jeanine's recent trip to the Amazon with a shipload of scientists. The sale of his Mercedes at the weekend to a footballer. The weather, cold for this time of year – or was it hot? It can't have been hot, because it was snowing when he arrived at the Camões. When Jeanine had arrived, too. 'I haven't seen snow like that for ages,' she said, 'not at Christmas time.' The conversation petered out and they sat in a sad and confused silence, each waiting for the other to speak.

He shrank deeper into his chair. He was bursting with questions, and yet all he could think of asking was one more banal thing that had nothing to do with her father, the subject they were here to discuss.

This time she did not reply, but looked rueful.

He cleared his throat. He needed to get it out of the way. He should have done so immediately – what he had promised himself he would do without fail, first thing, soon as she sat down, had not a complicated feeling restrained him.

Before he could say anything, she blurted out: 'Listen, I'm sorry.'

He gave Jeanine a vacant look. 'What for?'

She raised her hand as though lifting a veil. Her expression more serious than the girl with the calf-eyes drawing him.

'I apologise for not turning up last time.'

He looked blinkingly at her as she explained.

In short, everything he had steeled himself to tell Jeanine: how the lawyers had instructed her not to make contact; how she had wanted to telephone, but did not have his number; how she had felt it inappropriate to burden Rui with the message, so that she had pictured Andy in a position more or less identical to the one in which he had imagined her, waiting on his own in this Portuguese restaurant for someone who was never going to show up etc., etc.; and how the uncertainty about her father that he had planted instead of vanishing had deepened, resulting in her decision, which Bennett & Blaxworth had greeted with horrified amazement, not to contest the will.

The funny feeling that came humming out of his bones. 'I never made it here that evening, either.'

'You didn't?'

'No.'

'You weren't sitting here, cursing me?' still cagey.

'No.' He felt himself unbinding.

His eyes found hers. They looked at each other.

He hailed Rui, who was heading for the kitchen – was it Andy's imagination that he no longer limped? – and with Jeanine's consent ordered a bottle of Vinho Verde.

Amália was singing 'Disse-te Adeus e Morri'. Was it his imagination that the *fadista* had developed a celestial voice?

He gazed around the room at the honeycomb of faces and back to

Jeanine. Emerging from the black bin liner inside which he had been swishing about for longer than he dared to remember.

She had crossed her arms and was staring at him in a thoughtful way.

'So, Andy Larkham, you didn't know my father.'

'No.'

'He didn't write a book.'

'No.'

'He never read Montaigne.'

'Not as far as I know.'

'Then what were you doing at his funeral?'

He quickly told her. He felt such a relief.

She nodded to herself. The riddle resolved.

He waited for her to ask more, but she stared down at her wrist and started toying with her bracelet.

'You had something you needed to tell me,' he said.

She tilted back. Red-and-green reflections pulsing on her face. Her defiant look had returned. 'Yes – about my father's money,' and took a breath, but across the small round table he was holding up his hand.

'Listen,' with a spring in his voice, 'I'm aware why you should think it's tainted, but it's not.' Again, he looked her in the eye. 'I need to tell you something. Your father is not the man you thought he was.'

She fended him away with her familiar glare. 'So you keep saying.'

'I mean it even more.'

In a boneless gesture in time with the fado, her hand moved back and forth over the tablecloth.

What's she thinking? surprised that she did not listen when he mentioned her father. He began to talk about Maral, but her eyes looked frightened, and an instinct told him that Jeanine had been taught by her mother never to trust a word that 'Mary' said.

He had not got very far when he was interrupted by the girl with the calf eyes plucking at his sleeve. Her broad, dimpled face reminded him for some reason of his sister, who had telephoned two nights before with the news that she was expecting a baby.

'My mother says you dropped this.'

'Thank you,' accepting the loose page.

The girl resumed her seat, folding her arms to obscure the tablecloth.

'What is it?' Jeanine asked, perplexed.

He scanned the sheet of paper that the girl had returned to him.

'It's the penultimate page of your father's autobiography.'

She took the news calmly. 'Written by you?'

'That's right. This isn't what your father wrote. I wrote it.' He lifted

247

the holdall onto the table and withdrew the manuscript. 'Sorry it's taken so long.'

She gave the title page a look, part-asteroid, part-fascination.

'*The Trials of Christopher Madigan*,' she read.

'I guess it's what you might call a self-examination.'

'Why "trials"?'

'It was the original meaning of the word "essay". But it's an apt word to describe his life – at least in my opinion.' The pleasure it gave Andy to talk about him was unexpected. He patted the mound of pages the way his father used to pat his head. 'See what you think.'

She turned a page. 'Who,' she wanted to know, 'is Stuart Furnivall?' What did he have to do with her father?

Andy told her.

She listened. 'And this other person?' pointing to the name of the second dedicatee.

'My best friend. Without his help, I never could have written it.'

Her face assumed a terribly sad expression. 'How do I know it's the truth?'

He did not have time to elaborate, because Rui was splashing out the Casal Garcia for him to taste.

'Why don't we talk about this later?' Andy said. 'Once you've read it?'

'You're right,' she nodded. 'I can read this later.' And scooped the manuscript back into the holdall, putting it down on the next chair and her handbag on top of it.

'Delicious, Rui,' Andy said, after smelling the cold tart bubbly liquid and swirling it around and taking a sip. 'Quite delicious.'

'But, Mané, you've got him to a T!' exclaimed the girl's mother at the next table.

5

ONE THING HE WANTED to know: 'Why didn't you challenge the will?'

Slow to drink her wine, Jeanine told him about the process that Andy had initiated in Hortense Avenue. The seed he had germinated when – grabbing at a straw – he had begun to describe a man considerate, honest and wise. As Andy filled in the blank with a tender portrait of his teacher, something unbelievable and bewildering had occurred: if only for a second, Jeanine had stopped hating her father.

'Of course, this was just the start. It didn't happen at once.'

Andy's homage was open to so much interpretation; the person he evoked impossible to reconcile with Jeanine's long-entrenched impression of a rapacious, licentious and tyrannical bolter. She had attacked and questioned this new identity, and gone away full of self-doubt, exposed to emotions she had never expected to feel, and also thinking that it was possible her father had had a friend. From the cold grey embers of her dislike, she had seized this tiny warm coal, until gradually, gnawingly, with the fertile promise of something undivulged, Andy's version took hold and began to seep through her, until it pulled at her heart. The upshot was: she had respected her father's decision – 'perhaps the first decision of his I was able to respect', she reflected, her wryness disappearing.

Rui refilled their glasses, then produced from his red jacket a pad and a pencil that he scratched behind his ear, waiting.

'What would you like to eat?'

Andy had never felt so ravenous.

6

HE HAD THE BEST conversations with Furnivall.

Over the years many of his teacher's remarks had bubbled back into meaning, into a delayed explosion of sense of something not understood or ignored at the time.

'*You won't catch big fish unless you're prepared to get snagged on the bottom.*'

'*Ah, progress. The Gadarene swine made progress – rapid progress.*'

'*Yes, Larkham, run. You can't walk through a game of rugby.*'

'*It's hard work being anyone.*'

Once, voicing an abrupt thought, Andy asked him: 'At what point do you decide who you are? I mean, at what point are you going towards this person; at what point are you going away?'

'That's not the right question.'

Puzzled. 'Why not?'

'You need to ask: how can I be who I am? Discover that and you'll be fine.'

He persisted. 'What if you'd like to be other than who you are?'

'Then you make too much room for the wrong sort of person to slip in.'

Andy had come to understand certain things about himself, not least the various people he was not. All that sunny delusional thinking when he was ambitious to be Someone Else – he could not have been more mistaken. His evidence? Sitting across the table and looking with dark shining eyes into his face. And he thought of the image that he had nurtured in his most secret depths, of a couple floating together on a dimensionless sea.

'Fado', it came back to Andy, was Portuguese for fate. Those excruciating songs that Amália kept singing, to which Jeanine was gently swaying her head, like a young woman trying to remember the words of a song that all of a sudden Andy realised he knew: they boiled down to the same tune.

7

'LOOK AT ME, ANDY. No, over here.'

He did as she asked.

'Maybe I was too quick to judge, too harsh,' her eyes alive and meaningful. 'I thought you were awful the first time we met.' He had seemed young, inexperienced, heading at a determined, canted angle away from himself. 'Then when I received your letter, I thought: *At last. Someone's being honest.*'

She went on, not in a voice used before: 'My father can wait. What about you?'

'Me?' He said it twice, pathetically.

She laughed and he felt found out. Her sonic laughter went through him.

'Do you have family? Where did you grow up? Who are your friends? I know nothing about you.' Was it his imagination that her eyes added: *Your hopes, your fears, your likes, your dislikes?*

Even as he began answering, something happened. He was visible – suddenly – to himself. In focus. After a few sentences, it made him happy to speak. He talked in a manner he had not felt in a while, animated. He used words that he wanted to say and had never found; but they were as nothing to what she was able to express simply by sitting there, listening to him. Until he never wished to be anyone else again. It was extraordinary. He did want to be Andy Larkham.

Jeanine heard what he had to say without interrupting. No longer staring at him as though he were a sky she watched with distrust. Her gaze lingered; her smile did not vanish so quickly. He felt her brown eyes sweeping through him, seeing all that there was to see.

The arrival of the main course gave Andy an opportunity to ask questions. And as she talked about herself, her voice was warmer, with more rhythm than he remembered. She's grown up as well, he thought, she's less judgmental. For the first time, he was seeing her in fine weather. He knew that everything she said was true. He did not know how he knew.

They had finished their main course when he had this unusual, strange sensation – the soft beginning of an emotion that he had not experienced before, but that he could liken only to an absence of fear. It was absurd that he should be feeling this way – he had met her but four times – and he could not say what triggered it or if it was a trick of the wine.

He looked sternly at her, afraid and suspicious of this feeling that spread from his face into his chest, making it difficult to breathe. What it was like to feel like this, he had never imagined.

Rui, who had wheeled over a two-tiered trolley of desserts, was admiring her bracelet. 'What's that?'

She hesitated, and after a moment said: 'For good luck.'

Luck? This was not luck. After everything, it was nothing short of a miracle she was here – a miracle she was talking to him. But he needed more miracles if he was going to convert the mysterious heat and light radiating through him, and which he longed to continue, into a vital and enduring relationship. Easier to acquire £17 million than to win the woman you wanted, especially after such a messy start. What had happened to Jeanine was traumatic, and the notion that anything could be resolved on the basis of a single conversation was, of course, absurd. Her involvement with Andy would follow a more ragged path. The fact that she had showed up at all was the first step of many. At last, though, he was playing an honest game. One with no assured outcome, but which was the only game worth playing. For the first time, he was playing with his heart wide open.

It would be a few days following their dinner before Jeanine felt strong enough to read the story of her father's life, and was subsequently prepared to talk about the man she had known as Kes Wakefield, her father as Don Flexmore and her mother as Carl-Andrew Purcell. 'He was everything you have my father say,' and her way of not looking at Andy stopped him from asking more. Another occasion, she said: 'He only kissed me before he did something dangerous. Whenever one of us wanted to have sex, the other backed off. I used to say to him: "When you look at a woman you smile, but you don't listen." It got so bad, I made him come with me to a Pranik healer, who scrubbed away at our auras, throwing our black stuff into a bucket of salt water, so that what was left was a lot of blues and greens. The healer claimed to have X-ray vision. He maintained that Kes had a spirit on his shoulder, a jealous woman ruining it all, that's how it came out, but if you ask me the jealous woman on his shoulder was another man.'

Their relationship never recovered from her decision to cut off relations with her father – a decision vehemently opposed by Kes and which would result in Jeanine not being able to touch her trust fund until her father was dead. 'I couldn't explain this at the time. I realise now it wasn't so much the money Kes was after: he seemed to *need* my father in his life.' A month after her twenty-first birthday, Kes kissed Jeanine goodbye; he had an assignment in West Africa. 'I never heard from him again.' He had vanished like the profile he had created on Facebook to lure teenage boys and girls, and which she discovered on his laptop: a construct of quotations from L. Ron Hubbard, favourite novels and food, pet hates (Nicolas Cage, Michael Winner, crayfish), and wild loves (Trini Lopez, Jo Malone perfume, two goldfish – Fanta and Orangina). Another three years before she learned that he had perished in a plane crash on an island off Guinea-Bissau. 'His end – or what for a long time I thought was his end – was banal. His Cessna was coming in to land and the wind flipped it over and he was burned to a cinder. He was importing cocaine from Colombia.'

Only later was there any doubt that he had died. Interpol had sent out one of their best undercover men to rootle through the ashes of Kes's last aircraft, an Englishman called Joseph Silkleigh, who discovered that this was the fourth such accident in the self-same Cessna and that Kes had been living off insurance payouts all these years.

'Silkleigh did finally nail him – in Melbourne. He currently resides in a Supermax prison in Goulburn. For now.'

8

THE RESTAURANT HAD EMPTIED. The waiters had stripped the paper tablecloths and laid out the tables for the morning, and to the mild astonishment of Rui, Andy and Jeanine were still talking.

Rui had allowed them a further half-hour's grace. He finished rubber-banding the receipts in the till and came over, on his way straightening a chair.

'We're closing, *senhor*,' with immaculate regret turning down Andy's request for two more coffees.

They folded their napkins and stood up and walked to the front of the restaurant, where Rui waited with their coats. He held them for Andy and Jeanine to put on.

Rui unbuttoned his red jacket and hung it up. Andy watched him switch off the Christmas tree lights, and then the lights in the room and the last thing he switched off was the fado.

'Goodnight, Rui.'

'*Boa noite, senhora, senhor.*'

Outside, the snow was coming down sideways. The air current shifted, and the snowflakes, like particles of light, flew up from the ground as though out of it.

The frosty air was so cold that she let out a gasp.

'What would you like to do now?' she asked.

So that was the situation. And if he could not remember his exact reply, Andy did recall how the winter street jostled with young men and women not much different to them, each heading off in their own direc-tion to face whatever the darkness was about to bowl at them, some to be deceived, some to deceive, some to break up, some to come together for the first time.

ACKNOWLEDGEMENTS

Murray Bail for the idea; Robert Sykes of Parker Bullen for giving it legal legs; Vergine Gulbenkian for helping me to understand Armenia; Rob Libby for turning up at the right time; Mike Rikard-Bell and Bill Howroyd for their experiences of the Pilbara; Don Forrest and Judith Street for memories of Perth; the late Angela Geraghty for details of a bush fire; Gillon Aitken, Niko Hansen, Nigel Horne, Christopher MacLehose, Charlotte Metcalfe, Nick Robinson and Rachael Rose for comments on the text. I would like also to thank Jonathan Beswick, Piers Litherland, Ronnie Lloyd, Ellen O'Halligan, Julia Pilgrim, Susan Richards, Amanda Shakespeare, David Willis and Francesca Zaenglein. Above all, I am grateful to Peter Washington for his red pen, my wife Gillian for her unstinting support and my editor James Gurbutt for his loyalty.

This is a work of fiction and not one of the characters is a real person; nor is Carpe Diem based on any publishing house. Krikor Makertich's discovery was sparked by an interest in the 1952 flight of Lang Hancock, well told in Neill Phillipson's *Man of Iron* (1974) and Richard Duffield's *Rogue Bull: The Story of Lang Hancock, King of the Pilbara* (1979). I would also like to pay tribute to Michael J. Arlen's *Passage to Ararat* (1975) and Terence Cave's *How to Read Montaigne* (2007). The quotations from Michel de Montaigne are taken from the Everyman Library edition of his complete works (2003), translated by Donald M. Frame.

AUTHOR BIOGRAPHY

Nicholas Shakespeare was born in 1957. The son of a diplomat, much of his youth was spent in the Far East and South America. His novels have been translated into twenty languages. They include *The Vision of Elena Silves*, winner of the Somerset Maugham Award, *Snowleg* and *The Dancer Upstairs*, which was chosen by the American Libraries Association in 1997 as the year's best novel, and in 2001 was made into a film of the same name by John Malkovich. His most recent novel is *Secrets of the Sea*. He is married with two small boys and currently lives in Oxford.